Provoked

BENSON SIBLINGS

BOOK ONE

SARAH BAILEY

Please note the spelling throughout is British English.

Cover Art by Sarah Bailey

Published by Twisted Tree Publications
www.twistedtreepublications.com
info@twistedtreepublications.com

Paperback ISBN: 978-1-913217-03-7

To Dante & Liora

Thank you for showing me love can blossom &
thrive under the strangest circumstances.

Chapter One

LIORA

When my father asked me to come on his business trip to London, he'd told me it was for us to spend some time together as father and daughter. The first time he'd taken me anywhere without Mum. Whilst he had meetings during the day, I'd visited the Natural History and the British Museums, spent time wandering Oxford Street and had gone to see Buckingham Palace.

It'd been years since I'd stepped foot in England. We were Scottish through and through. Stewarts. A bloodline steeped in history, except my offshoot didn't amount to much.

My father worked with tartan all his life. He lived and breathed the patterns for each clan, the fabric. It was his calling. His first love after my mother. His clientele was prestigious. Nothing but the best for Angus Stewart. And yet, he seemed on edge during our time in London.

The night before we were due to return to Edinburgh, he took me to dinner. His nervousness set me on edge. His eyes darted left and right as if the shadows hid what was ailing him so. I wanted to ask but knew better. He never spoke to me about his business dealings.

We caught a black cab after dinner. I expected us to return to the hotel, but the driver stopped outside a nondescript building. Dad paid and helped me out of the car.

"Now, lass, don't speak a word to anyone," he told me as he rang the doorbell.

I never expected him to take me with him on a business outing, but something in his voice told me this was much more than that. Fear laced his tone.

Who are we meeting and why?

The door opened. A man in a neat suit with a bald head greeted us.

"Mr Stewart, we have been expecting you."

Dad nodded, taking me by the arm and drawing me into the building. The bald man led us through the hallway and up one flight of stairs. He opened a door to our right. As soon as we walked in the room, my hair stood up on end.

A man with greying dark hair and piercing blue eyes sat at a long table. Behind him, stood two more men in suits. The room was only lit by a single light above the table. One of them came around and pulled out a chair for me and my father.

"Angus, it is a pleasure," said the man with greying hair.

My father's expression told me pleasure was the last thing on his mind.

We both sat. I folded my hands in my lap.

"Shall we talk business?" Dad said.

"Why, of course."

I drowned out their voices, not interested in what they had to say. Something else caught my attention. In the corner of the room, bathed in shadow, a younger man leant against the wall. He was watching my father and the older man. I couldn't see his features properly, but his shirt was unbuttoned at the top and he wore no tie. This struck me as odd considering all the other men were formally dressed.

Who is he?

As if tugged by the thread of my thoughts, I found his eyes on me the next moment. I could just about make out they were blue. Something about them reminded me of the man talking to my father. Was this his son?

He regarded me for several long moments. I couldn't look away. The hairs on the back of my neck prickled. None of the men in this room bar my father were warm or welcoming. They left me feeling as though we were in a den of wolves who were waiting to devour us whole.

The younger man shoved off the wall. My eyes tracked his progress towards the man with greying hair. When he came into the light, I noticed his hair was as black as night. He had an air of danger surrounding him. His unbuttoned shirt was light blue and his suit, dark grey.

When he leant down to whisper something in the man's ear, he stared right at me. I could see the stark resemblance between father and son. His gaze pinned me to my seat, all my senses telling me to run far, far away from him.

His father's eyes flicked over to me and I wanted to bolt. He was terrifying. His gaze cold and calculating. Whilst his son looked at me with an air of possessiveness, his eyes reminded me of a tiger about to maul its prey. My palms began to sweat. I felt stripped to the core.

Then the father looked up at his son and nodded once. The deadly smile which appeared on the younger man's face gave me the distinct impression what happened next had everything to do with me.

I tore my eyes away and glanced at my father who'd gone as white as a sheet. What was wrong with him? Did he understand the silent communication between father and son?

The son straightened and walked around the table. Putting his hand on my father's shoulder, he said something to him I couldn't make out.

"The lass is only eighteen and at Uni," my father hissed.

The son held up three fingers. My father didn't relax, but he looked resigned.

"Fine."

"Now that's settled, how about we have some whisky to celebrate? Just like old times," the older man said, clapping his hands together.

My father nodded but did not look happy about the prospect. I wondered why since having a wee dram after dinner was one of his favourite pastimes.

The younger man walked behind me back towards his position by the wall. I felt his gaze scorching my skin through my clothes. They'd been talking about me. What had the three fingers meant? What did any of this mean? I didn't understand.

My father indulged in a tumbler of whisky with the older man before he rose and pulled me up with him.

"Don't forget, Angus. Three years," the older man said.

My father stiffened.

"Three years," he replied.

He hustled me out of the room without saying goodbye.

"What was that about?" I asked when we were outside and in another black cab.

"Never you mind, lass."

I did mind. I couldn't think why my father knew such men and what they wanted with me.

Three years later

I shook myself as I walked across the stage for my graduation ceremony. Four years of hard work had paid off. I had a First in BSc Biological Sciences (Zoology) from Edinburgh University. I shook the hand of the Principal, giving him a nod and a smile before I walked the rest of the way across the stage.

As I sat back down, I wondered why I'd even thought about that night. It felt like a lifetime ago when I'd gone on that trip to London with my father. The three years they'd mentioned were up. They'd been up for a month and nothing had happened. I supposed it was stupid to think it had anything to do with me.

The ceremony drew to a close. I fought through the crowd to find my parents and my boyfriend, Harrison, waiting for me. His brown eyes twinkled when he spied me. We'd been together for two years, having met on a night out with the girls. My parents loved him. And me? Well, I loved him in my own way, but I couldn't help being on edge. Waiting for the other shoe to drop. Perhaps it had something to do with that night in London.

Nothing is going to happen to you, Liora. It's in the past.

Harrison kissed my cheek as I drew near.

"Och, my wee baby girl, I'm so proud of you," my mum, Heather, said, enveloping me in a hug.

"Thanks. I didn't trip, that's a plus."

My dad ruffled my short blonde locks, grinning. I'd always been a tad clumsy. I didn't take after him with his red hair, but my mum with her green eyes and long blonde hair.

"She's a superstar," Harrison said.

I felt my face heat up. Accepting praise never came easy to me.

"I take it Declan didn't bother showing up," I said.

"Oh, you know your brother, always busy with this and that," Mum said.

He'd never taken an interest in anyone but himself. *Prick.* I chose not to comment. She always made excuses for him. Harrison wrapped his arm around me and squeezed. He knew how much it annoyed me.

We spoke for a while longer before he gave me a kiss, saying he'd see me at the pub later. Mum and Dad had arranged lunch at an upmarket restaurant. It passed peacefully. Mum beamed at me. Dad seemed quiet and withdrawn.

When we'd finished, Mum excused herself to go to the bathroom. My dad eyed me warily for a moment.

"Liora, there's something I need you to do for me."

I frowned.

"I'm sorry, lass. Please believe me."

"What is it?"

"Say bye to your Ma. There's a black car waiting outside. Go with the lad and don't ask any questions."

My hands shook. What did he mean go with the lad? Who was he talking about?

"Dad, what are you saying?"

"I can't say more. Just be a good lassie for your Da."

"But Dad…"

"Liora, do as I say."

I was about to press him further when my mum arrived back at the table. Dad nodded at me. He'd told me to say goodbye. Was this goodbye for now or goodbye forever? I couldn't help the cold sweat beading at the back of my neck. I stood up, giving my dad a kiss on the cheek.

"Liora, are you off?" Mum asked.

"Sorry, Mum, can't stay longer."

She smiled, got up and gave me a hug.

"I'm so proud of you."

I tried not to think about what I was walking into. Something in my dad's eyes told me I wasn't going to like it. I picked up my bag and shrugged my coat on. Giving them both a wave, I took a breath and left the restaurant.

As my dad said, a black car sat outside. A man held the door open. He was wearing sunglasses and a dark suit.

"Miss Stewart."

"That's me."

He half bowed to me and indicated the interior of the car.

"Please get in."

Despite feeling like I would regret getting into the vehicle, I did as he said. There was a driver, but the other seat next to me was unoccupied. The man in the suit shut the door, came around the car and got in beside me. I popped my seatbelt on and clutched my bag to my chest as the car set off.

"My name is Brent. I'll be escorting you home."

I nodded at him. It dawned on me the next moment. Home was not going to be the flat I shared with Gwen. And my suspicions were further aroused when we ended up driving towards the airport.

"Where are we going?"

"London."

I froze, my fingers curling around the door handle. What did he mean London? Why were we going there? What had my father done?

"Why?"

"I'm afraid I can't answer that."

I sat back, watching the houses pass by. What could I say to that? Nothing. Brent left me with the impression he wouldn't answer any pertinent questions. Dad said go with him. So I would. Didn't mean I had to be happy about this turn of events.

I fumbled with the clasp of my bag, pulling out my phone.

"What are you doing?" Brent asked.

"Just making up an excuse for my absence tonight."

He eyed me for a long moment.

"Let me see it before you send it."

I was about to object but thought better of it. I wasn't sure Brent would let me send a message otherwise. I didn't want

Harrison to worry. Would I even see him again? My throat felt tight all of a sudden. Would I ever see anyone I knew again? Why did this entire thing fill me with dread? What was going to happen to me when we got to London?

I shook myself. I needed to get my head on straight. Until I knew where exactly in London Brent was taking me, I had to keep it together. I tapped out a message to Harrison.

ME: No pub for me, ate something bad at lunch. Sorry! xxx

I showed it to Brent who nodded. I pressed send. I got a response less than a minute later.

HARRISON: Aww, do you need me to come look after you?

ME: No. I'll be fine. Have fun.

HARRISON: Miss ya xxx

Brent insisted on seeing what I'd said. I wasn't about to tell Harrison that my father had sent me off with some random man I didn't know to London. God knows what fate awaited me when I got there.

The rest of the journey was silent. We were dropped off near the front of the airport. Brent pulled a suitcase out of the boot and I realised it was one of mine. When had this been packed? Who let him into my flat and touch my stuff - or had my father done it? Either way, I was unnerved.

I followed him inside. Arriving at a desk which didn't seem to have an airline marked on it, the lady took the bag and spoke to Brent for several minutes. Next, he dragged me through security and then straight to the gate. I realised the plane sitting waiting for us was not from a commercial airline.

That's a private plane.

What?

When I got on board, there were four seats facing a table and two seats facing each other. The hostess greeted us with a warm smile.

"Welcome on board, Miss Stewart."

I nodded at her, unsure of what to say. I'd never been in a private plane before. And why did she know my name?

"Please sit wherever you like."

I sat down on one of the separate seats, whilst Brent took the table. I strapped in and tried not to think too much about who would have the money to pay for a private plane to escort me to London.

We took off twenty minutes later. During the flight, the attendant gave us some refreshments. I chose to have juice rather than drink any alcohol. I wanted a clear head to prepare for what was coming next. I was certain I needed my wits about me.

Landing at London City Airport an hour later, Brent escorted me off the plane. As soon as we received my bag, we were outside and he was herding me into another car. I really wanted to know what this was all about.

The journey took about forty minutes. We stopped outside a large townhouse. Brent came around and opened my door. I slid out of the car and looked up at it.

"This is home," he said in answer to my unspoken question.

Home.

Provoked

This place didn't remotely feel like home. More like the place I was going to be held against my will for the foreseeable future. I'd come quietly just like my dad had told me to, but that didn't mean I was going to stay silent forever.

I followed him up the steps and through the front door. He carried my suitcase up two flights of stairs before opening a door and placing it inside.

"You need to wait in here."

"Are you going to tell me why?" I asked.

"No questions, Miss Stewart."

I walked in and Brent shut the door behind me. I'd stepped into a large bedroom. It was very masculine. The walls were painted a midnight blue except for one accent wall in grey. There was a huge bed with dark grey sheets. I wheeled my suitcase further in and set it by the desk near the corner. I didn't dare look in any of the huge floor to ceiling wardrobes with black doors.

Sliding my coat off and placing it on the chair, I took my heels off. They were pinching my feet. I wasn't sure what to do or how long I'd have to wait for whoever wanted me here.

Looking around, there wasn't much else to see. A laptop sat on the desk, open but not turned on. The bedside tables were dark wood. One had a fancy alarm clock on it, but nothing else. No pictures. Nothing that told me anything about the owner.

I slumped down on the end of the bed. I wished Brent had answered my questions. At least I'd have some idea of what I was doing here.

The door opened and in strode someone I never thought I'd ever lay eyes on again. He shut it firmly behind him.

Dressed in a blue shirt, the first two buttons undone and the sleeves rolled up with black trousers was a man I'd only ever seen once. A man from three years ago. The one with blue eyes and midnight black hair.

His eyes landed squarely on me and he smirked. My heart pounded in my ears, drowning out all other noises. I gripped the sheets below me. What had my father done? Why had he made me come here? I was in the den of a lone wolf. There was no doubt in my mind this bedroom belonged to him.

This can't be happening. What the hell is going on?

His eyes swept down my outfit. I hadn't changed out of the green dress I'd been wearing for my graduation. I felt exposed.

When he took a step towards me, I scrambled away onto the bed. It only made him smile wider. He shook his head.

What does he want with me? Was this what they meant by three years?

"Hello, Liora. It's nice to finally meet you."

Chapter Two

DANTE

The girl huddled on the bed, her chin length blonde hair surrounding her like a halo. Pity her innocence wouldn't save her. I could feel her terror seeping into me. Little did she know fear fed me. I wanted her scared.

"It's you," she whispered, her voice betraying her slight Scottish lilt.

It was the first time I'd heard her voice. It did things to me. I'd always loved the accent, but on her, it sounded so much sweeter. Perhaps it was the anticipation or it was just her. All I knew was I wanted to hear it again.

"Glad you remember me."

She frowned.

"What do you want?"

I'd waited three years for this day. When I could finally have what was promised to me.

"You."

She froze in place. Her mouth stayed firmly shut. I could see the wheels turning in her head at the implications of what I'd said.

"Now, you best do as I say, girl."

I looked down at my nails.

"You see, you are my gift."

I stalked towards her, coming to a standstill at the end of the bed. Her forest green eyes stared back at me, pupils constricted.

"But if you choose to deny me or disobey me too much, then I'll give you back. Trust that he is much, much worse than me."

"Who are you people?"

She had no idea why she'd been taken. What she was given to my father for, nor why he'd given her to me. *Good.* Angus wasn't meant to spill the beans.

"You don't get to ask questions."

"Why should I even listen to you?"

She would learn from her mistake. I knelt on the bed and crawled towards her. She tried to escape, but I grabbed her leg and pulled her underneath me, pinning her hands down.

"I am your master and nothing you say or do will change that."

She struggled in my grasp. I sat on her legs to stop her moving. Her eyes met mine.

"What's your name?"

"That's none of your concern."

Her green eyes grew wider. Her form trembled beneath me. Soon I'd have her trembling for a very different reason. As my pet, she'd do exactly as I told her or she'd be punished.

"What are you going to do with me?"

"So many questions. In time you'll learn those won't get you very far with me. I'll allow this one since you do need to understand the rules."

I pulled her hands up above her head, lacing one hand around her wrists. I trailed a finger down her cheek.

"There is only one rule between you and I. Obey or be punished."

"Wh… what?"

"You will obey me in everything. No buts. No arguments. Nothing. If you are good, you will be rewarded and if not, you will be dealt with appropriately."

"Why?"

I smiled at her.

"Because, Liora, you are mine."

Her mouth opened and shut twice. She had the prettiest bow lips, just itching to be kissed. I wouldn't, but the temptation was there all the same. As much as I wanted this girl and had done since the moment I laid eyes on her, she had lessons to learn first.

"Why won't you tell me who you are?"

"You haven't earnt that information… yet."

She was about to open her mouth again, but I put my hand over it.

"No more questions."

Her eyes flashed with irritation. I hadn't meant to invade her personal space, but something about her drew me closer. She'd lost some of that youthful glow, but she was still the same girl. Three years older and I wondered if she was wiser.

Did she remember every detail of that first day like I did? The way she'd inspected each occupant of the room with sharp intelligence. How she'd unconsciously shifted back when my father laid eyes on her as if she knew he was deadly and should never be messed with.

I'd known she was smart given her grades at school and now she'd received a First for her degree. What I wanted to know is why she'd chosen to study zoology. To be honest, I wanted to dig into her mind and find out everything about her. The things I couldn't learn from regular updates about her progress.

I released her mouth, hoping she would take my warning seriously. I wouldn't answer any further questions. She had to earn them.

"Can you get off me, please?"

I should've expected that.

"Mmm, since you asked so nicely."

I rolled off her, onto my side and propped myself up by my elbow. She turned her head towards me but didn't move away. I could feel her appraising me, wondering how I would react if she bolted. She swallowed, perhaps realising it would be a bad idea.

"Cat got your tongue?" I asked.

"You said no questions."

I grinned.

"So you can take instruction?"

"I didn't think I had another choice."

She pronounced the word 'didn't' more like 'didnae'. Her accent was like music to my ears. It drew me in. I resisted the urge to touch her again.

"There's always a choice."

She frowned and shifted away slightly but didn't say another word. I sat up, watching her squirm underneath my gaze.

"You either obey or you find out what type of punishments I have in store for you."

"That's not a choice I want to make."

A part of me wished she would test the boundaries. Perhaps later.

"No? Fair enough. Tell me, why did you come willingly?"

"What do you mean?"

"Brent told me you didn't fight him when he brought you here."

She looked conflicted for a moment before she sat up and faced me.

"My dad told me to go with him. Didn't want to make a scene or disappoint him."

Did she idolise her father? No. That wasn't right. It was because she wasn't the type to want attention brought on her.

"You remember the day we saw each other three years ago."

"Yes."

I reached out, taking one of her hands. The need to touch her after all this time drove me. I could no longer resist. She flinched but didn't pull away. I turned her hand upwards and traced lines down her palm. She looked like she wanted to ask me what I was doing and yet her mouth remained closed.

"What do you remember about it?"

"Everything." Her eyes fell on our hands. "You look like your father."

A fact I hated, but that was neither here nor there. My fingers drew circles around her wrist, moving higher. I felt her freeze, her muscles locking up at my touch. Did I repulse her?

I could feel the heat of her skin against mine like sparks of electricity. I wondered if she felt it too and that's why she'd reacted the way she did.

"Does this bother you?"

Her green eyes met mine. Her gaze inscrutable.

"Yes."

"Why is that?"

She pulled her wrist out of my grasp, holding her arm to her chest.

"I don't know what you want and… I have a boyfriend."

That little fact was not lost on me. It needed to be remedied, but I wouldn't tell her just yet. Let her live in the fantasy that she could go back to him for a little longer. I'd rip that away from her just like everything else. And she knew what I wanted. Her. She just wasn't ready to accept it.

"I know you do."

Her eyes flashed again. I could tell it drove her crazy not being able to ask me questions.

"And yet you still took me and now you say I'm yours. I'm not a piece of property."

"Property? No, I told you, you're my gift. I only ask for obedience. You're not a slave, but I suppose you could call yourself my pet."

"Pet? I'm not a pet either. I'm a human being. I don't belong to anyone."

I struck, one minute we were seated, the next I was on her again. I kept her hands pinned with one of my own, leaning

18

down, I buried my face in her neck and breathed in. A gasp left her lips.

"Wrong, Liora." I nipped her ear. "You belong to me."

She struggled in my grasp.

"Get off me."

"No."

"I'll scream."

I raised my head, staring down at her.

"Go ahead. No one will come and you'll leave me with no choice but to discipline you. Not quite what I had in mind for our first evening together, but I'll enjoy it nevertheless."

The fire in her eyes died in an instant.

"You'd enjoy hurting me?"

And now I really did have to discipline her. Asking me questions and struggling instead of allowing me to touch her without complaint, neither of those were permitted.

"I never said I'd hurt you."

"You implied it."

I smiled. Smart girl. If she expected pain, then pain is what she'd receive.

"I think you need to learn a lesson about what will happen if you continue to step out of line."

Having her beneath me, trembling with fear caused a reaction in me I wasn't prepared for. I wanted to rip away her clothes and have her whether she wanted me or not. I'd never taken anyone against their will. Was I really so much like him that I wouldn't care if she struggled, cried and told me to stop? That pulled me up short. I was not him. I couldn't be.

I released her, shifting off the bed and pacing away. Those thoughts were not allowed. Liora had to want me first. And she would. I'd felt her unconscious reaction to me being on top of her. Her hips angled towards me, her legs falling open rather than staying shut. Her body wanted mine even if she didn't know it yet.

I couldn't punish her in the way I wanted to. Not when I couldn't keep myself under control. There were other methods. Ways of teaching her to obey.

"Get up," I told her.

She shuffled off the bed and stood.

"If you behave yourself, you will earn the right to have things, such as contact with your family, your own room and perhaps, eventually I will allow you to do what you love and work with animals."

Her eyes widened.

"For now, I want your phone."

She hesitated for a moment before walking over to where she'd left her bag on my desk and fished it out. Stepping towards me, she held it out. I took it from her.

"Passcode?" I asked.

"Six, eight, four, two."

I unlocked it and checked her messages. What Brent told me was correct. She'd only messaged her so-called boyfriend to tell him she wouldn't be out this evening.

"I will tell you if he contacts you."

She nodded, eyes downcast.

"Over there is the bathroom."

I pointed towards a door in the corner.

"This room is where you'll stay except for meals and when I allow you out with me. In case you hadn't cottoned on already, this is my bedroom."

Her eyes caught mine, abject horror on her face.

"You expect me to sleep in the same bed as you."

She framed it like a statement instead of a question so I let it slide.

"Did you expect otherwise?"

Her face went bright red.

What just crossed her mind?

"You're not going to want me to… to…"

"To what?"

She squirmed, clearly uncomfortable. I smiled when I realised what she was thinking. It was clear on her face.

"Are you trying to ask me if I expect sex from you?"

She looked away, fidgeting with her hands.

"Yes."

Despite my earlier urges, I was determined not to make her think I was a complete monster. I might not be the good guy, but I was not and would never become like *him.*

"Forcing myself on unwilling women does not hold any interest for me. Rest assured I won't touch you like that unless you ask for it."

"I have a boyfriend," she mumbled.

Something she didn't need to remind me of. If she continued to bring him up, I'd make her break it off with him today rather than waiting until she was in a better frame of mind to accept it.

"You think that matters to me?"

"It should."

I grabbed her hand and pulled her towards me.

"It will never matter because you're mine, not his."

I saw the realisation on her face. She tore her hand away and shoved me, glaring.

"No. No. You can't make me do that. I won't. You don't get to make that choice for me."

That little outburst was unwelcome and now I was angry. She wouldn't like what I was going to do next, but she'd learn she couldn't say no to me.

"Don't I? You seem to think you can negotiate with me. You're wrong. I was going to wait, but now you've just pissed me off. It's time you realised how this works between us."

I unlocked her phone again and pulled up the camera. I stepped towards her and dragged her against my chest, pinning her there with one arm. She stared up at me in shock. I raised my other hand with the phone, placing us in the exact position for a perfect selfie as I leant towards her.

"Smile, Liora."

Before she had a chance to look at what I was doing, I took a photo. My forehead met hers before I took another one. I turned my face towards the camera and smiled, snapping a further photo. I let her go, stepping away and checking my handiwork. The photos looked rather intimate and just the effect I was going for.

"What did you do?" she demanded.

"Don't you want him to know how happy you are with me?"

Her eyes widened and her mouth fell open.

"No. No, you can't send him those."

"You don't get to make demands and tell me no."

I opened up her messages and composed something as she launched herself at me. I stepped back, holding the phone out of her grasp.

"Please, don't."

ME: I'm sorry. I didn't want to do this over text, but I've been seeing someone else and it's over between us.

I attached one of the photos to the message. The one with our foreheads touching. It was the only one where she had her eyes closed and you couldn't see her expression of shock. I didn't hit send quite yet. She jumped at me again.

"I suggest you stay still if you don't want me to break his heart."

She froze in place. She only came up to my shoulder so keeping the phone from her was easy. I brought it down and showed her the screen. Her expression soured.

"That's heartless."

"Do you think I have one?"

"No, but you can't say that to him. He doesn't deserve it."

"Watch me."

I hit send. Her face dropped. I expected her to retaliate and have a go at me, but she didn't. She turned away from me, walked over to the bed and sat down, staring at the floor. Her phone vibrated in my hand. He was calling her.

"Do you want to speak to him?" I asked.

"After what you just did? No," she said, quietly.

I rejected the call. Didn't matter to me either way. It was done. Now she couldn't use that pitiful excuse to stop me from doing what I wanted with her. She probably thought I was being cruel for the sake of it. It was better for her not to have false illusions about what life with me would be like or cling to hope that I'd let her go.

"Get up and come with me."

Her phone vibrated several times in my pocket. She stood but didn't look at me when she walked over. I pulled her phone out as I opened the door and strode out.

HARRISON: Are you serious?

HARRISON: I don't believe you. Talk to me. What's going on?

HARRISON: Please answer the phone.

HARRISON: Liora, why are you doing this? Answer the phone. You're not seeing anyone else. I know you.

She followed along after me as I took the stairs.

"Are you sure you don't want to speak to him? He says he doesn't believe you. Perhaps we need to give him further evidence, hmm?"

"If you want to," she replied, her voice void of any emotion.

I'd only said that to get a rise out of her. What was wrong with her? Why wasn't she fighting back?

I stopped on the next landing and she barrelled into the back of me. I turned to find her rubbing her face.

"I didn't think you meek."

That made her look up at me, eyes narrowing.

"You took me away from my home. You broke up with my boyfriend for me. You keep telling me I belong to you and

24

that I'm only allowed to do what you say, when you say it and that if I don't, you'll punish me. Excuse me if that's a lot to process in one go."

She had a point. We knew nothing about each other. I might have learnt things about her life, but that didn't mean I knew the girl inside. That would only come from being around each other for an extended period of time. I had to remember to be patient.

"Don't dawdle."

I turned away and continued down the second flight of stairs to the ground floor. Her feet were almost silent on the carpet, but I could feel her behind me.

I led her through the kitchen where the staff nodded at me and out into the large conservatory which housed an informal dining area. Pulling a chair out for her, I waited. She sat down, staring at the knives and forks on the table. I sat next to her at the head of the table.

"The staff will take care of meals for you and anything else you need. Outside of my room, when you're not with me, Brent will be with you."

She looked up at me, green eyes full of conflicting emotions. Hurt and resignation stuck out the most. I understood both those things, more than she knew.

One of the chefs came in, which stopped her replying to me. Dinner between us was silent. I didn't try to engage her in conversation because she looked dejected and tired. I supposed she'd had a long day what with her graduation.

I took her back upstairs when we were done and left her to get ready for bed. Her father had packed a suitcase for her. The rest of her things would be sent down at a later date.

When I went back to my bedroom an hour later, she was huddled under the covers and didn't raise her head. I stripped down to a t-shirt and shorts before clambering in next to her. I made sure to keep my distance and turned out the light.

I found myself unable to get comfortable knowing she was right there. The girl I'd wanted for so long. I had her, but I also didn't. What I wanted from her she wasn't yet ready to give me.

I gave up after five minutes, rolling on my back. That's when I heard it.

Liora was crying.

For some reason, all I wanted to do was allow her to cry on me. So I could become her source of comfort. That urge was unwelcome.

And I knew from that moment onwards, I was completely and utterly fucked.

Chapter Three

LIORA

I hated myself for being weak, but I couldn't stop the tears soaking the pillow. My day was ruined. It was meant to be my proudest moment and in many ways it was. Everything that happened afterwards sucked. I'd known deep down when my father told me to go with Brent, I would somehow end up here with Nameless.

Whatever reason he had for not telling me his name, it still grated on me. I needed a name. At least I'd know who I was dealing with. Nameless decided I wasn't ready for such information.

My heart ached. I just wanted to understand. I didn't exactly hate him. A part of me knew this situation was caused by our fathers, but he didn't have to go along with it.

I sniffled, trying not to make too much noise. I was most upset about what he sent to Harrison. I could deal with everything else, but that was uncalled for. He could've let me do it in a nice way. Except he told me not to question him and

I'd ignored that. Then I stupidly argued with him. He warned me and I should've taken him seriously when he talked about punishment. Still, Harrison didn't deserve to be told that way.

I rolled on my back and stared up at the ceiling, tears still running down my face. Something warm covered my hand, fingers entwined with mine.

Wait, what is Nameless holding my hand for?

He didn't speak. His skin warmed mine, sending tingling sensations up my arm. I'd never had a reaction like this to another person. Earlier when he'd stroked my skin, it'd made me uncomfortable because of the strange stirring it gave me in my stomach.

Why wasn't his touch repulsive to me? Why did I feel like shuffling closer to him?

His thumb ran down mine. Instead of being soothing, it made my skin burn hotter. My tears abated, replaced by alien feelings and unwanted urges. The silence between us became suffocating.

"I don't like not knowing what to call you," I whispered.

"When you've earned it, I'll tell you," he whispered back.

"I can't ask you how I do that."

"I think you just did."

I tensed, waiting for him to get irritated by my question. His thumb ran over mine again. Here in the dark, in bed with him and holding his hand, I wasn't so terrified of him. I wanted to know the man who'd waited three years to have me.

"If you'd been listening, you'd know how already," he said.

"Behave myself, do what you say and please you."

"You're welcome to please me, but it's not a requirement."

The way he said please sounded dirty. I felt my face heat up. Did he think I meant please him sexually? He told me he didn't expect that from me. *Unless you want it,* my brain helpfully reminded me. Did I want that? What was I even thinking? I shouldn't want to have sex with him.

What about Harrison?

What about him? We were over. Nameless had seen to that. And honestly, I didn't know how I would ever sustain a relationship with him when I was here with another man. One I apparently belonged to.

I found myself shifting closer to the middle of the bed, pulled by some invisible force between us. I looked over at him as he rolled onto his side.

"What are you doing?" he asked.

"I don't know."

And I really didn't. I needed something. The ache in my chest needed soothing. Could Nameless give me that if I let him? I wondered where on earth my common sense had fled to. Should I even be contemplating allowing him in at all?

So I did what anyone else would never do in this situation. I shifted closer and lay on my side, facing him with our bodies only inches apart. Our joined hands were trapped between us. I could just about make out his features. He let out a breath.

Why the hell had I moved so close to him? Was I certifiable?

"What do you want, Liora?"

Was I going to be honest?

"I'm confused. My chest hurts. I don't know how to process, handle or cope with this situation. And I really don't know why I'm telling you this or why I came closer."

He reached up, brushing my hair from my face and tucking it behind my cheek. His fingers lingered. The pads leaving fire in their wake. I turned my face into his touch without thinking. Nameless came closer, his breath dusting across my mouth.

"Do you want me to take your pain away?"

His lips brushed across mine as he spoke, sending jolts up and down my spine.

"Why would you do that?"

"Your welfare is my responsibility. And if I'm going to be entirely honest, I don't think I can stop myself kissing you right now."

Any thoughts I had about him doing that were stolen by his mouth on mine. It was the softest of touches, but my lips burnt. He cupped my face, holding me still. I found myself responding, kissing him back.

A low groan escaped his mouth. He pressed it more firmly against mine. My free hand curled around his hip. A part of me knew this was incredibly fucked up. Especially since only hours ago I'd been Harrison's girlfriend. The rest ignored it because the larger part of me wanted to kiss Nameless in that moment. Whatever reasoning I had for that I didn't like to think.

He pulled away, his breathing a little faster. Letting go of my hand between us, he readjusted and tugged me into his embrace. Having his body flush with mine stirred more of my senses.

Just as he leant towards me to kiss me again, I jolted awake. The sunlight streamed in through the gap in the curtain. I felt groggy and disoriented.

What was that? A dream?

I turned towards Nameless. He was staring up at the ceiling. No. Last night wasn't a dream, but was the kissing?

"Did you kiss me last night?" I blurted out without really thinking.

He turned to me, his eyes wide and confusion apparent on his face.

"What?"

His reaction told me everything I needed to know. I'd dreamt that part. My face burnt.

"Nothing, it doesn't matter."

"I think I'd remember if I kissed you, Liora."

He frowned momentarily, then his eyebrows shot up. He pointed at me.

"You had a sex dream about me."

Excuse me?

"I didn't have sex with you in it."

He smirked.

"But you did dream about me kissing you… And judging by your expression, I think you enjoyed it."

I put my hands over my face and buried it in the covers. This could not be happening. Why did I dream about him kissing me?

I loved Harrison, didn't I?

Didn't I?

Christ, what is wrong with me?

My relationship with him was over. Nameless had decided that for me.

"What did happen?" I mumbled.

"Last night? You cried yourself to sleep. I didn't touch you."

31

So I'd imagined our conversation too. Could this get any worse?

"But now I'm quite jealous of dream me."

I peeked out at him.

"Why?"

"He got to kiss you."

I scowled and huffed.

"Be jealous all you want, dream you is the only one who's ever going to have that pleasure."

I scrambled out of the covers and hopped off the bed. I needed to get away from him. My body felt hot and bothered by that dream and having him right there was not helping matters either. I felt his eyes on me as I walked around the bed and across to the bathroom.

I'd been in here last night, but it hit me again. He really did have the most amazing en-suite. A huge Victorian style bath sat by the window looking out over the conservatory and the small garden. The shower could probably fit four people inside. Tiled in dark blue, it fit its owner well.

I felt something rest on top of my head and two hands banded around my waist. He was leaning his chin on me.

What the…?

"Gawping?" he asked.

I tried to shift away, but his hands kept me pinned to him. I felt his chest almost flush with my back.

"Which part do you like best?"

Was he talking about the bathroom? I pointed at the bath. His hands around me tightened.

"It fits two."

My face burnt again. Was this going to be a regular thing? Him making suggestive statements and me blushing over the implications. And why on earth did thinking about bathing with him cause such a flurry of activity in my stomach?

Mind out of the gutter, Liora.

"I don't remember asking about that."

His thumbs traced circles around my sides. His proximity made me very aware my dream was based in reality. My skin felt far too hot where he was touching it through my clothes.

"No, but it is important. Would you like to put it to the test?"

"And have a bath with you? I think not."

"Neither of us has to be naked to do so."

I swear my face couldn't burn any hotter. My tongue stuck to the roof of my mouth. He leant down, his breath hot against my ear.

"It would allow us to get to know each other better, don't you think?"

I trembled. Not only was I stupidly tempted by what he'd suggested because I wanted to learn things about him, but my insides were molten.

"I'll take your silence as acquiescence."

"I… I…"

His chuckle reverberated around my skull. He released me before stepping around me and walking towards the bath. He flipped the taps on and poured in bubble bath.

Christ, what did I just agree to without really agreeing to it?

He stepped by me again, going back into the bedroom. A minute later, he handed me a dark blue t-shirt. I stared down at it.

"I'll leave you to put that on. Make sure the bath doesn't overflow."

He pressed me further in the room and shut the door. I lifted the t-shirt to my face and inhaled. It smelt like him. I'd noticed the faint scent of the detergent used on his clothes yesterday when he'd been up against me mixed in with his cologne. Citrus and sandalwood. Why the fuck was I smelling his t-shirt?

Shaking myself, I stripped out of my sleep shirt and shorts, keeping my underwear on. No way was I letting him near me without them. Didn't need him getting any ideas. He said he wouldn't touch me intimately unless I wanted it, but I didn't trust Nameless.

I pulled his t-shirt on. It swamped me. I eyed the bath, but it wasn't full enough yet. I pulled the door open. He was fiddling with his phone outside it. Looking up, he grinned at me.

"That suits you."

I rolled my eyes and walked further into the bathroom. I flipped off the taps and waited for him. I should object to what was about to happen, but the threat of him punishing me loomed. He shut the door behind him.

"If you can get through this without disobeying me, I'll answer one question honestly. Think carefully, Liora. Don't waste the opportunity."

I didn't need to think about it. The thing I wanted more than anything else was his first name. I needed an identifier that wasn't Nameless.

He stepped in the bath and put his hand out to me. It didn't escape my notice he hadn't taken his t-shirt off, but he was now only in boxers. I let him help me in the bath. He made me face away from him before pulling me down. The water soaked our clothes in an instant.

Seated in between his legs, my back to his front and his arms wrapped around me, I felt tense. He was right about the bath comfortably fitting both of us. It was long enough that he could stretch his legs out whilst sitting up.

"Relax, I'm not going to bite," he said in my ear.

I tried to. I'd never had a shower let alone a bath with someone else before. We were both clothed, but this felt very intimate.

"I haven't done this before," I admitted.

He drew lazy circles with his fingers around my stomach.

"No? Mmm." His nose nuzzled against my ear. "I wonder what else you haven't done. Perhaps you'll allow me to expand your horizons further."

I shivered despite the heat of the bath. His voice sounded more like a purr. Seductive. His hands ran lower, grazing over the tops of my thighs just below where his t-shirt ended. I tried not to flinch.

Just let him touch you. He won't do anything more.

I wished I could believe that. I wanted his name. The need to know it outweighed any objections I might have.

"What made you choose zoology?" he asked.

That was an easy question.

"The first time I remember my dad taking me to Edinburgh Zoo, I was enamoured by the big cats, penguins and meerkats. I told them I wanted to be a zookeeper when I grew up and it's been that way ever since. We've always had cats. Their current one is called Theodora. She's this huge white Persian with a squished face. She barely fits through the cat door. I keep telling them to put her on a diet."

My heart felt tight thinking about my mum and dad.

"We didn't have pets when I was growing up. Perhaps it's time to remedy that."

I looked up at him. Was that for my benefit?

"I can see the question you want to ask written all over your face."

I shrugged. I wasn't going to ask it outright. I needed to earn an answer from him.

"I told you already. Good behaviour will be rewarded. If we don't get to know each other, how will I know what to give you?"

He had a point. It was thoughtful of him to want to give me things I would appreciate. That little titbit of information intrigued me. Who'd have thought Nameless would be considerate.

"Getting to know you is kind of hard if I'm not allowed to ask you anything."

He chuckled.

"Shall I tell you something about me then?"

I nodded, wondering what he'd reveal.

"I have three younger siblings. Jennifer and Fiona are twins and James is the baby. Yes, you will meet them one day and no, they won't know the truth about how you came to be with me."

What would he tell them then?

Siblings.

That reminded me of my own.

Declan.

I didn't miss him at all. As far as I was concerned, he could get fucked.

"I don't get on with mine."

"Me either."

I hadn't expected that. Why did Nameless have issues with his brother and sisters? Another question I knew he wouldn't answer.

The longer we stayed in this bath together, the more I relaxed into his hold. He'd moved one hand back on my stomach. The other was entwined around one of mine. I wasn't sure when it happened, but I didn't mind it.

Maybe I could do this. Be his... pet. I didn't like that word, but what else could I call myself? It depended on how far he'd take this and what else he expected from me.

Knowing sex was off the cards made it easier to ignore what was sticking into my lower back. I was careful not to shift around too much. He clearly wasn't embarrassed about it in the slightest. I suppose I should be flattered he found me attractive.

I tried not to think about how handsome he was. Definitely older than me, but I was sure he'd not reached thirty yet. He still had a sort of boyish charm about his face. His eyes were the colour of the clear Caribbean ocean. My dad took us on regular holidays to Antigua, Barbuda and Jamaica. He'd always come home with sunburn, whilst Mum and I would get a soft, natural tan.

And his short dark locks? My fingers itched to touch them. An urge I needed to keep a lid on. I wasn't going to let him know I wasn't immune to him. Nameless was so different to

Harrison and Max, the boy I'd dated throughout high school. Different in a good and a bad way.

"I'll let you in on a secret, Liora," he whispered in my ear. "I've often thought about what it'd be like when I finally had you with me."

I wanted to ask if I lived up to his expectations. If I was everything he wanted. What kind of man waited three years to have a girl he was going to keep as a pet?

"You're beautiful, but that's not why I wanted you. I watched how you looked at each person in that room. How you assessed us. So much intelligence behind your eyes."

His fingers danced across my stomach. I squirmed. Mostly because of how close his fingers were to somewhere he said he wouldn't touch me. And them being there made my heart thump and my core throb in anticipation.

Christ, what is he doing to me?

"I want to know what goes on in your head. I want that more than anything else you could give me. Although, I won't deny my interest in your other… assets."

His fingers ran up my stomach and brushed the underside of my right breast. I shuddered involuntarily. So he does want to sleep with me. Why wasn't that as abhorrent as it should be?

Be honest, Liora, you don't find it abhorrent at all. You wanted him to kiss you in your dream.

I told my brain to shut up. That bloody dream.

"So, if you ever want to make your little dream last night a reality…"

Did he just read my mind?

I squirmed again. The truth? I was curious if reality matched up to my dream. He didn't need to know that.

"Not happening."

His breath tickled my ear.

"You say that, but I can read your body. Don't think it hasn't escaped my notice that your nipples are hard."

I looked down at my chest.

Fuck, he's right.

Even though they were mostly submerged in hot water, they strained against his t-shirt. I almost crossed my arms over my chest, but that would be admitting far too much.

"And I wonder what's going on between your legs. I can only imagine how wet you are."

I almost bolted out of the bath and his arms. The only thing keeping me there, the desperate need to know his name.

He'd hit the nail on the head with that statement. I could feel it despite the water. His words, his fingers and his hard cock pressed into my back had done a number on me.

I shouldn't feel this way about him, yet I did. I felt it the day we met when his gaze burnt my skin. And I felt it stronger now.

Was this why I'd always been reluctant to let myself go completely with Harrison? Was it because I'd been waiting for Nameless just as he'd been waiting for me?

"Too bad you'll never know."

He laughed, his chest rumbling against my back.

"Mmm, I think you've earnt your question."

Had I? Did he mean it?

I sat up and turned to him. He looked entirely serious. His blue eyes twinkled. The only way I'd know is if I asked.

"What's your name?"

He smiled very slowly, cocking his head to one side as if he was trying to work out why, of all things, I needed that answering.

"Dante."

I sounded it out in my head. It fit him. Nameless had a name. And that name banded itself around my heart.

"Dante," I repeated aloud.

He closed his eyes momentarily as if his name on my lips was something to savour.

"Your accent…"

He opened his eyes. They shone with mischief.

"Say it again."

I stared at him. Why would he want that after keeping it from me?

"Dante."

He reached out, tucking his hand behind my neck and pulling me closer until our breath mingled.

"Say it just like that every day for the rest of our lives and you'll make me a very happy man."

It wasn't so much that his mouth was inches from mine which made my pulse spike. It was the fact he'd said the rest of our lives.

Dante was planning to keep me indefinitely.

And that both terrified and excited me at the same time.

What the fuck had my father gotten me into?

Chapter Four

DANTE

I watched her from across the table. She nursed her cup of tea between two hands, staring out the conservatory window. Dressed in a pale green blouse and jeans, she looked beautiful. That girl could light up any room she was in.

And the way she says your name.

I had to lock that thought down. Earlier in the bath, that really fucked me up. I hadn't expected her to ask for my name. I gave my word I'd answer a question from her honestly. I'd grown up being told your word was law. When she asked for it, I had no choice. And now I wanted to hear it from her lips again.

Whilst most people pronounced it Dan-tae, she said it more like Don-tae. Her accent already had me under a spell, but this was worse. I found myself drawn to her in ways I couldn't explain.

What the hell would he think if he knew how I really felt about my gift?

He'd make you hand her over to him instead.

I couldn't allow that to happen. Liora was mine. I'd have to teach her how to behave around him. How to make him believe she was obedient and answered only to me. And I had to do it soon because he'd be expecting me to bring her to see him.

I wanted her to want me. I wasn't like him. Forcing her wasn't in my DNA. When we were alone, I could treat her the way I wanted. With him, there were rules. The longer I waited to tell her, the harder it would be for both of us. Still, she'd only come to me yesterday. I could give her a little time to adjust.

I was so fucking happy she was finally here. The girl who'd haunted my dreams and invaded my waking thoughts for the past three years. If only it was under different circumstances.

She turned to me, forest green eyes wary. I could hardly blame her for being suspicious of my intentions. She should be. I hadn't done anything untoward in the bath, but I'd wanted to. Having her so close to me, touching her through my t-shirt, the temptation had been there. She knew I desired her, hiding it would've been pointless when my cock had been pressed into her back.

She needed time to come around to me after I'd ended things for her with that boy. Her dreaming of me was unexpected. Deep down, did she want me to kiss her? I'd have to continue to seduce her if I was going to find out.

"I like your house," she said. "What I've seen of it. Especially this room."

The conservatory was one of my favourite parts too. It'd been a bitch to get planning permission, but ultimately worth it. Money was no object when you were the son of a designer and fashion mogul. Liora didn't know who we were because my father refused the media photos of him. I stayed away from public life, unlike my brother and sisters. Privacy was important to me. She'd find out who we really were soon enough.

"You can see more if you wish. Brent lives in the basement, but the rest is all mine."

I had bought the house nine years ago when I was only eighteen. I'd done it to keep James and the twins away from him. It didn't stop him coming after us. And now we pretended we were happy families. What went on when we were kids wasn't spoken about. He had other outlets for his temper now.

James, Jen and Fi didn't know the whole truth. Instead, the twins doted on the monster and James hated me. Karma was a fucking bitch. Protecting them cost me everything.

Everything except her.

"I'd like that."

Her tentative smile caused a myriad of emotions, but I ignored every single one of them.

"Finish that and you can have a tour."

Would it always be this easy with her? I was sure she'd fight me more than she had. Was she biding her time? Or was the mere threat of me hurting her for any indiscretion enough to stay her hand?

Fuck. I wanted her to fight me. Should I really be thinking about how I could provoke her? My touching her in the bath hadn't done anything, but then I'd seen the determination in her face when I said I'd reward her with an answer. Was she really so eager to learn my name that she'd let me get away with anything? What would happen when she had no incentive to behave?

A plan formed in my mind. How far could I take it before she snapped? And when she did snap at me, I was going to enjoy teaching her a lesson. I wasn't above manipulating her to get what I wanted. I'd do it in a heartbeat.

She set her cup down and stood. I grinned. She had no idea what she was walking into. I rose, came around the table and took her hand. She looked down at our entwined fingers but said nothing.

I walked her back through into the kitchen. I let her look around properly. The staff were only here to clean and cook for me five days a week, mostly. There were times when I sent everyone away except Brent. He was my bodyguard and I supposed a friend. He knew the truth of my relationship with my family and how I'd acquired Liora.

The kitchen had dark granite countertops and stainless steel cupboards. All the appliances were built in. It wasn't that I couldn't cook or that I didn't have time. Laziness played a part in it, but mostly I just didn't enjoy having the house to myself.

Now she was here, things would be different. My pet. Except she was more than that to me. So much more. I wanted her to be my companion, my friend, my lover and ultimately, if she came around to the idea, I wanted her to stand beside me as my equal. But those things couldn't happen whilst he was around.

She looked back at me when she'd finished inspecting the appliances. Her eyes told me she wanted to ask something.

"If you have a question about this room, then ask it."

"I like baking. I was wondering if it'd be okay for me to do so. I know I have to earn things, but you said you wanted to know how to reward me if I'm good."

She liked to bake. Her father hadn't told me that.

"The staff aren't here at the weekends."

"Is that a yes?"

Her eyes shone with anticipation and excitement. How on earth could I say no?

"Two conditions. One, I can revoke the privilege at any time and two, I get to sample the goods."

She nodded, smiling.

"Well, I can't eat it all myself."

Fuck. She was adorable. I put my hand out to her. She came willingly, her eyes shining as she took my hand and looked up at me. I could not allow myself to get sucked into her happiness no matter how infectious it was.

The only other room on this floor was the formal dining room at the front of the house, which never got used. I took her up to the first floor and showed her the living room. A huge TV dominated one of the walls, which were painted eggshell blue. My incredibly comfortable sofa faced it and two others faced each other. A couple of armchairs sat by the fireplace.

She let go of my hand, moving over to the sofa and running her fingers over the dark grey fabric. I hadn't forgotten my urge to provoke a reaction.

I came up behind her and pressed her into the back of the sofa, my hands splayed out over her stomach. She stiffened. I dropped my face into her neck, inhaling the scent of lavender and heather that seemed to follow her around.

"I thought this was a tour," she said.

"You're having a tour of your new home and I'm having a tour of you."

My hand moved higher, brushing the underside of her breast. I pressed harder into her back, making it impossible for her to escape me. I skimmed around her breast until my hand found its way around her neck. That made her tremble in my grasp. And fuck, did I want to bend her over, tear down her jeans and sink my cock into her.

"Dante…" she whispered.

"Are you scared?"

"You have your hand around my neck, am I not supposed to be?"

I chuckled. She'd just slipped up and asked a question. My fingers tightened.

"You know questions aren't permitted."

"I don't like your rules."

She wasn't meant to. She was just supposed to obey without question.

"And you think that will change anything?"

"No."

She struggled against me, clearly unnerved by what I was doing. I said nothing, merely held her in place.

"Please, let me go."

"Did I not say you can't make demands of me?"

She struggled harder. I was a fucking bastard, but I didn't care. I wanted her to fight me so I could punish her. The need pulsated in my veins, overriding my desire to fuck her.

"Get off. I don't like this."

"You don't have to like it."

She brought her arm up and elbowed me in the ribs. I grunted but didn't let go.

"That wasn't very nice," I growled in her ear.

She tried again, but I was wise to it. I dragged her away from the sofa and flipped her around to face me. Her eyes were dark with anger.

"What is your problem?" she spat. "I get that you think I'm your fucking pet, but this is not cool. I've done everything you asked me to this morning without complaint. Why the hell are you suddenly being an arsehole to me? What did I do to deserve that?"

She shoved me back and stormed away. I stifled a smile. She hadn't done anything other than be the victim to the urges I kept hidden from the outside world. I paced away towards the armchairs and sat in one of them.

"Come here, Liora."

She turned to me, her eyes still blazing with fury and confusion.

"Why the hell should I?"

I cocked an eyebrow.

"Do you think you should be speaking to me like that?"

Her mouth opened and closed. Then her shoulders slumped. She knew she'd walked right into my trap and there was nothing she could do to stop any of it. I saw it written all over her face.

"You're a prick," she muttered.

I chose to ignore that comment and waited. She put one foot in front of the other, her eyes downcast as she came over to me. I pointed at her crotch.

"Take your jeans off."

Her eyes went wide.

"What?"

"Take them off."

"But you said…"

I looked up at her.

"I'm not going to fuck you. I told you I won't touch you like that unless you ask for it."

She hesitated before her hand went to the button. She undid it, unzipping the fly and tugging them down her legs. Her eyes met mine and she wanted to know what happened next.

"I want you to bend over my knees."

She frowned. Shuffling closer, she did as I asked. I shifted her so she was in the right position. Her head dangled down, her hands planted on the floor.

"I expect you to take this without complaint. I won't lie, it will hurt."

I placed one hand on her lower back, keeping her in place whilst I tugged down her underwear, exposing her luscious behind. My cock was rock hard in anticipation. I'd have to deal with it afterwards. Right now, it was about punishing her.

The first strike made my palm sting. She cried out, tensing. Her right cheek blossomed red. The sight of it made me harder. The second strike was just as hard as the first.

Fuck. This was incredibly satisfying. I shouldn't want to hurt her. Inflicting this sort of pain on another person shouldn't make me hard. I knew it wasn't normal. Growing up the way I did, I was never going to turn out right.

Four more strikes left my hand throbbing. She gasped, a sob escaping her throat, but didn't tell me to stop. I wasn't holding back. This is how I would punish her in the future after I revoked her privileges. I drew a line in the sand. Now she'd understand I was serious about obedience.

The next slap across her cheeks, made her cry out again. She gripped my calf in one hand, fingers digging in. Three more and I'd stop. I ran my hand over her behind and she flinched. It really was a fucking beautiful sight. I slapped her again. Her skin was so red, raw and everything I needed at that moment.

I wanted to draw it out longer, but I knew she was suffering even if she refused to tell me. So I struck her again, twice in quick succession.

My breathing was laboured and my cock pulsated and strained against my jeans. Shit. Now her punishment was over, I desperately wanted to fuck her. Seeing the result of my handiwork made my need worse.

I stroked her skin, my other hand leaving her back. She whimpered, flinching again. I released her, leaning back in the armchair.

"You can get up now."

She stayed where she was, gasping for air. I wasn't going to hurry her along even though I needed to be away from her before I broke my word and fucked her anyway.

"You... You..." she whispered.

She shifted, whimpering again as she raised her head to me. Her face was wet with tears.

"That hurt."

"It was meant to."

She shifted off me, wincing as she stood. Staring down at me, her eyes went wide and she blushed. I couldn't exactly hide what was happening between my legs. Liora needed to know who I was. This was as good a place to start as any.

She didn't say anything, tugging her underwear back up and hissing as it touched her tender skin. I reached down and picked up her jeans before standing. There wasn't much point her putting those back on.

I took her hand and started tugging her towards the door.

"Slow down, it really hurts."

"I know it does and if you want me to take some of the pain away, I suggest you come along quietly."

She whimpered the whole way up the stairs to the second floor. I took her into my bedroom, dumping her jeans on the bed. I left her there whilst I went into the bathroom and plucked the arnica cream from the cabinet. I'd become well acquainted with using this on myself. It would help her.

She was shifting on her feet when I walked back out. I sat on the bed and beckoned her over. I spun her to face away from me and tugged her underwear down again.

"What are you doing?"

"Do I have to tell you again not to question me?"

"No, I just…"

"Let me make it better than you can have a go at me about it if you wish."

She twisted to look at me, her forest green eyes full of confusion. I shook my head, opening the cap and pressing some cream out onto my palm. I tugged her closer, keeping my other hand on her waist to hold her still. I gently rubbed the cream into her tender skin.

When I was done, I pulled her underwear back up and released her. She turned to me, her expression not exactly full of hatred for me, but she didn't look happy either.

"You want to ask me what that was about, don't you?"

She nodded.

"Go ahead. You have my permission to say what you want for the next ten minutes and there won't be any consequences. I think you've learnt your lesson today."

She fidgeted for a moment, eying me warily.

"You deliberately provoked me so you had a reason to do that, didn't you?"

I knew she'd worked it out and I wanted her to. Her intelligence was part of what made her so damn attractive.

"Yes."

"Why?"

"Because I wanted to."

"That's not an answer."

I leant back against my hands.

"I think you know why I wanted to."

She shook her head, turning away.

"I don't understand you at all."

"Do you want to?"

Pacing away, she wrung her hands. I couldn't see her face and it bugged me. What was she thinking?

"Yes, I do. I want to know who you are behind that mask you like wearing."

My heart stuttered in my chest. Intelligent and far too discerning for her own good. I wanted her to see me even if it would destroy everything in the process.

"Come here."

She turned around and looked me in the eye, determination on her face.

"Not until you tell me why you liked hurting me, and don't try lying to me, Dante. If you want me to trust you, then be honest and don't bullshit me."

Why did she say my name? That made it completely impossible for me to think straight. She wanted honesty. Could I really do honesty if it meant she trusted me?

There were already so many secrets between us as it was, but I needed her trust if this was ever going to work. If we were ever going to survive him without it blowing up spectacularly in our faces.

"You want to know why it turned me on when I spanked you?"

"Yes."

"There isn't just one reason. What excites me isn't normal. Causing you pain gives me pleasure. You whimpered and held onto me but didn't object. I like seeing the way your skin turned red under my palm. I like the control. I even enjoy the sting of it on my own hand."

She took several steps toward me. Reaching out, she took my hand, turning it over to expose my palm. It was still a little red.

"Have you always been like this?"

"No."

'I wasn't going to tell her what triggered it. I didn't talk about those things to anyone.

"You wanted me to come over here."

I stood up and looked down at her. Her face was still tear streaked. I reached up, wiping them away.

"Why are you so calm about this?"

She stared at me for a long moment.

"I wanted to be annoyed with you. I wanted to shout at you for hurting me, but that wouldn't really get me anywhere or help me understand what this is."

"This?"

"This thing between you and me. You see, I don't think you want a pet. You want much more than that from me."

I smiled, cupping her face.

"What makes you say that?"

"I don't think you're really the type of person who wants a girl to obey you completely. I might have only been with you less than twenty four hours, but that much is clear to me."

When I said to myself last night that I was completely and utterly fucked, it'd been before she said that. Now I knew Liora was going to be far more trouble than I ever imagined. Fucked didn't quite cut it. Well and truly screwed beyond belief? That didn't either.

There were no words for how much she would mess with my life and drive me crazy.

"What type of man do you think I am in that case?"

"You want to provoke me so you can punish me over and over again. You need that. Tell me I'm wrong."

"You said you wanted honesty, so I won't lie to you. Your time is up, but I will give you this parting gift."

I ran my thumb over her bottom lip which trembled.

"I will provoke you and punish you. I will push you way past your limits. And I will enjoy it. But there's one thing I don't think you realise, Liora. Do you want to know what that is?"

She nodded slowly.

"You're going to enjoy it too."

Chapter Five

LIORA

I lay on top of the covers on my stomach in just a long sleep shirt. I couldn't stand to have anything else against my skin. I really, really wanted to hate him for doing it, but I couldn't. In those moments I'd learnt far more about Dante then I had in the past twenty four hours. And I wanted to know more.

I'd clearly lost the plot. Why would anyone be intrigued by a man who got off on inflicting pain?

There was far more to Dante than just that. Somehow, I found myself drawn to him instead of repulsed. Shouldn't I want to run away from someone who'd physically hurt me?

He might have hurt you, but he soothed you afterwards. He made it better.

I buried my face in the pillow. Why the hell were my feelings towards him so damn complicated? It should be simple. I should want to get as far away from him as possible.

Instead, I wanted to be closer. The war going on in my head drove me crazy.

I wondered where he was. It was getting late. Why did I care where he was?

Christ, get a fucking grip, Liora.

I hadn't been able to sit down all day, which made everything difficult. His mood had lightened considerably after that incident in the living room. Almost as if it had made him feel better.

What the hell happened to him to cause his need for inflicting pain? Was he going to do it to me again? I shuddered. The answer to that question was very much a yes. He'd told me as much.

The door to the bedroom opened. I didn't look up, but I heard him moving about and felt it when he settled down on the bed. Silence ticked by for several moments. He knew I was awake because I hadn't turned the lights out.

"You know, he's been blowing up your phone all day."

Harrison? Why had I forgotten about him?

Well, obviously because Dante decided you two should have a bath then he spanked you. Those were far more pressing matters than your ex-boyfriend.

My brain could really go and do one right now. I sighed. I supposed I had to deal with the mess Dante had caused. I owed Harrison that much.

"I should probably speak to him."

He tossed me my phone, which landed by my head. I sat up on my elbows. I checked some of the messages he'd sent.

HARRISON: Please talk to me.

HARRISON: I just want to understand. Everything was fine between us.

HARRISON: Please, Liora. Don't shut me out.

HARRISON: Who is that person in the photo? Tell me the truth.

HARRISON: Are you really seeing another guy?

I couldn't read any further messages. I had to fix this somehow and it had to match up with what I'd already said. Or should I say what Dante had told him.

"I'm going to send him a voice note."

Dante looked over at me with a raised eyebrow. I noticed he was only in a t-shirt and boxers. His long legs spread out on the covers as he sat up against the headboard. I swallowed.

The fact he was so attractive?

A big fucking problem.

Even though I was still in pain, the sight of him forced me to confront something I didn't want to admit. I, on some level, desired him. My body responded to his proximity as if it knew I belonged to him.

You know what my body could do?

Get fucked.

"I won't contradict what you told him."

He waved a hand at me as if to say fine, whatever. I pressed down on the button, flipping it up so it would keep recording without me having to hold my thumb down on the screen.

"Listen, H, I'm sorry. I never meant to hurt you, but it's the truth. You need to believe me. Thank you for being an amazing person to me even though I'm not worthy of it. I need you to stop texting me because you're not going to get any more answers. Don't go around my flat because I'm not there anymore. I've left Edinburgh and I won't be coming back."

I sent the voice message. I spied Dante rolling his eyes from the corner of mine. I wanted to provoke him just as he had done to me earlier.

"Did you want me to tell him that he never satisfied me in the bedroom and how much you give me pleasure instead?"

He turned to me with a smirk on his face.

"Well that's not exactly the truth now, is it? You haven't said yes yet."

I almost breathed a sigh of relief when he didn't bring up the fact that I'd asked him a question and how that wasn't allowed.

"I already told you this morning that's never going to happen."

His eyes trailed down to my mouth. My phone vibrated. I looked down at it.

HARRISON: You're not the person I thought you were. Have you lied to me for two years?

ME: No. I've always cared about you, but you have to accept what I'm telling you. Goodbye H.

I locked the screen and shoved it away from me. When I looked up, Dante's face was right next to mine. I was so startled, I froze in place.

"I don't think you know what you really want when it comes to me," he said, his voice low.

I didn't like how he read me so well. I shrugged.

"If you say so."

"I want to play a game."

My eyes found their way to his mouth. The one I'd dreamt about kissing. The one I wanted on me if I was to admit the truth to myself.

"A game."

"Truth or dare, Liora."

I raised an eyebrow. Was he serious?

"If I agree to play it with you, I get to ask questions."

He grinned.

"Of course, that's if I pick truth."

Why was he still so close to me? My skin prickled. I had a feeling I knew exactly why he wanted to play this with me, which meant I couldn't under any circumstances pick dare.

This was ridiculous. Playing such a childish game when we were full grown adults.

Dante wanted to play so we'd play.

"Truth."

"Why did I kiss you in your dream?"

I rolled my eyes, shifting back from him.

"You asked me if I wanted you to take my pain away and when I asked why you'd do that, you told me my welfare is your responsibility, after which you admitted you couldn't stop yourself kissing me."

His eyes flickered with amusement. I wondered if it was because it was something he would say or if my subconscious had just made shit up.

"Truth."

What should I ask him? There were too many things. I could ask him about his father and mine, but something told me that subject was off-limits.

"How much do you want me to say yes to you?"

He arched his perfect eyebrow. He knew the meaning behind my words.

"How much? I'm not sure that's quantifiable. Don't forget I've already waited three years for you. I can wait some more."

I swallowed. His expression told me he knew I'd give in.

We'll fucking well see about that.

"Truth."

He watched me for a moment before he asked the next question.

"Are you attracted to me?"

My face felt hot in an instant. Damn him. Why did I agree to this idiotic game? That was something I didn't want him to know.

"Yes," I mumbled, looking away.

When he said nothing for a long moment, I peered at him from the corner of my eye. His expression was deadly. Like I'd revealed something he could use against me and was planning to.

You stupid fucking idiot.

Hadn't I realised by now he was never going to play fair with me?

"Dare."

And now I had literally no idea what to say. Dare him? To do what exactly? Then an idea formed in my head.

"Okay, I dare you to go a whole day and night without laying a hand on me. That means you can't touch me at all."

That made him scowl. If he wasn't going to play fair, neither was I.

"And if you don't, then you have to go an entire week as a forfeit."

His scowl deepened. I smiled at him. He'd wanted to play and he didn't tell me there were any rules about what I could and could not ask of him.

"Fine, but that only starts tomorrow morning."

I nodded, my grin growing wider. I wasn't sure if Dante could manage that considering how much he insisted on touching me and we'd only been around each other for a day and a half.

I was about to say truth again when he put his hand up.

"This is going to get very boring if you keep sticking with truth."

"I don't trust you. I know what you'll dare me to do."

His scowl turned to a smirk.

"Really now? Why don't you live a little and find out if you're right?"

Christ, he doesn't half make things difficult.

If I chickened out, he'd win. Would it be so bad?

"Dare."

"So she does take the occasional risk."

"Just get on with it."

"I dare you… to touch me."

Wait, what? I thought he'd dare me to kiss him.

"Where specifically?"

His eyes sparkled. He pointed to his face.

"Here."

Next to his stomach.

"Here."

And finally, he pointed to his crotch.

"Or here."

Why the hell wasn't I surprised that was one of the options?

"Keep in mind, it has to be with your mouth."

And there was the fucking kicker. Fine. He didn't specify where on his face I had to kiss him.

"Come here then," I said.

I was too sore to move over to him. That happened to be entirely his fault. He did as I asked, coming closer until our faces were almost touching again.

"Where's it to be?"

"I think you know where I pick."

He grinned.

"Go on then."

I leant towards him, turning my head enough so I could kiss him on the cheek. Except Dante had other ideas. When I was less than an inch from his face, he turned towards me. My lips caught the edge of his. Electricity crackled across my mouth, sending jolts down my spine. I froze against him, entirely unable to move or breathe.

Everything screamed at me to shove him away. I couldn't. Hot waves of desire clashed inside me, searing through my body at an alarming pace and causing my core to throb restlessly.

It was at that moment I realised Dante wasn't breathing either. He was frozen like me. One of us had to move. To break the contact and whatever fucking sorcery this was between us.

Turns out, both of us had the same idea. I turned into his mouth just as he turned into mine. Lips clashed together and all thoughts of what was right or wrong flew from my head.

His kiss was entirely gentle at first as if working out what the fuck the two of us were doing. Should we even be kissing each other?

This wasn't like my dream. Dante made me feel things I'd never felt before from that simple touch. His mouth glued to mine caused fireworks in my chest and stomach. Wave after wave of hot, searing lust made me tremble and melt.

As if pulled by some force, I cupped his face, holding him closer. He growled, the low rumble in his chest battering me with waves of passion and possession. Right then, I was Dante's and I surrendered to it.

He cupped my face with both hands, deepening our kiss. Mouths melded together. He tasted my lips, sucking the bottom one between his. He tasted like honey and wine. And I wanted more.

Except this was entirely fucking wrong. I should not be kissing him let alone enjoying it.

My hand dropped from his face and I pushed at his chest instead. He released me. Both of us panted. His eyes were dark with desire, lust and confusion. I was sure mine reflected the same thing.

That kiss stripped me of everything I knew about myself. Disarmed me on every single level. I barely recognised myself. And judging by the look on his face, he wasn't prepared for it either.

"I don't want to play this game anymore," I whispered.

"Neither do I," he whispered in response.

That was about the most honest thing he'd ever said to me. I stared at his mouth. His lips had been so soft and he'd tasted so good. My brain told me to stop it, but my body had other ideas. My body wanted Dante so much, it decided to override the command. I winced as I shifted closer to him. His expression grew wary.

I reached out, running my fingertips over his mouth. His lips were wet from our kiss. I leant closer until only my fingers separated our mouths.

"Tell me why I'm considering moving my fingers."

His eyes met mine, so many emotions swirling in those blue depths.

"I don't know, Liora. Why did you kiss me back?"

A question I had no answer for. He'd engineered it so we'd kiss each other, but I doubted he'd known what would happen when we did. Wildfire still rampaged through my veins. My skin burnt, not just from his spanking earlier but because it wanted his hands on it. The pads of his fingertips brushing against places they shouldn't.

I needed to break the spell between us. I needed to stop wanting his mouth on mine again. I needed to stop wanting Dante. He was dangerous and unpredictable.

I pulled back and turned away from him onto my side. If I kept staring at him, I'd do something I might well end up regretting.

Dante terrified me. Not only because he was irritatingly cocky, arrogant and enjoyed winding me up, but he held some strange power over me. I had to keep my urge to be close to him at bay. Especially after that kiss. The kiss which set my entire world ablaze. And I really hadn't had enough. I wanted to taste him properly. Have his tongue wrapped around mine.

Stop. Stop. No. Enough.

I felt him shift away and then the lights went out. I wasn't going to get in the covers because the weight of them would hurt. I tried to focus on anything else but the man lying next to me, but I felt his heat seeping into my back. That heat got closer when he moved.

I felt his hand on my waist, his thumb running circles around my side. I didn't stiffen, if anything, I melted. I couldn't help it. His kiss had torn down my walls and left me vulnerable. I needed time to seal those feelings and urges away. He didn't press himself against me, but his face burrowed into my neck.

"Tell me the truth," he whispered. "Did that fuck you up just as much as it did me?"

Under the cover of darkness, I felt as though our secrets could be laid bare to each other. The dark could keep those safe. In the light of day, things would be different.

"Yes, it did."

His lips trailed along my neck and up my jaw.

"Will you let me stay here with you until morning? I'll stick to the terms of your dare come daylight."

I flipped over so I faced him. My arse smarted, but I ignored it. I took his hand and placed it back on my waist. I could just about make out his features.

"Yes."

"Come closer, Liora."

He shifted his other arm under me as I moved towards him. He tucked my head under his chin and pressed me against his chest. He was solid and warm. And heck, I didn't mind him holding me. His scent filled my nose. The fire in my veins didn't dim. It pulsed, restless and wanting.

"I want you to let me hold you like this at night. Whatever happens during the day doesn't matter. We draw a line through it. Can you do that?"

I curled a hand around his waist. I wasn't sure what this was or what was happening between us, but what he suggested didn't feel like he was trying to manipulate me. His voice was tentative. His tone full of stark honesty. This wasn't a demand. It was a request. One I could say no to and he would respect my wishes.

So I made up my mind. I drew the battle lines between us. "Yes. I can."

And then I put up my white flag and gave in.

Chapter Six

DANTE

Being around her was pure fucking torture. I had to leave her in the bedroom because every moment my fingers itched to be on her skin. And my lips wanted hers so much, it burnt.

I really shouldn't have kissed her. What had started as a game to get her to let me, turned into a nightmare. Not only had that damn kiss ruined me, not being able to touch her at all made me want to beat someone into a pulp.

I paced the living room, dragging my fingers through my hair. Everything backfired spectacularly in my face. Liora was far too fucking wise to my tricks.

"You look like shit."

I turned at the sound of his voice. Brent stood in the doorway, grinning at me like a fucking fool.

"Don't you fucking start."

He walked in and leant against one of the sofas.

"Has she been giving you trouble?"

"Yes and no."

His grin got wider. Brent knew too much about me. Right now, I didn't need his shit.

"You built her up far too much in your head. I'm not surprised she doesn't match up to your fantasy version of her."

No, she didn't. She was so much more than I ever imagined she would be. I loved and hated it at the same time.

"You don't know anything about her."

"And you only know what her father told you. Tell me, D, what else did you expect? That she'd just let you walk all over her? She might have come willingly, but there's fire behind her eyes. A smart girl like her shouldn't be around the likes of you."

I clenched my fists, gritting my teeth. If he was anyone else, I'd have kicked him out for that comment. He was not helping my mood in the slightest.

"You know very well what it cost me to have her so if you've not got anything productive to say I suggest you shut up and fuck off."

He shook his head.

"What's gotten into you?"

"Nothing."

I paced away. He wouldn't believe that for a second. Staring out the window at the road below, I took a deep breath. I needed to calm down. Get my head on straight before I had to face her again.

"You weren't this worked up yesterday. I distinctly remember you being cheerful."

"That was before."

He didn't know I punished her, but he knew something made me happy.

"D…"

"Mind your own fucking business."

I heard him sigh.

"If you're not going to talk to me then you should talk to her."

Was he insane? How could I when she was the sole reason for my current disposition.

"I kissed her."

"And?"

Did he not understand? How could he? I'd never experienced a kiss like that before. One that tore my insides apart and gutted me because I wanted her so much. She hadn't said yes yet, but she would. I was determined to make sure she let me fuck her.

"And it fucked me up, Brent. I can't be around her today. You have to look after her. I don't trust myself."

I stopped caring it was cowardly. If I saw her, I'd take her and she wouldn't forgive me. Not only was she still in pain, she didn't need me ruining everything completely. Brent was right. She shouldn't be around the likes of me, but she was mine and I wasn't letting her go.

"She won't like that."

"Too fucking bad. Her own fault for daring me not to touch her for a day."

"Dared you? Don't tell me you decided to play that with her."

"I know it was stupid now. Just go make sure she has lunch. I can't see her."

69

I turned to him. His amusement had faded.

"You really are suffering today."

I nodded.

"Okay. I get it. She can't see you like this."

He looked down at his hands.

"I didn't come in here to talk about her. I have a message."

I stiffened. There could be only one person that was from.

"The charity gala is in two weeks. He doesn't expect you to have tamed her completely, but she has to behave herself in public."

I died a little inside. Not only did I hate these events, I'd have to deal with him watching us all night.

"James and the twins will be there so you have to tell her who you really are before then."

He'd expect me to pass her off as my girlfriend to them and everyone else.

"Oh wonderful, just what I needed."

Brent shrugged.

"Just relaying the message."

And now my life just got a hundred times more complicated. She and I had to come to an understanding and soon.

What went on here was one thing, but in the outside world, she had a different role to play.

One I was pretty sure she'd hate.

I didn't go back and see her. I stayed away all day and night, sleeping in what used to be the twins' room, but was now the guest bedroom. She would tell me I hadn't played fair. If she knew what dark thoughts I had about her, she'd understand.

I opened the door silently. She was laying on her stomach on the bed, her head on the pillow. Seeing her made me hard instantly. I stalked towards the bed and crawled over her. Tugging up her t-shirt, I stared down at her bare behind. The redness had faded. I pushed it up further, exposing her lower back.

"You didn't come see me again yesterday." Her tone was accusatory.

"Does it still hurt?"

"A little. Don't change the subject."

I leant down and kissed the base of her spine. She stiffened. Shit, she felt so soft. My fingers ran circles around her skin.

"You never specified I had to be around you."

I kissed her skin again. She twitched and relaxed just a little.

"But you didn't even come to bed."

I raised my head. Had I upset her?

"Did you miss me?"

She looked back at me. Her expression told me she did, but her mouth remained shut.

"You did."

Her eyes narrowed.

"Don't presume to know how I feel."

I chuckled before resuming my progress up her spine with my lips. I'd missed her. The way she felt. Her skin on mine. I tried not to think about how she wasn't wearing any underwear and if I pressed her legs open, I could see her.

"I think we missed each other."

"Brent told me you were busy."

Busy sorting myself out so I could be around her again.

"I might live a life of luxury and idleness, but I still have responsibilities."

It struck me. She wasn't objecting to me kissing her back. Two days and she'd already become comfortable enough around me to accept I needed to touch her. Liora had this way about her that surprised and delighted me. Strong, fierce and so fucking smart.

"Well, I know money is no object considering you brought me here on a private plane."

"If you're good, I'll make sure you have everything you could ever want."

"What if I don't care about things and possessions? What if I want something real?"

I froze.

"What do you mean?"

"Money doesn't mean anything to me, Dante. All I want is to be able to do what I love, but you stand in the way of that."

I sat up on my knees, staring at her. I wanted to make her happy. It would make her amenable to me. There were just things she didn't understand.

I grabbed her waist and forced her onto her back. She cried out.

"Hey, it still hurts."

I pinned her hands down on the bed, leaning over her.

"Let me make something clear. You have a role to play. Outside this house, you will obey me in everything. You will not talk back to me or question my decisions."

Her eyes flashed with confusion.

"If you don't, he will take you from me and trust me when I tell you that you do not want that under any circumstances."

"Who will?"

"My father."

Her eyes went wide with fear. Even though she'd seen him once, she knew he was someone you didn't want to know or be anywhere near.

"He scares me more than you do."

"I scare you?"

"Sometimes. Like right now."

I eyed her for a moment. Her hands trembled beneath mine.

"You should be scared. I won't go easy on you if you choose to disobey me outside of this house."

"What about inside?"

I should tell her off for questioning me but getting my point across was far more important.

"That depends entirely on how much you let me do to you. I want you willing, Liora. I want you to want me. Don't think you can try and fake anything with me. I'll know."

She appraised me for several long moments.

"I never told you I wanted you to kiss me."

"You didn't have to."

The way she was staring at my mouth set me on edge. I wouldn't do it. I wouldn't give in.

"What do you really want from me, Dante? We've established I'm not really your pet."

I'd told her already. What more did she need me to say?

"Haven't you been listening?"

"I have but I don't get it. I don't get you."

My eyes roamed down the length of her. I took a breath when I realised her t-shirt had ridden up past her crotch. My head whipped back up to hers.

No. Fuck. No. Shit. No. I didn't see anything.

Except I had and I was in pure fucking hell. I released one of her hands and tugged her t-shirt down, all too aware of how much I ached with need.

"Don't look at me like that," she said. "I was covered before you came in here and pulled my t-shirt up."

"You should've said something."

"Should I have? You were too busy telling me I have to obey you yet again."

I tore away from her, getting off the bed and running a hand through my hair. My cock strained against my jeans. It hurt. It really fucking hurt.

"Get dressed. I can't have you half naked around me."

I heard her jump off the bed.

"If you hadn't decided to punish me then I wouldn't have been too sore to put clothes on."

I wanted to turn around, but she'd see exactly what I was struggling with if I did.

"Just get dressed."

"What's wrong, Dante? Can't control yourself around me?"

"Don't test me."

"If you can't have me half naked, what about fully?"

What the hell?

I spun around, about to tell her to cut it out, but she was standing there with nothing on. My mind went into overdrive. She looked like a fucking goddess. Her head held high, completely unashamed in her own skin. And hell, everything about her was perfect. Perky breasts, her nipples darkening and hardening under my gaze. My eyes roamed lower. She was a natural blonde.

Holy fucking hell.

"Christ, Liora, what are you playing at?"

I strode towards her, pulled the duvet off the bed and covered her up. The image of her naked seared into my brain.

She stared at me, her forest green eyes full of challenge. I couldn't fucking make head nor tail of why she'd done it.

"Do you want me to punish you again? If you keep this up, make no mistake, I will make sure you can't sit for a week."

"I don't care if you do."

She was determined to fucking provoke me. What was this? Her own brand of punishment because I left her alone all day yesterday or was it that I didn't give her the satisfaction of seeing how much it killed me not to touch her?

My fingers twitched. She hadn't taken the covers from me. I was done. I couldn't take the way she was looking at me. If she was going to insist on behaving like this, then so fucking be it.

I threw the covers back on the bed and pressed her down on it, my hands wrapped around both her wrists.

"You think this is funny? I'm not playing games with you today, Liora."

She stayed quiet, observing me without fear. I leant towards her.

"Do you want me to take you against your will? Do you?"

"No."

"Then tell me what the hell you're doing right now."

It was a long moment before she answered me.

"I don't know."

She looked away from me.

"I wanted you to come back yesterday," she whispered.

"Why?"

This girl was so unpredictable. I had no idea where the hell I stood with her. She looked up at me again.

"Because for some reason I still want to know you."

The frustration and anger died inside me. I rested my forehead against hers and released her wrists. She reached up and curled a hand around my jaw. And shit, having an ounce of affection from her felt so good.

"I wanted to get back at you for finding a loophole to my dare."

She sighed, her whole body going slack against mine.

"Are you going to punish me?"

I should. What she'd done was completely out of order.

"Yes."

"Okay."

I moved off her and sat up. Having her naked beneath me did nothing to help my need to have her. She slipped off the bed. Instead of running away from me and covering up, she nudged my legs apart and lay across my knees in an act of complete submission. My palm twitched.

"How many do you think you deserve?" I asked.

"Isn't that up to you to decide?"

"Give me a figure."

She gripped my calf.

"Twenty."

"And why is that?"

"Ten because I disobeyed you and a further ten for deliberately provoking you."

Her logic was sound enough. Twenty strikes. I was looking forward to each one. What I was not going to enjoy is the aftermath. The need to find a release. The only person I wanted that from was her. My hand would hurt too much for self-pleasure.

Suck it up and get on with it. Stop acting like a pussy.

"Count for me then."

Liora took each one. Whilst her voice began to falter when we reached fifteen and her fingers dug into my leg, she kept counting.

"Sixteen."

Slap.

"Seventeen."

She let out a strangled cry at the next one. I must've hit a sensitive spot. She took a rasping breath.

"Eight...teen."

Again, I struck her. The sting ran up my fingers. My hand throbbed.

"Nineteen."

Her arse was so red. I knew bruises would form this time.

Slap.

"Twenty."

I laid my hand on the bed, needing a break just as much as she did. Neither of us moved for a long moment. When she shifted off me onto her knees, her face was blotchy and tear streaked.

"Lie down on your front for me."

I put my other hand out and helped her up. She shuffled onto the bed, breathing heavily. I'd left the cream on the bedside table. I applied a generous amount to her raw skin. She whimpered even though I tried to be gentle.

I fetched a clean t-shirt of mine and helped her put it on. Having her clothed took away some of the immediate urge to pin her down and fuck her. It was still there, pulsating in my veins. Would she ever let me?

"Do you need me to do anything else for you?" I asked.

"No."

I sighed. She was lying. She wouldn't meet my eyes. She hadn't eaten today. I left her there whilst I stalked downstairs to the kitchen. After hassling the chef, I came away with a tray for her. I set it on the bed when I got back upstairs. She looked up then.

"You need to eat."

She moved up onto her knees. The pain she was in very apparent on her face. I slid the tray over to her. I watched her as she dug into fruit and yoghurt.

Sliding the tray back to me when she was done, she didn't move to lie down again. I picked it up and set it on my desk before returning to her. Her expression was full of caution and shyness radiated from her. It concerned me considering how unashamed she'd been to show her body off to me earlier. She had nothing to worry about on that score. I was well and truly hooked.

"I feel like there are too many sides to you and I get whiplash from how often you switch between them," she said quietly.

Perhaps she was right. I did wear many masks to survive different situations.

"What side do you want now?"

"I don't want a side. I want what's lurking underneath."

"So you admit you want me."

"I didn't say… Don't twist my words."

I moved closer, her knees pressed against my thigh.

"You just said you want the real me."

"And you made it sound sexual."

I grinned. Well, that couldn't be helped. She had got naked in front of me. Sex was very much at the forefront of my mind.

"You made it sexual the moment you decided to take your clothes off."

She spluttered, shut her mouth and scowled. I shook my head. I really had to go deal with my cock, but I didn't want to be away from her. I reached out, tucking her hair behind her ear.

"I'm not hiding now."

Her bottom lip trembled as I stared at it. I didn't remove my hand, instead brushing my fingertips down her jaw.

"I know you're in pain. I shouldn't want you, but I do."

Her hands twisted in her lap. She didn't look away from me.

"And I don't think you're immune to me either."

My fingers brushed down her neck and over her collarbone.

"Why don't you stop lying to yourself and me? Perhaps if you did, this wouldn't escalate into pain and punishment. Don't you want pleasure, Liora? I can give that to you. I will give it to you."

I stopped short of touching her breast. My hand hovered over it, waiting for her response.

"You want me to sleep with you when I'm barely a few days out of a two year relationship."

Her statement made me feel like an arsehole. I was used to feeling that way. I'd had enough grief off James over our father. And yet her boyfriend had nothing to do with us except for me forcing her to break it off with him.

"Don't bring him into it when this is about you and me. You want real. This between you and me, that's real. I know you feel it. You can't deny it, not after the way you kissed me."

"You kissed me first."

"We kissed each other."

The truth was it had been mutual. We'd both moved at the same time as if pulled by a cord binding us together.

"I can't lie on my back. It hurts too much, Dante."

Hold on a second, did she mean…?

"You don't have to."

I shifted away, sitting up against the headboard and put a hand out to her.

"I never said—"

"Just come here and sit on me before I make you."

She crawled towards me, swung one leg over mine and straddled me. Having her on top of me made the ache worse.

I reached between us and unbuttoned my jeans just to get some relief from the pressure of them against my cock. Her eyes went wide. I realised what she was thinking. I raised an eyebrow. Had I not told her enough times I wouldn't fuck her until she said yes?

"I'm only going to kiss you."

Before she had a chance to reply, I tugged her towards me by her neck and planted her lips on mine. That's when everything flew out of my head, just as it had last time. All I could feel was her and the crackle of electricity which flowed between us. Her hands landed on my shoulders.

Liora kissed me back and it was fucking wonderful. I could taste the fruit she'd eaten on her lips. So damn sweet. She moved closer, her body brushing against mine. From the moment we'd laid eyes on each other, we'd shared an instant connection. And she couldn't contain or deny the pull.

It wasn't me who deepened the kiss, but her. As her tongue met mine, a small groan left her throat. That was it. I was fucking lost. My self-control shot to pieces.

One hand pressed against her lower back, the other ran up her side and cupped her breast through her t-shirt. She arched against me when I ran my thumb over her nipple. Not only did she not pull away, one of her hands cupped my face and the other dug into the hair at the back of my head.

I wanted her with a desperation which completely threatened to undo me. My fingers itched to be on her bare skin. Intense, pulsating desire laced my veins. My cock throbbed restlessly, seeking the warmth and wetness of her pussy.

"Liora, say yes," I whispered against her mouth.

She merely kissed me harder, her fingers digging into my face. I was going to snap. My hand left her breast. I had to know if she desired me as much as I did her. No sane person could cope with such an overload of sensations and be able to resist the urges.

I traced a line down her stomach towards her thigh. I exposed her to me although I didn't look down. My fingers danced up her inner thigh. Finally, they met her soft curls. She shuddered, clutching me tighter.

I ran my finger down her pussy and groaned. Heat radiated from her. And she was so fucking wet I could barely hold it together. Pulling away from her mouth, I stared at her. Her breathing was as heavy as mine, her pupils dilated and her lips glistened.

"I'll make you come if you reciprocate," I said.

"I…"

"Touch me and I'll touch you."

To reiterate my point, I circled her clit with one finger. She whimpered, biting her lip.

"Touch me."

I hadn't meant it to come out like a command, but it did. She hesitated, her hands twitching.

"If you don't then I'm going to leave you here and deal with it myself. I can't kiss you and not need more."

She leant away from me and looked between us. Tentatively reaching down, she brushed her fingers along my length through my boxers. It jerked at her touch and I stifled a moan. What the hell was I thinking? Having her touch me was going to be fucking torture.

"I will if you take them off," she whispered.

She got off me and waited, her eyes expectant.

"Completely off?" I asked.

She bit her lip again and nodded.

"You know if I do that there won't be any barriers between us."

"I know what it means."

I slid off the bed and took my jeans off. I hesitated at my boxers and turned to her. Something about this felt off.

"You're not ready."

She looked up at me.

"What?"

"You don't want to do this, Liora. You're doing it because I want it."

"I…"

"Do not lie to me."

What the fuck was I doing? She'd just offered herself up on a plate to me. It didn't feel right. None of it did.

"I've never slept with anyone after two days of knowing them. With Max, we were together for two years because we were only fourteen when we started dating and with Harrison, it was two months before I let him anywhere close to me. I've let you kiss me and touch me and we barely know each other."

Her eyes fell on my crotch.

"I won't deny I want you on a physical level, Dante. It feels like a volcano is trying to erupt inside me whenever you touch me. I've never wanted anyone in the way I want you and that scares the crap out of me. So no, I don't want to because I'm terrified of what this means."

The brutal honesty from her cut me to the core. All my desire evaporated in an instant. If it had been anyone else, I might have ignored what she said and fucked her anyway. This was Liora. The one I wanted, needed for life.

I knelt on the bed, grabbed her by the shoulders and tugged her into my chest. I held her there, my face buried in her hair.

"Then I'll just have to make you trust me enough to let me in," I whispered.

And no matter what other bullshit that we had to endure because of my father, I would do what I could to let her see the real me too.

Chapter Seven

LIORA

I didn't think for one second he'd stop after he'd touched me so intimately, but Dante had a habit of surprising and confusing me at the same time. He just held me until I wrapped my arms around his back.

This man made me feel things I wasn't ready to feel. Admit things I wasn't ready to admit. And told me he'd make sure I trusted him. I didn't think that would ever happen. How could I trust a man like him? One who hid behind so many masks. One who made me vulnerable with a simple kiss and touch.

Who was I kidding? Kisses between Dante and I were not simple. They were like two planets colliding, exploding in a ball of flame and destruction. Wildfire catching a forest leaving only chaos and ruin in its wake. How could I ever resist such temptation when it consumed every part of me? That kiss we just shared made me weak. It made me dizzy and if he hadn't broken it, I would've given in. If he hadn't commanded me to touch him, I would've drowned in him completely and given him everything.

He didn't need to know that. Didn't need to know how close I'd been to throwing caution to the wind. I had to shut down these emotions and desires raging inside me.

I pulled away from him abruptly. The sharp slap of rejection flickered over his face for a moment before he schooled his features.

I'm not rejecting you. I want you.

The words were on the tip of my tongue, but I kept silent. I'd already told him I desired him on a physical level, but I knew that's not what he wanted. Dante wanted access into my mind and if I gave that to him, perhaps he'd let me into his. Except letting him in would be a huge mistake.

He jumped up off the bed and paced away to the bathroom. With his back to me, I couldn't see his expression. And I desperately wanted to know what was going through his head after my admission.

His hand was on the door handle, but he stopped when I spoke.

"Where are you going?"

He stiffened but didn't turn around.

"To deal with the problem you caused."

What did I cause?

"What problem?"

He turned his face to me. There was a mixture of agonising desire and irritation painting his features.

"Up until you decided to drop that little bombshell on me, I was sure you'd reciprocate. Now I have to deal with matters myself."

He didn't give me a chance to respond. He ripped the door open, walked inside and slammed it shut behind him. I heard the lock click.

Bombshell?

Did he mean me admitting wanting him terrified me? Didn't he want the truth from me and to know me? I'd never been more truthful about my feelings or emotions with anyone before. In the space of a couple of days, Dante had access to parts of me I never showed anyone. Everything screamed at me to stop letting him in, but my need to understand Dante overrode my common sense.

And deal with what himself?

You turned him on, you big idiot. He wanted you to touch him, to make him come.

The funny thing was, I had wanted to do that too. He'd been the one to stop because he'd assumed I was saying it was okay for us to have sex. What I'd really wanted was unfettered access to his cock so I could learn how to touch him in the way he liked. Trying to please the man who took me and told me I was his was just about the most batshit crazy thing I could think of doing, but a part of me wanted to do it all the same.

It's what led me to get off the bed and storm over to the bathroom door. I banged on it twice.

"I never said I wouldn't reciprocate."

The words were out of my mouth before I could stop them. I heard nothing from beyond the door.

"I would've touched you if you'd just let me instead of jumping to conclusions. I still will if you come out here and talk to me."

Would I?

What the hell was I saying?

The thought of touching him made my core clench and my insides grow molten. I wanted Dante to kiss me again. I wanted his hands on my body, branding me with heat. I just didn't want to have sex because I wasn't ready for the fallout it would surely cause inside me.

I was at war with myself. One part of me accepted I was his and the other, the rational part of me, rebelled against the very idea of his ownership.

"I know you can hear me."

I got no response at all. It frustrated me no end. And when I heard the shower turn on, I stomped away. That's when the pain decided to resurface, reminding me Dante had physically hurt me. His punishments weren't something I should welcome. And yet I'd told him exactly how many times he needed to hit me for my transgressions.

I didn't understand myself around him.

I wasn't the girl who liked someone who got off on pain, was I?

Did I even like Dante?

I wanted to kiss him, but actually liking him as a person? That was an entirely different ballgame because I knew literally next to nothing about him. I didn't even know his last name or who his family really were. I knew they must be rich because why else would he be able to afford all of this, but as to how they got rich? Who knew. Would he ever tell me?

What had he said about me learning things about him? I had to earn them. I had to think about how I was going to do that.

Firstly, I was going to put clothes on even if it killed me because standing here in his t-shirt wasn't doing me any favours. I could smell Dante on it. It flooded my veins with heat which pulsated restlessly, seeking a release. One I knew only he could give me.

I ripped his t-shirt off and threw it on the bed where it taunted me with the scent of its owner. Citrus and sandalwood. Fuck him and his smell invading my nostrils and causing all sorts of unwanted feelings. I turned away from it and opened one of the cupboard doors.

He'd provided me with an entire wardrobe full of new outfits. Ones which I was in no doubt were to please him rather than me. I didn't question why all the clothes were my size. I had a feeling my father had been complicit in giving Dante information about me. Whether it was forced or not, I didn't care. He'd still done this to me. Put me in this insufferable situation.

The dresses he'd bought would save me having painfully tight clothes against my heated and sore skin. I selected the least revealing set of underwear. I swore Dante just wanted me trussed up in a bunch of sexy lingerie for his perusal. *Dick.*

I hissed as I pulled on the underwear. It stung like fuck, but I ignored the pain, putting the bra on. I selected a navy sundress, tugging it over my head. I brushed my hair next, making sure it sat right. Did Dante like my hair short or would he prefer it long? It'd been shoulder length the day I'd met him three years ago.

Christ, why the hell do I even care?

The bathroom door opened. I hadn't noticed when he'd turned the shower off. When I turned around, Dante stood in the doorway. His black hair was damp and he was only dressed in a robe, but it was wrapped so tightly around him, I couldn't see any part of his chest. His eyes met mine and his expression gave away his irritation.

"Do you even understand what you're doing to me?" he asked, his voice vibrating with urgency and need.

"What I'm doing to you? What about what you're doing to me?"

I wanted to shut down all my thoughts about how sexy he looked standing there with wet hair. My body thrummed at the sight of him. He'd worked me up and I hadn't had a release.

Had he?

Isn't that what he said he'd do in the bathroom?

Had he enjoyed thinking about me naked whilst he stroked his cock?

Enough. I have to stop thinking about him and his cock.

It didn't matter that touching him through his boxers had flooded my body with longing. Why was my body going haywire in response to him? Why did I grow wet and wanting for a man I barely knew? And the worst thing my body did to me? Dante punishing me was strangely erotic rather than abhorrent.

Should I want the sting of his palm?

No.

Did my body care about what was right and wrong?

No.

Fuck my body and fuck my desire for him.

He stalked towards the wardrobe, ripped the door open, pulled out clothes and walked back into the bathroom leaving so many unspoken questions and answers between us. The door rattled on its hinges when he slammed it shut.

I should've quaked in fear at his display of frustration, but I didn't. I straightened my spine and waited. When he finally emerged, his hair was still damp, but he was dressed in jeans and a plain black t-shirt. His blue eyes hardened when his gaze fell on me.

He stalked towards me, backing me up until I hit the wardrobe door. I winced at the wood pressing into my overly sensitive and sore skin.

"I'm trying to teach you how to survive what's coming, Liora, but you don't seem to understand that," he growled.

"What do you mean? What is coming?"

He reached up and wrapped a hand around my neck. I swallowed but didn't stop him.

"When I told you I'd introduce you to my family, I meant it. I have no choice. My siblings don't know how I acquired you."

Why was he bringing this up? I didn't think he'd lied to me about me meeting them.

"You have to convince them we are together."

Wait, what?

"Why on earth would I do that? We're not a couple."

His fingers tightened, his expression turning deadly.

"Wrong. What have I told you before? Obedience is how you survive. He expects this of us, so you will do what I say."

He?

His father. On some level, I knew this always came back to that man.

"So what, you and I just have to do what he says? Bullshit."

What was I doing? Dante's father terrified me. I should just do what Dante said and stop questioning him. The rational part of my brain had apparently gone on holiday and the bold, idiotic side of me had taken the reins instead.

"If you value your sanity, then yes. Do you want your body and mind broken? Because that is exactly what he'll do if you don't fucking do what I say."

I trembled, my palms beginning to sweat. What kind of monster was his father? And what had he done to Dante? I was sure the man with his hand wrapped around my throat had suffered because of his father. There was something in his eyes that spoke of immeasurable pain and sorrow.

"No," I whispered. "I don't want that."

"Then stop fighting me on this. Play your role. Two weeks from now, convince him you're mine. Convince them we're happy together."

"What's happening in two weeks?"

"A charity gala. Before then, I expect you to earn the right to know who we are."

I swallowed. He loosened his grip, his fingers running down my neck and tracing the line of my collarbone.

"How?"

"Stop asking questions and start doing what I tell you."

I hated that was his go to response. More bullshit from him. Hadn't I already provoked him enough today? He'd punished me with his hand once. What other ways would he do it if I continued to push his buttons? What else did Dante have up his sleeve?

"I don't want to."

Provoked

His eyes flashed. I knew I was in trouble. So I did what I could to mitigate his reaction. My hands came up and I tugged his face towards me. His mouth landed on mine, causing sparks to fly between us. Even when he tried to pull away, I gripped his face tighter and pressed my tongue against his lips, demanding he let me in.

He ripped my hands off his face and pushed me back into the wardrobe. His blue eyes were wild with anger and desire.

"You are playing a dangerous game," he growled.

"Am I? I thought you enjoyed playing games with me."

"Right now? No. I'm warning you, my patience is wearing thin. If you want me to throw you on that bed and rip your clothes off then be my fucking guest and continue."

Two separate reactions to what he'd said had me freezing. One part of me wanted to bolt and the other wanted to tug him against me and let whatever it was between us take over. My body tried to arch into him, but I kept my joints locked in place.

Everything about Dante assailed my senses. The power and control. His incredible scent. His mesmerising eyes and the way he looked at me with such passion and possession. All of it lit me up like an inferno. Desire coated my veins. My body primed itself for his.

Yes. Yes, I want you to throw me on the bed and fuck me with wild abandon.

I wasn't ready for the intensity.

"You have to stop looking at me like that," I whispered.

"Explain. How am I looking at you?"

Words flew out of my head. He pinned me there, unable to form sentences and completely at his mercy. There were far too many sides to this man. How was I ever meant to keep up? How would I ever know the true Dante who hid behind walls, masks and radiated heat, sin and suffering?

"Like… Like you're a starving lion and I'm your prey."

His lips curved up into a cruel smile.

"I am starving," he replied, his voice a purr. "I want to devour you whole. I've waited too long to have you. I want inside you."

He lifted a hand, pressing a finger to my head.

"Here."

His finger brushed over my mouth.

"Here."

He trailed it down my jaw and neck. As if my body couldn't become more aroused, wetness coated my underwear. His eyes flickered with darkness. Darkness he wanted to drown me in. Pull me under and take possession of every inch of my soul so I would become as twisted as him.

His fingers trailed over my breasts, not bothering to avoid them. I arched into his touch. His smile grew wider. He knew exactly what this was doing to me.

Damn him. Fuck him. I wish I never met you, Dante.

Fingers brushed over my stomach, causing it to twist and turn with longing and need. My core throbbed. I ached to be filled. Mastered. Branded. I wanted Dante to claim every part of me as his own.

Christ, what the fuck is happening to me?

His fingers danced across my pussy, not quite touching me.

"And here."

Dante was finally clear about what he wanted.

My mind, my words and my body.

Translation: he wanted every part of me.

He'd told me that before, but it only fully registered now.

"You can't have any of it."

His smile only grew.

"No? Mark my words, Liora. They'll fall to me one by one. I think I know what will come first."

He gripped the hem of my skirt, trailing it up my thighs until he exposed my lingerie clad pussy to him. He kept his eyes on mine as he held the dress up with one hand and trailed his fingers over me with the other. A low growl, which was almost a purr, left his lips.

He leant towards me, his mouth brushing against mine.

"You're going to let me fuck you and you're going to want it as much as I do. Perhaps your words will fall next, and lastly, your mind will be mine. You won't be able to resist. Ultimately, I will win."

He didn't let me talk. His mouth commanded mine as his fingers found my clit through my underwear. I bucked, trying not to surrender but utterly failing.

And as I decided to kiss him back, his phone rang. The sound piercing through our lust filled haze. I wanted to thank and curse it at the same time.

He pulled away from me, his eyes dark with irritation at the interruption.

"Stay right there," he said, his voice rough and gravelly.

As if I could move after what he'd done to me. I'd collapse in a heap on the floor if I tried.

He strode over to the bedside table and snatched up his phone.

"Hello."

The next instant, his face grew serious. Irritation and resignation slipped in, twisting his features into something unrecognisable. He straightened, his expression darkening by the second. Whoever it was, they had altered the mood dramatically.

"I understand."

He tucked the phone into his pocket when he was done. He'd barely responded apart from the occasional 'yes' and 'no'.

When his eyes met mine, they were cold. The man who wanted to own me was gone. I didn't know the stranger who'd replaced him.

"Brent will bring you down for lunch. I have to go."

And he left me standing against the wardrobe, a trembling mess of sexual arousal.

What the hell was that?

Chapter Eight

DANTE

Fuck my father. I hated him more now than I'd ever done before. And I really fucking despised the man.

His reminder that Liora was payment for a debt rang in my ears. The fact he knew I was struggling with my insatiable need for her drove me fucking insane. It made me painfully aware we were being watched. Brent and I may be friends, but he was still under my father's payroll. I didn't have to ask him to know he'd told my father Liora wasn't obedient yet. That she was causing me to lose control.

The problem was Zach had known from the moment I asked for her. When I bargained with him to have her, it was because I wanted her. It had nothing to do with her father's debt. I didn't care what Angus Stewart had done. All I cared about was having his daughter. Possessing her. She was mine from the moment I laid eyes on her.

My father's plans differed from mine. Liora was a transaction between the Bensons and the Stewarts. A blood debt. He wouldn't kill her, but she would stay with us for the rest of her life. And he'd given her to me. A gift for my so called obedience. A gift which came with conditions. Ones I hated. But having Liora was worth all of it. And she'd never know the sacrifice I'd made.

The cost should be too high. A sane person would never entertain the idea. I wasn't sane. And I really didn't care about my mental state. I kept that under control. Yet Liora was insistent on unravelling me piece by piece. Instead of me possessing her, she was trying to own me. And she was fucking winning.

I needed space and distance to give myself a fucking chance to keep her where she belonged. Unless I had a part of her I could hold on to, this was going to be impossible. And she wasn't ready yet.

She admitted to wanting me physically, but that wasn't enough. She had to be mentally ready to accept her body was mine. That was the first part I needed. If I had her body, I could have her voice, her thoughts bared to me. Then I'd have her mind.

Until then, I had to stay focused. I had to keep myself from giving in to her needs. Her wants. I was damn sure she wanted my mind too even if she didn't know or want to accept it.

I put my hand on my face, trying to reign in the tidal wave of insanity threatening to burst through. That was a mistake. I could smell her arousal on my fingers from when I'd touched her.

Holy fucking Christ.

I resisted the urge to stick them in my mouth so I could taste her. Instead, I walked into the guest bathroom and washed my hands thoroughly. I lamented the loss of her on my skin, but it couldn't be helped. I'd storm back in my room and pin her down if I allowed myself to indulge further.

I looked at my face in the mirror. His eyes stared back at me. I hated the connection. I couldn't see myself without seeing him too. The monster. The man who'd fucked me up. Made me the way I am for better or worse.

I walked out of the bathroom and went in search of Brent. I found him in the kitchen, laughing with one of the chefs. When he saw my face, his dropped abruptly. He indicated with his head we should take this into the conservatory. I followed him and shut the door behind me.

"Why the fuck did I just get a lecture from Zach?"

Brent had the fucking cheek to shrug his shoulders.

"I haven't spoken to him since yesterday."

I stared at him for a long moment. If he hadn't told my father, then who had? I turned away and looked out at the garden.

"What did he say?" Brent asked.

"Usual bullshit about me getting my act together along with the reminder Liora is a family debt and I should treat her accordingly."

"And you're surprised he's interfering? You know Zach."

Sadly I did. All too fucking well. I ran a hand through my hair. My patience had run out. I couldn't let myself slip up any further. Especially not around Liora. Christ, I'd almost fucked her.

"He expects me to put her in the playroom and beat the defiance out of her."

"Are you going to?"

I turned to him. I don't know why he bothered asking me that question when he knew the answer.

"Are you going to tell him if I don't?"

He grinned, his teeth gleaming.

"I don't fancy getting in between the two of you."

I could hardly blame him. He'd patched me up enough times after incidents with my father.

"Have you shown her it yet?"

I raised an eyebrow. Yes, I was really going to show the girl who was terrified of me the room where I'd enjoy inflicting pleasure and pain within days of her arriving here. Good fucking plan. Not. I'd done enough damage already.

"You're a funny man."

Brent was a twat of epic proportions and he knew it.

"I'm just saying, you're better off being honest with her from the outset, D."

I wanted to throw him out of the house on his ear for such an idiotic suggestion. He really had no fucking clue about women. And he didn't know Liora.

"I'll show her when I'm good and fucking ready to."

He put his hands up in a gesture of 'okay, okay, chill out'. I'd got my point across. What I did with Liora would be on my terms and my terms alone. Fuck what my father said. He didn't know her either.

You don't know her yet.

I knew her a damn sight better than Brent and Zach. I knew simple kisses from her brought me to my knees. The way she said my name made my pulse spike and my cock twitch. Her smile lit my world on fire and that was just the tip of the iceberg. She was so smart and capable.

A niggling doubt crept into my mind. What if Brent was right? Should I show her? Would she hate it knowing that's what I needed from her?

"Bring her down here," I said, looking out the windows again.

"Whatever you say... boss."

I stuck my finger up behind my back to which I was greeted with a hearty chuckle before I heard his retreating footsteps. She was probably wondering why the fuck I left so abruptly. Not that it was any of her business, but the way I left her all worked up like that. It hadn't been my intention.

Perhaps it would work in my favour if I made her desire me to the point of madness. Where she couldn't hold back any longer. Then she'd snap and let me fuck her the way I wanted to. The thought of being buried in her sweet pussy made me hard all over again.

Get a fucking grip.

I'd told her I was going to sort myself out in the bathroom, but I found I couldn't when I got in there. Not when she told me through the door that she would've done it for me. How was it possible to want someone as much as I wanted her? My hands on her soft skin. My mouth on hers. Bringing her to climax over and over again. I wanted to know what noises she'd make. I wanted to hear her calling out my name in the heat of the moment.

If Zach knew I wanted to bring her as much pleasure as I did pain, he would've never let me have her. It was only because of me that he'd even called in the debt in the first place, so quite frankly, he could get fucked. Liora was mine now. I wouldn't let him take her. My father would never ruin the girl who belonged to me.

"Here you go, D," Brent's voice called from the doorway.

I turned to find Liora standing in front of him, looking markedly put out. Brent gave me a nod before retreating and shutting the conservatory door behind him. I beckoned her over with a curl of my finger. She took several steps into the room, stopping just outside of my reach. Her hands fisted in her skirt.

"Are you sore?" I asked.

Her eyes flashed with irritation.

"I don't know why you're bothering to ask. It's not like you care about how much you hurt me."

I took one long stride and closed the distance between us, gripping her face and turning it up towards me.

"You think I don't care about you?"

"I'm your pet, aren't I? A slave to your needs. So, why would you care?"

Her words sucker punched me right in the gut.

A slave? She's not a fucking slave.

My other hand curled around her back and pulled her against me. I caressed her face with my thumb. She swallowed. I could feel her pulse thundering in her neck under my fingertips.

"Pets are more obedient than you, especially dogs. Loyal to their masters."

"Too bad for you I have no intention of being loyal or obedient."

My grip on her face tightened. We were going around in circles. I had to break this fucking ridiculous cycle.

"Come with me. We never did finish your tour."

I let her go only to grip her hand and tug her towards the door with me. There were two rooms she needed to see, both on the same floor as my bedroom. Maybe, just maybe she'd stop fucking provoking me every moment we were together if she knew.

Liora didn't protest to being dragged up two flights of stairs. I stopped outside the room which would be hers if she wanted it. If she behaved. I'd tried so hard to make it perfect for her. I took a breath and opened the door.

She walked in after me and stopped in her tracks, pulling me to a halt. Her eyes bugged out. It was decorated in soft greens. Her father had assured me those were her favourite colours.

The wallpaper behind her bed had a forest pattern across it. Pale green trees on a grey background. The fourposter bed was white, each post made from birch tree branches. The duvet and pillowcases were grey with a pale green tree pattern across it to match the accent wall.

There were several black and white prints on the walls of her favourite animals. The rest of the walls were painted in a slightly darker green to her bed, but it was still light and airy. A vanity table sat with a huge mirror on one side of the room and a chaise lounge was opposite the bed. I'd had a window seat installed in the bay windows, the fabric matching her bedding.

I looked at her whilst she took it in. Her mouth was hanging open, green eyes welling with unshed tears.

"I was going to wait longer before I showed you this room," I said, my voice soft.

"It's... beautiful," she whispered.

"Your father told me what you like. It took me a long time to decide on each thing in this room."

Her eyes met mine.

"You designed it for me?"

I nodded. Would this be enough to show her I cared? The thing was, I really did care about her. Her wellbeing. Her happiness. Her willingness to give herself over to me. I cared about it all. Zach probably thought he'd beaten all the sentimentality out of me, but my father didn't know me as well as he thought he did.

"You have to earn it first, just like everything else, but yes, I chose everything personally."

Her hand tightened in mine as she took a step towards me. She reached out and took my other hand, turning the palm over and running her thumb down it.

"Thank you, Dante."

My heart stuttered in my chest.

"You're welcome."

Her eyes were still trained on our hands, but the next words out of her mouth gave me a strange feeling inside my chest.

"I'm not supposed to ask you for things, but... Can I... Can I kiss you?"

I didn't fucking know what was up or down any more. Her asking for permission to kiss me was completely at odds with the behaviour I'd come to expect from her.

"Why?"

She shifted on her feet, still not meeting my eyes. Her cheeks stained red.

"We were interrupted before. I didn't kiss you back and I... I want to."

I pulled my hands from hers. She wanted to kiss me back. Wanted me. I tried not to think too hard about the way my heart raced in anticipation of her lips on mine. Her features fell, hands dropping to her sides.

"Okay," she whispered. "I understand. I haven't earnt the right to ask you for that."

"You can decide whether or not you still want to kiss me after I've shown you the last room."

Her head whipped up to mine then, eyes wide with curiosity and confusion.

"You mean...?"

I smiled, reaching out and cupping her face.

"Do you really think I'd say no to having you kiss me, Liora? I assure you, no is not in my vocabulary when it comes to your lips on mine."

She closed her eyes, turning into my hand as if savouring the ounce of affection I gave her. The connection between us flared and solidified. Who was I fucking kidding? Her and I were two flames drawn together, burning for each other.

"Why wait?"

"You'll see why."

I needed to know if she'd still want me after discovering the extent of my needs. My darkest desires. The ones which fed me unlike anything else. I could neither control or hide what I needed. It wasn't just about sex. I could enjoy sex without the need to inflict pain. This was a different matter entirely.

I let go of her face and took her hand instead, drawing her out of the bedroom I'd created for her. I walked her across the landing to the other side of the house. I took the keys from my pocket and selected the right one. Unlocking the door, I opened it and gestured to her.

Liora looked at me and then into the dark room beyond. I let go of her hand when she moved towards it. I took a step into the doorway, leant against it and flipped the lights on. Her sharp intake of breath was the only reaction I got from her. I couldn't see her face.

Nicknaming this the playroom was Brent's way of taking the piss. It wasn't a sex dungeon with leather and red walls. The walls were actually painted a dark grey. One of them had a dark wooden cross mounted to it with metal loops to attach cuffs. A seemingly normal bed sat in the centre of the room. It had metal posts and places you could attach restraints. On the wall behind it, various whips hung. I had other things within the drawers off to the side.

"Do you have questions?" I asked.

She walked further into the room and ran a hand down one of the bed poles. She next inspected the whips on the wall and finally the cross.

She turned to me.

"No."

I raised an eyebrow. I thought she'd want to know why I had this room and if I intended to have her in here regularly. She walked towards me and rested her hands on my chest, staring up at me with wide eyes.

"Can I kiss you now?"

I didn't reply. My hands were in her hair the next moment and my mouth crashed against hers. I took and she gave. She really did fucking give. Her mouth opened and our tongues clashed with together. Her small hands wrapped around my neck, pressing me closer.

I lost all sense of control. How many more times would we end up in this position today? Three fucking times I'd got sucked into the girl in my arms. I pulled away, breath ragged as I ran a thumb over her glistening bottom lip.

"For a girl who claims she doesn't want to sleep with me, you have a funny way of showing it."

Her face grew red, even the tips of her ears were pink. Her forest green eyes flickered with desire even so. I pressed her backwards until her calves hit the edge of the bed. With one hand on her shoulder, I pushed her down onto it. She hissed when her sensitive behind hit the mattress. I crawled over her, running my fingers down her collarbone.

"Have you changed your mind already?"

She shook her head. I hadn't expected her to.

"Tell me what you think of this room."

Her eyes darted to the side, eying the wooden cross.

"I don't know what to think," she whispered.

"Does it scare you?"

Her eyes met mine again. There was a strange sort of determination in them.

"Should I be? I know you like pain, Dante. I'm not shocked or surprised by what's in here."

She might not be surprised, but I was. Surprised by her calm reaction. I supposed I shouldn't be considering how calm she was about other things I'd revealed to her.

"There is a fine line between the good sort of pain and the bad."

"Good sort?"

I continued to stroke her collarbone.

"Mmm, there can be pleasure in pain."

"Pleasure for you or me?"

I smiled. Her naivety was a blessing and a curse.

"For both of us."

She let out a huff.

"What makes you think I enjoyed it when you… punished me?"

I shook my head.

Sweet, innocent Liora, you really have no idea.

"That wasn't meant to be pleasurable." I cupped her cheek. "I could've brought you in here to punish you, but I didn't. This room is for pleasure."

She was silent for a long moment. Simply appraising me with a quizzical expression on her face. I didn't move to touch her further even though I wanted to. I desperately wanted to tug her dress up, push her underwear aside and plunge inside her. Having her in here did things to me.

I wanted to fuck her more than I wanted to cuff her to the cross and whip her, but the temptation was there all the same. I could strip her, cuff her and have my way with her. Except I couldn't. The need to have her want those things overrode everything else.

"Who are you really, Dante?"

I licked my bottom lip. If I answered that question honestly, it would open up Pandora's Box and no one needed that in their life. No one needed to hear about the fucked up bullshit I'd been through. I didn't want her to look at me with pity or feel sorry for me. Hell, she'd probably think I was a victim. That's not how I saw myself. Fucked up perhaps, but never a victim.

"Who am I? Your master."

She frowned.

"But if you want to know where or should I say who I come from… I told you, that's something you have to earn."

"How? Don't tell me I have to obey either. I want to know what you expect me to do."

I supposed that was fair.

"Perhaps instead of obedience, you can earn it by answering my questions honestly. I want what's inside your head."

"Then ask."

I released her and sat up. Having her body against mine was not doing me any favours. I leant against one of the poles, staring at her. She shifted up onto her elbows.

"Who do you think my family are?"

She cocked her head to the side.

"My father said yours is a business associate so I assume something to do with clothing or fabric. The fashion industry perhaps."

Clever girl.

"What do you know about your father's business?"

She shrugged.

"Next to nothing. Honestly, I don't know why he brought me with him on that business trip three years ago. He said it was so we could spend time together, but now I think it was all because of this."

109

She waved her hand between us.

"I don't know why he gave me to you."

"Do you want to know?"

She looked at me as if the answer to that was obvious.

"You think I'm not curious about why he handed his only daughter over to a man to use as his pet?"

A normal person would be curious. I had a feeling Liora's need to know bordered on desperation.

"Naturally you are." I paused, biting my lip. "I have one more question."

"Yes?"

I leant towards her and took her hand, pulling her up into sitting position. My face was close to hers. I could feel her breath across my cheek.

"Are you curious about the cross, Liora? Do you want to know what it'd feel like if I chained you to it and whipped you until you begged me to fuck you?"

I'd seen the way she looked at it. Her eyes kept falling on it as if she couldn't quite work out if it aroused her or not. Her lips parted, pupils dilating.

"You'll learn it will feel good, the sort of pain I'll give you. That's why you'll beg. You'll be so aroused, you won't be able to stand the thought of not getting fucked to within an inch of your life."

She didn't look away from me. Her breathing sped up a fraction. I could see her chest rising and falling.

"Yes," she whispered. "I am curious."

"Good. When you're ready, I'll show you."

I leant back, breaking the spell between us. She blinked rapidly as if coming out of a trance. Fuck. It felt good to disarm her so thoroughly with a few words.

She'd answered all my questions honestly. She'd obeyed. Liora earnt the right to know who I was.

"My full name is Dante Ajax Benson."

She stared at me for a long moment before she put a hand to her mouth.

"Does that mean your father is Zachary Benson?" she whispered through her fingers.

I nodded once. Her hands shook, her face going pale. I knew her view of the world had been flipped upside down. Bensons was a household name. My father's designs were sought after. He was well respected in the industry.

And he was a monster behind closed doors.

A monster who would stop at nothing to destroy this budding relationship between Liora and I if he had any idea of how deeply it ran.

"But… your father is… Oh my god."

My father was and always will be my worst nightmare.

And now he'd just become Liora's too.

Chapter Nine

LIORA

I stared at myself in the mirror. Dante had left the dress out on the bed for me whilst I was in the shower. He was nowhere to be seen when I got out, but there was a note tucked into the box.

Wear this and don't forget the shoes.
Dante x

I really wasn't sure how he'd known it would be perfect for me. It was almost the exact colour of my eyes, forest green and lace with little capped sleeves. Whilst it covered my chest completely, my back was almost bare except for the lace detail at the sides. It cinched in at the waist and flared out, hitting just below my knees. He'd even left me appropriate underwear to go with it. A backless bra and black lacy underwear. My heels were ridiculously tall and black to match the small purse.

When I'd opened the box, my heart had been in my mouth. I supposed this was the benefit of being a pet to a man whose father was a famous fashion designer. I shivered at the thought of Zachary. When Dante finally revealed who his family was two weeks ago, I'd barely been able to get my words out. Everything about that day completely overwhelmed me.

I had two weeks to unpack my feelings about it because he left me alone for most of it. He made no apologies for it nor gave me any indication as to why. More often than not, he didn't come in until I was already asleep and left before I woke up. He'd not kissed or tried to touch me. I was beginning to wonder if he was avoiding me after all he'd shown me.

Brent and the staff had been taking care of me, which I appreciated, but a part of me found myself missing Dante. It was completely insane given who he was. I dreamt about his blue eyes and the way his voice sometimes sounded almost like a purr. It reminded me of a majestic tiger hunting down its prey. I really had to stop comparing him to animals. I had to get that man out of my head.

Except I couldn't.

Especially not after we'd gone in that room across the hallway. The bedroom with no windows. I'd given it a nickname. The Den of Sin. I hadn't told him about that, but it felt appropriate to me.

I shivered thinking about what he'd said to me in that room. I couldn't help being curious about that cross on the wall and he'd noticed it. Nothing got by Dante.

I had no idea why I'd suddenly become so fascinated by the thought of him whipping me. Perhaps, deep down, on some level I'd enjoyed his punishments. It concerned me that I'd get turned on by the pain he so obviously wanted to dish out.

There was a knock at the door. I turned to find Brent standing in the doorway. His eyes roamed over me appreciatively.

"Don't you scrub up well, Miss Stewart."

I rolled my eyes, feeling my cheeks growing hot at his compliment.

"I told you to call me Liora."

He grinned, putting out his arm to me.

"Come along, he's getting impatient."

I narrowed my eyes as I walked over to him.

"Is he? Serves him right for ignoring my existence for two weeks."

Brent's eyes shone with amusement as I placed my hand in the crook of his elbow.

"D is complicated."

"No shit," I muttered under my breath.

I'd gotten used to Brent. He was chatty, which was a little annoying at times, but at least he talked to me unlike Dante. I wanted to give him a piece of my mind, but he was never around for me to do so. And now tonight, we had this charity gala and dinner where I'd have to pretend to be his girlfriend. The thought of it caused my stomach to clench. A part of me wanted to piss Dante off and act out, but the other part, the rational part, knew that would be a mistake. He'd warned me his father would be watching us. There was no way I was getting on Zachary Benson's bad side. His father terrified me to my very core.

"You really do look nice," Brent said, pulling me out of my thoughts as we descended the first flight of stairs.

"Thank you. Do you think he'll like it?"

Why the fuck did I just ask that? I don't care what Dante thinks.

Except I did. I really, really did. I wanted him to see how perfect the dress he'd picked out for me looked on my body. I wanted him to know how much I appreciated him taking the time to choose it. I just wanted Dante to pay attention to me. This lonely feeling inside cut me to the core.

"Well, he is a man, so most likely."

"Brent…"

He looked down at me, his eyes bright with mischief. Even in heels, most people towered over my five foot four frame.

"D won't say anything, but just watch his eyes. They'll tell you everything you need to know. Trust me, Liora, no one can fail to notice how stunning you look."

I spied Dante pacing with an impatient stride in the lobby as we walked down the last couple of steps. His eyes snapped up to us.

"You took your time," he said.

Brent took my hand out of his elbow and pushed me towards Dante, who stopped a couple of feet away from me. His magnetic blue eyes roamed across my figure, taking in every detail. Then he put his hand out to me. I stepped forward and took it.

"Get her coat," he barked at Brent as he rubbed a thumb across my knuckles.

His bodyguard had been right. He didn't say anything aloud. His eyes did the talking for him. They burnt me with the sheer intensity of his desire and appreciation of my appearance. He pulled me closer, tucking my hair behind my ear with his other hand.

"You ready?" he asked in a low voice.

I nodded, unable to speak past the knot in my throat. This was the only thing he'd spoken to me about in detail. How to conduct myself at this event. He'd told me his sisters, Jennifer and Fiona, were twenty five and both worked for their father and his brother, James, was a year older than me. He'd explained enough about them and his father for me to blag my way through the evening.

I took Dante in. His tux was immaculate and moulded to his toned body, making my mouth water. I swallowed, trying to will myself to say something.

Brent brought my coat and helped me into it. Dante led me out to the car and got me settled in the back before climbing in next to me.

I stared at the partition between us and the driver, unsure of what to say. I was sure at least ten minutes had gone by when I felt his breath on my ear.

"I'm glad it fits you," he murmured.

"What does?" I squeaked.

His hand brushed over my thigh.

"The dress. Do you like it?"

My pulse went into overdrive. I could hear it pounding in my ears.

"Yes, thank you."

"Do you remember what to say about how we met?"

I nodded, swallowing. His fingers caught my chin, turning me to face him. His blue eyes were dark with a heady cocktail of lust. The smile on his lips accentuating his handsome face. And my lips craved the touch of his.

"You look like you want to ask me something," he said.

"Where have you been?" I blurted out without a thought to what the hell I was saying.

He seemed amused by my question rather than annoyed.

"Why, have you missed me?"

I felt my face burning. I didn't want to admit it to him. The truth was I had. He'd made me want him.

His eyes flicked down to my mouth.

"I… No. You didn't answer my question."

His smirk was downright irritating and yet I found myself quite unable to pull away or tell him where to go.

"You're not a very good liar." He brushed his knuckles across my jaw. "Tell me, what did you miss the most?"

"I didn't miss anything."

"No? I think I need to remind you, don't you?"

Dante's mouth met mine before I had a chance to respond. His lips caused an inferno inside me. It coiled in my stomach, razed through my veins and intoxicated me completely. His hand curled around the back of my head, whilst the other went to my waist underneath my coat, trailing fire in its wake.

My lips parted on instinct, allowing him access. His tongue drove between, curling around mine. I adored the way he tasted like berries and honey. I pressed closer, my hand circling the back of his neck. I'd really missed his kisses even though we'd only shared a handful of them.

"Christ, I fucking want you," he growled.

I barely had time to process the words. He pressed me backwards until I was half squished up against the door, his hand pushing up my dress. His breath was hot against my ear, his teeth grazing the lobe.

"You're going to have to tell me to stop if you don't want the first time I fuck you to be in the back of a car."

How on earth had this escalated so quickly? His fingers darted between my inner thighs, trailing their way upwards until they met my lacy underwear. I jolted under his touch. I could barely move with him pinning me to the seat and my head wedged between it and the door. He stroked me and I completely lost the ability to breathe. I gripped his shoulders, struggling to maintain any sense of composure.

"I want to take my time with you, draw out every ounce of pleasure until you're a trembling mess below me, whimpering and begging for a release."

I dragged air into my lungs, trying desperately to think of a response.

"Tell me, how would you like me to fuck you the first time? In my bed or would you prefer it if I tied you up and whipped you first?"

I arched into his fingers, still brushing against my clit. I couldn't think straight. How did he expect me to answer that when he was commanding every inch of my body with one simple touch?

"Dante," I whimpered. "Please."

What the hell was I begging for? I needed to get a grip. I was never like this about sex. Never. Not once had I felt this level of need and urgency to have another person between my legs.

He pulled me down the seat until my head was resting on it. My dress was bunched up around my waist, knees bent and he was between my legs. His blue eyes were like pools of never ending darkness. They spoke of his need for me and I was sure mine said the same thing.

How did he manage to keep his distance from me for two weeks then completely unravel me within the space of ten minutes? I really didn't understand him or his many, many masks. All I knew is I was pent up with all kinds of intense lust and desire for the man staring down at me.

"You're so beautiful," he whispered, his mouth inches from mine.

"So are you," I replied, the words falling out of my mouth without my consent.

He smiled and it met his eyes. My mouth went dry at the sight of a real, genuine smile from him. My heart did several backflips in my chest. He trailed kisses up my jaw until his mouth met my ear again.

"The bed or the cross, Liora. Which is it to be?"

If I could've answered him, I would've. The problem was I really didn't know. I wanted to have sex with him, denying that to myself was pointless. I should want him to take me in his bed, but the thought of him whipping me sent a shiver down my spine and heat flooded my veins further.

"I can't answer that," I whispered, settling for complete honesty.

"No? Do you want both? Shall I fuck you first, before I whip you and fuck you again?"

I took a breath. That's when I realised the car had stopped moving. There was a knock on the partition followed by a cough.

"Mr Benson, we've arrived," the driver said through the intercom.

Dante muttered something under his breath, pulling away from me. Whilst I felt like jelly, I couldn't stay half lying on the seat with my underwear on show. I shifted away from him, sitting up and tugging my dress down. I fumbled with my purse, pulling a mirror out and checking my appearance. I looked a mess.

Dante stared at me with amusement. He reached over and brushed my hair down, making sure it wasn't sticking up. I re-applied my lipstick and gloss and adjusted my make-up until I looked presentable again. I eyed Dante for a moment. He had lipstick on his face from our kiss. I held back a smile.

"What?" he asked, eying me warily.

I pointed at his cheek.

"You have something…"

He snatched the mirror from my hands and grunted when he saw what I meant. I tugged a pack of tissues out of my purse which I always kept on me for just in case moments. I handed him one and he gave me a nod before wiping the lipstick off.

"Leave your coat in the car," he told me.

He reached over and knocked on the partition. I slipped it off as I heard the driver door open and a moment later, the door next to me swung back. I climbed out with the help of the driver and Dante got out the other side.

The flash of cameras almost blinded me. Dante was at my side, wrapping his arm around my waist and herding me into the building. He ignored the calls of the reporters and strode through the doors. I hadn't realised the press would be here.

I hoped I wouldn't be plastered all over social media as the mystery woman on Dante Benson's arm. What if all my Uni friends saw it? What if my parents saw? What if Harrison did?

My heart sunk. I shouldn't be thinking about him. I still felt awful about the way we'd broken up. Harrison seeing me with Dante on social media would confirm what I'd told him though. It'd make it clear I was seeing someone else. Perhaps it would be a good thing.

Dante's hand around my waist felt like a brand on my skin as we walked through the lobby where there were a lot of people milling around. I'd barely had time to compose myself after the incident in the car. He scanned the crowd before making a beeline for the three sets of double doors. They led into a huge ballroom with tables laid out and a stage at the far end.

He scanned the seating plan for a moment and then his eyes flicked over to a specific table. There, standing next to it, was a man I recognised. Dante's father. There were two dark-haired girls who looked exactly alike and standing with his arms across his chest was a younger version of the man next to me.

I froze next to Dante who was trying to move towards them with me. He looked down at me with a frown.

"What's wrong?" he asked.

I turned to him.

"I'm not ready to meet your family. This is too much, Dante. How am I going to remember everything you told me? What if I can't convince them we're together? Your father… I…"

His brow smoothed out, his other hand coming to rest on my bare arm.

"Stop panicking and breathe."

I took a deep breath, trying to squash down the nerves coiling in my stomach.

"You are going to do this. You don't want to disappoint me, do you?"

I shook my head. Hell, I knew what would happen if I did. I winced at the memory of the bruises he'd left last time. The only small mercy about him leaving me alone for two weeks is there were no further punishments. If he wasn't around, I couldn't get into fights with him.

He tucked my hair behind my ear.

"I want to reward you and I think you want that too."

I swallowed. The look in his eye told me the reward I'd be getting was sexual in nature. Despite what happened in the car, I wasn't certain I was ready for sex with Dante. It felt like giving in. And I shouldn't give into him. Not if I ever wanted to get away from the man in front of me. Something told me that was wishful thinking. Dante was never going to let me go.

He took my hand, entwining our fingers together and gave me a nod. I let him lead me towards his family, my stomach sinking with every step.

"Hello, son," Zachary said, his piercing blue eyes falling on me.

Dante didn't respond, merely nodded at his father. The twins openly stared at me, their mouths twitching in unison.

"Who's your date?" one of them asked.

"Liora, this is Jen and Fi," Dante said, pointing at each twin in turn.

The twin's dresses matched except they were different colours. Jennifer was in red and Fiona in fuchsia pink. Their dark hair suited the colours. I didn't put my hand out to them.

"Um, hello, it's nice to meet you," I said.

"Are you Scottish?" Fi asked, her eyes going wide.

I decided the twins suffered from lack of tact. Dante told me they didn't have much between the ears when he'd described them to me.

"Yes, I'm from Edinburgh."

The twins exchanged a look and then levelled their gaze on their older brother.

"You've never brought anyone to one of these before," Jen said.

Dante shrugged, his fingers tightening in mine.

"Because any girl with sense stays away from him," James muttered.

I looked over at Dante's brother. He straightened when he realised I'd heard him, his arms dropping to his sides. He stuck his hand out to me.

"Sorry, I'm James."

I shook his hand, feeling a little awkward and wondering if Dante had heard him too.

"Liora."

"Don't mind my little brother, he hates forced family fun, don't you, James?" Dante said, eying the two of us with an amused expression on his face.

James scowled, rolling his eyes. This is what Dante had meant by not getting along with his siblings. I could feel the animosity rolling off James and the twins were whispering to each other behind their hands. I shifted closer to Dante, feeling uncomfortable. He responded by letting go of my hand and wrapping his around my waist.

Zachary had been silent during this conversation. I noticed the way he watched me. It was up to me to be a convincing girlfriend and I wasn't sure I'd been doing a very good job so far.

I reached up and straightened Dante's bowtie which was at a slight angle. I rested my hand on his chest, giving him a smile. His returning one made my pulse spike. He leant down, nuzzling my ear.

"I'm going to introduce you to my father now," he whispered.

I giggled, pretending he'd said something funny to distract me from the sick feeling I got in my stomach at his words. His hand pressed into my back as he ushered me towards Zachary Benson.

"Zach, I don't think you've ever met Angus' daughter, Liora," Dante said.

Zach? Does he not call him, dad or father?

"It's my pleasure, Miss Stewart," Zachary said, his eyes telling me it was the exact opposite of a pleasure.

I shook his hand. His grip was far too tight. I tried not to wince. It was most definitely a warning to be on my best behaviour.

"My business with your father is very important to me. I do hope you will look after my son," he continued. "He needs the right woman in his life."

The underlying threat in his voice made me tremble. If he had his way, I wouldn't be Dante's at all.

"Who's Angus?" Fi asked.

"A business associate," Zachary replied.

"Is that how you met?" Jen piped up, pointing at Dante and me.

"Yes," I said. "It was quite by accident. My father brought me to London after I finished Uni to celebrate. Whilst waiting for my dad, I walked head first into Dante who was just leaving your father's offices. To cut a long story short, he invited me to dinner and the rest is sort of history. I moved down after my graduation ceremony a couple of weeks ago so we didn't have to be apart."

I looked up at Dante, hoping my eyes showed my affection for him. This wasn't as hard as I thought it was going to be. Yes, I was lying about how we'd met and what we were to each other, but being next to Dante, who was stunning to look at, I felt a tiny ounce of pride. Even though this was pretend, I was still the only girl Dante wanted. He'd waited three whole years to have me with him. In a really fucked up way, that meant something to me.

"Hold on, are you saying you're in a relationship, like it's serious, she's your girlfriend?" James asked, his eyebrows raised.

"Yes," Dante replied. "Liora is special."

I could see the disbelief in his brother's expression. I wondered why James suspected us so much. Having Dante say I was special warmed my heart. Then I scolded myself for being such an idiot. I shouldn't want his compliments or anything else. I was here to play a part not get wrapped up in a fantasy.

"Dante's in luuurve," Fi sniggered behind her hand to Jen.

I wanted the ground to swallow me up. Love was not something which would ever enter the equation between Dante and me. I was glad he chose to ignore her comment, although his eyes darkened.

There was movement around us and I realised people were beginning to file in and take their seats. The twins and James moved towards the table. Dante turned me around, but Zachary caught my arm before I had a chance to move over to our seats. His breath was hot on my ear sending a chill down my spine.

Dante let me go when he saw his father had stopped me, walking over to the table without me. I felt completely exposed without him by my side. How could he just leave me at his father's mercy?

"You behave yourself this evening," Zachary hissed. "Don't think you can bat your eyelids at my son and expect him to go easy on you. You are our property and you will do exactly as he says. Are we clear?"

"Yes, Mr Benson," I whispered, swallowing hard.

"Come, come, Liora, we're family now, are we not? Call me Zach."

"Yes, Zach."

"Good girl. Now, run along to him and don't forget your place or there'll be consequences even he can't save you from."

He released my arm. I took several unsteady steps forward, needing to be away from him. Dante was waiting by the table, he pulled out the chair for me and I sat down. I was in between him and James with Zach seated to Dante's left and the twins beyond him.

I trembled all over. Zach's threatening tone completely disarmed me. I was in no doubt the consequences he spoke of would be horrific.

Dante leant over to me.

"You're going to tell me what he said," he whispered.

I nodded, looking down at my hands. I didn't really want to tell him, but Zach's words about obeying Dante rang in my ears. I was trying to behave for Dante, he just pushed my buttons too often. I couldn't help but explode at him with his stupid rigid rule about no questions.

He draped his arm across the back of my chair and rested his hand on my shoulder, nuzzling my ear.

"You're shaking like a leaf."

Surely, he knew I was petrified of his father. I turned to him, he was so close my mouth almost brushed against his.

"He threatened me," I whispered.

His hand on my shoulder tightened. Dante's expression turned grim. To the outside world, this likely appeared to be an intimate moment between a couple in love, but I knew better. He cupped my face with his other hand.

"With what?"

"Consequences you can't save me from."

"You believe me now."

I nodded. There was no doubt in my mind, Dante hadn't lied about how dangerous his father was. How he'd take me away from the man in front of me if I disobeyed or did something Zach didn't care for.

"I'll be good for you," I murmured. "I promise."

His smile made my heart thump. He brushed his lips against mine with the gentlest of touches.

"Good girl."

He pulled back and settled his gaze over at the stage. I tried to breathe but my body felt tight from his proximity. I shrank back in my chair and fiddled with the cutlery next to my plate.

"What did you do at Uni?"

I jumped at the sound of James' voice. Him directing a question at me was unexpected.

"I… Um… Biological Sciences. Zoology specifically."

"She got a First," Dante said.

I hadn't realised he was paying attention.

"You like animals and you're smart," James said. "Tell me again what you see in my brother."

Other than the fact one simple touch from him burns me to a crisp and I can't get the thought of him whipping and fucking me out of my head?

Dante's fingers dug into my shoulder. I bit my lip, holding back from telling him to stop it because he was hurting me.

"He makes me laugh and…" I faltered, my eyes falling on two people sat on the opposite side of the room.

What the hell?

When my mum's eyes met mine, she tried to stand, but my dad put a hand on her shoulder and whispered furiously to her. She gave him a look of complete bewilderment before he continued. Her face went pale and she looked down at the table.

"You are not allowed to speak to them," Dante said in my ear. "You haven't earnt that privilege, Liora. You know that."

I turned to him, completely forgetting my conversation with James.

"Why are they here?"

129

He indicated his father with a slight turn of his head. I looked at Zach, feeling dread wash over me.

"To show your father who you belong to now."

Chapter Ten

DANTE

I really wish my father hadn't decided to put the Stewarts on the guest list. I understood his reasoning, but Liora was still not ready to accept she was mine. This might just set everything back to square one.

"What if they come over? I can't just ignore them," Liora whispered, her green eyes wide with confusion and resentment.

This was not a conversation we should be having at the table. I wanted to take her outside and have it out with her, but I couldn't. The host was on the stage and the room was beginning to fall silent. Also, my father would thoroughly disapprove of me giving her space to talk back to me. He could fucking well deal. He'd caused this brewing shitstorm for me to clean up.

"We'll talk about this later," I replied.

I kept my hand on her shoulder, reminding her to remain obedient.

"Dante…"

"What happened to your promise just now?"

She shut her mouth and sat back. Her expression smoothed out and she plastered on a tentative smile. I almost breathed a sigh of relief. I'd let her shout at me if she wanted, just not now. When did I become so fucking soft over her? No, she couldn't have a go at me about this. She needed to learn. Learn she had to earn everything I gave her.

The image of her flat on her back in the car invaded my thoughts. When I'd told her how beautiful she was and she'd told me I was too. How she'd looked at me like I was everything to her in that moment. I wanted her to look at me like that all the time.

Christ, I really am fucked up about this girl.

I was going to fucking lose my shit if this evening set us back. She was so bloody close to letting me have her body. If she made me wait any longer, I wasn't sure what I'd do with myself. Except I knew I would never force her. I couldn't rape her. She really had to want me or I wouldn't be able to live with myself.

I felt her shift in her seat as the host started addressing the guests. I couldn't stand these functions, but Zach insisted we attend them. A show of happy families. I'd give my performance and leave with my pet in tow.

I dropped my hand from her shoulder and sat back, half listening to the host whilst I watched Liora. She was staring at the stage intently, her posture far from relaxed. Brent told me she was nervous about this event. It annoyed me she'd become buddy-buddy with him, but I could hardly say anything when I'd left her alone with him for two weeks.

Provoked

I'd had things to do in the lead up to this evening. My father insisted on finalising the details with Angus about Liora's permanent stay with us. As if we hadn't had ample time for this over the past three years.

She glanced over at me, her eyes curious as if she knew someone was watching her. Her hands were folded in her lap, but she moved one of them. Her hand sat on my knee, palm facing upwards. It took me a second to realise she was asking me to hold it.

When I hesitated, she looked at me again before pointedly looking down at her hand. I placed my own hand in it and entwined her fingers together with mine. Why the hell did she want to hold my hand?

It was when I noticed my father staring at us, it finally clicked. She was trying to behave as though we were a real couple. I couldn't hold back a smile. I appreciated her willingness to play her part even if it was under duress. I felt her hand trembling in mine. This whole thing made her nervous and uncomfortable. And I could hardly blame her.

The host droned on for what seemed like forever before the first course was served. Liora spoke in low tones to James as we ate. I half kept an ear out for what they were saying, but it was all very mundane questions about what Uni had been like for her and whether she missed Scotland. By the time the fish course came out, they were discussing music and I zoned out.

"She's a better actress than I expected," Zach commented.

"Who said she's acting?" I replied.

"Mark my words, that girl has no intention of submitting to your every whim, son. She can fool the twins and James, but not me."

I shrugged, taking another mouthful of scallop. What could I say to that? I wasn't going to use his methods. He knew that.

"Have you been teaching her?" he asked, blue eyes intent on me.

"I don't know what kind of progress you were expecting since you did keep me in the office for two weeks dealing with her father."

He sat back, giving me a hard stare.

"Touché."

"It's the truth."

"That may be the case, but I expect you to have a handle on her."

I clenched my fist under the table. He always tried my patience. I had a hard time keeping my cool around him. Liora's hand curled around my fist, fingers stroking and coaxing me to calm down. I didn't dare look at her, wondering how on earth she'd noticed.

"I will. You might enjoy broken birds, but I don't."

My fingers uncurled. Before she could take her hand away, I shifted it under mine and flattened it against my thigh. She could fucking well keep it there. Her touch gave me tingles in the base of my spine.

"Suit yourself. She is yours. Keep in mind she needs to stay quiet about how she came to be in your possession."

He was damn fucking right she was mine. I'd earned her.

134

"She knows her place, Zach. I've been very clear about the rules."

"I'm glad to hear it."

He turned to Fi who was sitting on his other side, ending our little talk. I glanced at Liora then. Her face was flushed, the tips of her ears pink and she bit her lip, her fingers flexing underneath mine. I knew that look. Trying to hide her embarrassment regarding her body's reaction to me.

I decided to have a little fun with it. I moved her hand further up. Her lips parted on a silent 'oh'. I smiled to myself. She needed to get over it and stop being ashamed of wanting me. Stop thinking she could prevent the pull between us.

I could see James talking to her, but I knew she wasn't listening. Her eyes darted to mine. I saw the cocktail of emotions, wanton need standing out the most. I'd given her a lot to think about in the car earlier. I fucking hoped she'd behaved this evening so I could reward her.

The waiters came around to clear our plates so I let her go. I watched her slowly remove her hand from my thigh, fingers flexing.

"Excuse me," James said, eying the two of us. "I didn't think Avery would show up."

As James rose, I glanced around and spied his best friend. She was sitting with a man I didn't recognise. Was this the guy she'd married? James mentioned something about it a while back. I could see tattoos peeking out of his collar and he was built like a brick shithouse. Not the type of man I expected. Avery had always been into the smart, sensitive types like my brother.

I'd known that girl since my brother brought her home from primary school. He'd been in love with her ever since even if he tried to deny it. I was positive they'd been fucking at one point, but I knew Avery would never give her heart to James. I think them growing up together put a dampener on that. She was aware of some of our family history after all.

Last year, some major shit went down with her family. Half of them were facing lengthy prison sentences for sex trafficking and various other charges. Many of the men involved had already been convicted. Daniels Holdings had been taken over by some company in the US. James told me the two of them were helping the women her family had kept recover from their ordeals. That was the last time I had a conversation with my brother that didn't involve us exchanging barbs.

I turned back to Liora. She sat peering around the room with curiosity in her expression.

"Did you have a nice chat with my brother?"

She jolted, head turning to me.

"He seems nice."

James was nice all right, too nice for his own good. Except that nicety didn't extend to me. Considering what he thought about me, hardly surprising.

"Don't get too cosy."

One of her eyebrows arched upwards.

"I'm not interested in your brother. He might look like you, but that's where the similarities end."

I smiled, leaning closer to her.

"So, you admit you're interested in me."

Her face flushed in that incredibly adorable way of hers.

"Don't put words in my mouth. Whatever it is you're thinking, just stop."

"Me? I'm not thinking about anything."

She gave me a disbelieving look. I chuckled. She really was far too easy to tease and fluster. So fucking endearing. And here I was again, feeling things about Liora I shouldn't. I needed to get my act together before my father noticed my innate fascination with this girl.

I felt a hand on my shoulder. Looking up, I found James' best friend staring down at me. James sat back in his seat, a smirk on his face. I don't know what he was so fucking pleased about.

"Hello, Dante," she said.

"Avery… how are you?" I asked, trying not to be irritated by the sudden interruption.

"I'm fine. James tells me you've met someone."

James had a loud fucking mouth on occasion. Apparently, nothing was off-limits between him and Avery. It's not as though I didn't get along with her, I just didn't need my affairs on broadcast.

"And what if I have?"

Avery laughed, slapping me around the back of the head. If it had been anyone else, I would've told them to fuck off, but from her, it was okay. She behaved more like my little sister than the twins ever did.

"Stop being deliberately obtuse and introduce me."

I rolled my eyes and looked over at Liora. She was staring at the both of us with wide eyes. In that moment, she looked like a little blonde angel with a halo of hair framing her face and my heart thumped.

"This is Liora…" I paused, wondering how exactly I should describe the girl who'd just turned up at our table. "Avery is James' best friend and spent so much time around our house, she practically grew up with the four of us."

Whilst that was true, James also spent a lot of time around the Daniels' house when they were kids. I had to drag him home on several occasions much to his dismay. I was only five years older than James, but after our mother died, I looked out for him. I really wished I could tell him what I'd done to ensure our father mostly left him and the twins alone, but I couldn't. Not whilst Zach was still alive.

"Nice to meet you," Avery said, sticking her hand out.

Liora took it, but I could see the trepidation in her expression.

"You too," Liora said, eyes intent on me rather than Avery.

"I hear you're off the market," I said, wanting to steer the conversation away from my relationship with Liora.

"Yeah… Oh, I should've brought Aiden over to meet you."

"I'm sure I can say hello later."

She smiled, giving my shoulder a squeeze. I noticed it didn't make Liora happy. Her eyes narrowed to slits.

Is she jealous?

"I should get back, looks like they're serving mains."

Avery gave me a wink and sauntered off. Like that helped matters. Liora watched her progress all the way back to her table where she kissed the cheek of the man I assumed was Aiden and sat down. He wrapped an arm around Avery.

Liora visibly relaxed and stared down at her plate as the waiter served her. Some posh sounding beef dish. I never really paid much attention to the menus at these things. There was some sort of magician act on the stage, which caught her eye whilst she picked at her food.

I wanted to ask if she was doing okay but decided against it. I had to be careful about how I treated her in front of my father. So I watched her silently instead, making a note of the way her eyes darted around the room, appraising the people surrounding us and wondered what she made of them.

The evening progressed as I expected. There was the charity auction, followed by various speeches and finally the band started up. Couples stood up and took to the dancefloor by the stage. My father had disappeared off to speak to his associates along with the twins. James was over by Avery's table. Liora sat with her arms crossed, watching the dancers.

"Do you want to join them?" I asked.

"Join who?"

I stood up, putting my hand out. I never danced at these things but I was willing to make an exception for her. She looked up at me.

"Come dance with me."

Her eyes lit up for the briefest of moments before they darkened again and she looked at her hands. What the hell was that? I reached down, grabbed one of her hands and pulled her to her feet.

"It was not a request."

I pulled her along towards the dancefloor. She didn't drag her heels, but she didn't exactly seem like she wanted to come willingly either. Reaching the floor, I tugged her into me, wrapping my hand around her waist. Her hand landed on my shoulder when I started to move to the song.

"Do you not want to dance?" I asked after the silence between us stretched on for too long.

"I'm not very good at it," she said, her eyes on our feet.

"Eyes up, follow my lead."

Her eyes met mine. Even in the four inch heels I'd given her, she still barely came up to my shoulder. I held her closer, needing her body heat on mine. Being around Liora made me fucking crazy.

"See, it's not so hard," I said when I felt her relax.

Her hand on my shoulder tightened.

"Why is that girl over there staring at us?"

I followed her eyeline and found Hannah Delaney staring at us with a scowl on her highly made up face. Her dyed platinum blonde locks shook as she whispered furiously to the girl standing beside her. Her clearly surgically enhanced breasts were pushed up in her mauve floor length dress. I rolled my eyes. She was the daughter of one of Zach's associates and I really couldn't stand the girl.

"Probably because she's had her eye on me since the dawn of fucking time."

"And you didn't go there?"

I turned back to Liora, eyebrow raised.

"You think she's my type?"

I moved her further away from Hannah's eyeline.

"I don't know what your type is. I mean she is blonde like me."

I chuckled, shaking my head.

"I'll let you in on a secret, unlike you, she's not a real blonde."

"How do you know?"

"I've known Hannah since she was a bratty teenager going through a goth phase."

Liora looked back in the direction of Hannah and her friend again.

"You're right, I didn't notice she has dark eyebrows. So, you really haven't been with her?"

I wasn't sure why she cared about who I had and hadn't been with. I knew her history, but that didn't mean she needed to know mine. However, I didn't want her thinking I slept with girls like Hannah.

"No. For starters, she's fucking annoying with a whiney voice. I have no interest in spoilt brats who can't keep their legs closed."

Liora bit her lip. I could see she was holding back a smile.

"So me making you wait is a good thing?"

I should've known she'd turn this back on me.

"Have you forgotten how long I've waited?"

She shook her head, a grin appearing on her lips.

"Do you enjoy teasing me? Because I'm telling you now, I expect you to deliver if you're going to start down this road."

The flush creeping up her neck almost fucking killed me. How could I ever resist her? I needed this night not to end in disaster. She needed to give in.

"Dante… I…"

The song came to an end. We stopped in the middle of the floor and clapped. Liora wouldn't meet my eyes. What had she been about to say? I wanted to shake it out of her but making a scene would completely fuck up the pretence we were a couple.

I looked away, noticing Hannah stalking towards me, her hips swaying.

"Go find James. I'll see you in a few minutes," I said to Liora.

She didn't say anything, eying the room before making a beeline for my brother who was still standing with Avery. I strolled off the dancefloor and met Hannah halfway.

"Dante," she purred, putting her hand on my arm.

"Hannah."

"Who's the girl?"

Her eyes darted towards where Liora was still making her way over to James. Fuck. She really did look stunning in that dress. Seeing her bare back did things to me.

"None of your business."

Hannah pouted, her hand tightening on my arm.

"You've never brought a date before."

"What's it to you?"

I really didn't care for her attitude. I removed her hand from my tux. The sooner I got this conversation over with, the sooner I could go back to Liora and perhaps take her home. I was fucking done with this event. Zach wouldn't expect me to stay until the small hours, nor did I fancy watching a bunch of rich pricks getting wasted on the free bar.

"Is she your girlfriend?"

"Again, I fail to see how that's any of your business."

"Come on, Dante, you know our fathers would be happy if we got together."

I swallowed back bile rising up my throat. There was no fucking way that was ever going to happen. The only girl I wanted was already in my possession.

"You know nothing about my father."

"I'm sure he'd like to see you settle down with a wife."

I almost laughed in her face. Zach might want someone to take over his fashion empire, but he couldn't care less about my happiness or finding me a woman. Besides, I already had one. She might drive me fucking crazy with pent up desire, but Liora was mine.

"I'm only going to say this once, Hannah. I have never been and will never be interested in you."

She grabbed my arm again, her expression darkening as her other hand ran up my chest.

"You don't mean that."

Her touch made my skin crawl. I stepped back out of her grasp.

"Stay away from me, and if you dare go anywhere near my girlfriend, I will make sure you wish you never laid eyes on her."

I didn't wait for her to respond, striding off in the direction I'd seen Liora go. My fists clenched at my sides. I hadn't meant to call Liora my girlfriend, but fuck, that little whiney bitch did my head in. I dug my phone out of my pocket and fired off a text to my driver telling him to bring the car around. I was fucking done.

When I reached Liora, I took her by the hand.

"We're leaving."

Her eyes went wide.

"Why?"

I didn't answer. I nodded at James who looked bewildered and dragged Liora away towards the doors.

"Dante… Why are we going?"

In the middle of the lobby, I was stopped in my tracks by Angus Stewart and his wife. Liora's eyes went wide and her mouth dropped open. I'd told her she wasn't allowed to speak to her parents. That didn't account for them ambushing us.

"Dante," Angus said. "May I have a word with my daughter?"

His wife looked confused, her eyes darting between me and her daughter.

"Anything you wish to say to her, you can say in front of me."

Angus sighed before he looked at Liora. She edged towards me, her hand tightening in mine.

"Lass, all I can say is I'm sorry. I hope one day you'll understand."

Liora simply nodded at him. She knew if she said anything I'd punish her. I was more than a little surprised by her obedience. Her mother broke free of Angus' hold and bundled her daughter up in her arms.

"I'm going to kill your father," she whispered, but it was loud enough for me to hear. "I'm so sorry, Liora."

Angus pried her off Liora and dragged her back.

"Heather, stop it. I told you, it has to be this way," he hissed.

I could see tears welling in Liora's eyes. Her bottom lip trembled.

"She had her whole future ahead of her. You've ruined everything. I'll never forgive you."

"Come on," I said to Liora, pulling her away towards the doors.

She looked back at her parents who barely noticed us leaving. They were still talking furiously to one another. The driver was waiting by the doors with Liora's coat. I took it from him and slipped it over her shoulders. We followed him out to the car and got in.

Liora didn't say a word to me. She sat staring out the window whilst silent tears slipped down her cheeks. I picked up her purse from the seat and pulled out her tissues, handing one to her. She took it without looking at me, dabbing her eyes before she screwed it up in her fingers.

"Liora…"

"Don't, Dante. Just don't."

I wanted to punch my father in the face. He'd really fucked things up for me. Why the hell did he have to invite her fucking parents?

The rest of the journey was silent. I sat seething whilst she continued to cry. This was an absolute mess. This charity gala was always going to be a challenge for the both of us, but I hadn't anticipated it going quite so wrong.

Brent was waiting in the hallway for us when we got back in the house. His grin dropped when he saw us. He took Liora's coat from her. He looked like he was about to open his mouth when I stopped him.

"Don't fucking ask," I grunted, taking Liora by the arm and leading her upstairs.

When we were in my room, I sat her on the bed, kneeling down whilst I took her shoes off. She looked tired and dejected. I rubbed her knee to get her attention.

"What?" she whispered.

"I didn't know they would be there."

"I don't want to talk about them."

"Should I help you out of the dress?"

Her eyes snapped to mine. I was taken aback by the anger in them.

"No. Don't touch me."

She batted my hand away, stood up and paced towards the wardrobes. I got to my feet, confused by her outburst.

"I know tonight was difficult—"

She turned on me.

"Excuse me? I'd hardly call that fucking difficult. It was horrible. Christ, you expect me to just be okay with the fact that your father threatened me. How can I be okay with any of this? My dad fucking gave me to you for whatever reason and is acting like he feels bad about it when he's clearly lied to my mum until now. And if that wasn't fucking bad enough, you told me there was nothing going on between you and that girl and yet she had her hands all over you."

I stared at her. The first two things I understood but did she really think I'd lied to her about Hannah?

"I'm telling you right fucking now, Dante. I won't share you with another girl."

Chapter Eleven

LIORA

The moment the words left my mouth, I slapped my hand over it. Dante's blue eyes widened. I couldn't believe I'd just said those words to him. That I'd let myself get so worked up over a stupid girl. I was already angry with my dad, but the only thing I could focus on was that girl with her hand on Dante's chest and how much it upset me. How I wanted to storm over and tear her stupid dyed blonde hair out by the roots.

You idiot. You fucking idiot.

Minutes ticked by in complete silence. Since when had I got so enraptured by the man in front of me? Why the hell would I get jealous over a girl he'd told me he had no interest in? Why was I jealous at all? It made no sense. I didn't like Dante, did I?

You do like him. You want him. You need him.

I told my brain to shut the fuck up, but the words rang in my ears. I'd liked dancing with Dante earlier, liked the way he felt against me. How he'd teased me and I'd flirted back. I'd forgotten for one moment I was his pet. I'd allowed myself to believe in the fantasy that we were something more.

His sudden movement as he strode towards me made me freeze in place even though I should've backed away. He grabbed me roughly then his lips were on mine, devouring my mouth with ferocity. I surrendered, gripping his tux lapels. He backed us towards the bed as his fingers trailed down my bare back.

"You're mine," he said between kisses. "Mine, Liora. I don't fucking want anyone else."

He unzipped my dress before pulling away from me. His hands went to my shoulders, slipping under the dress.

"Just you. Only you. I want you naked beneath me. I want to fuck you so hard you scream. I want to whip you until your back is raw. I want to chain you up and hurt you until you're begging for a release. I should fucking punish you for even daring to tell me you won't share me. News-fucking-flash, you live in my house, sleep in my bed and I fucking own you. You don't get to dictate terms to me."

He tugged my dress off my shoulders and it fell to the floor in a puddle at my feet. I moved to cover myself, but he grabbed my arms and held me in place.

"Dante…"

"Shut up."

My heart pounded in my ears. He reached out, carefully pulling away the stick on bra and tossing it aside. I'd been undressed in front of him before, but this felt different. Dante's eyes roamed across me in a predatory way. I knew exactly what he wanted because he'd just told me. All of it should scare me. On some level, I was absolutely petrified by the thought of him hurting me further, but the other side of me grew wet from it.

His hand went to his bowtie and he tugged it off, followed by his jacket. He unbuttoned his shirt, tossing that off too. He wore a plain white t-shirt underneath it. I could see the outline of his muscles. My mouth dried up. All the blood in my body felt like it was rushing to my core.

He kicked off his shoes and unbuckled his belt. Then he took my hand and pulled me over to the bed. He made me bend over it, legs spread wide. I still had my lacy underwear on, so I wasn't quite sure what he intended. I looked back at him as he looped the belt around his hand.

"As much as I want to fuck you, you've misbehaved. There'll be no pleasure this evening. Only punishment. Do you understand?"

"Dante—"

"Do you understand?"

"Please don't hit me with that," I whispered.

"Don't make me repeat myself again."

I could feel my legs shaking. I gripped the sheets, horrified by what he was about to do to me.

"I understand, but please... please don't hit me with your belt."

His blue eyes darkened, his expression a mixture of anger and lust. I knew he was going to enjoy hurting me. He abruptly dropped the belt, advanced on me and ripped the underwear from my body. I winced as the lace tore across my skin.

The first strike across my behind stung. I gritted my teeth against the pain as the next ones came in rapid succession. I gripped the sheets harder, so I wouldn't dig my nails into my palms.

I lost count of the number of times his palm met my skin. Tears ran down my cheeks. It had nothing to do with how much it hurt. It really did hurt like hell, but I wasn't crying because of that. I was turned on by him hurting me. I tried not to squirm and alert him to the fact.

It felt humiliating to be aroused by having Dante slap me so hard, he'd leave marks on my skin. Was this why I'd never really been that into sex before? I'd never managed an orgasm with Max or Harrison. I knew how to get myself off, but I rarely masturbated. Yet now, I ached for that release. I ached for Dante. I wanted him inside me. I desperately wanted him to make me come.

Instead of a whimper or a cry tearing out of my lips, it was a moan. I didn't dare look at him because I hadn't meant it to come out at all. My face felt like it was on fire. Hell, my behind was on fire because of his spanking.

He didn't slap me again. Instead, I found his hands pressed on the bed next to me as he leant over me, panting.

"You're not supposed to enjoy this."

"I don't," I whimpered, even knowing it was a complete lie.

"Shall I test that theory? Tell me, will I find you dry as a fucking bone if I touch you?"

I trembled, my legs buckling underneath me. I was so turned on, I couldn't hold myself up on the bed properly.

"Please…"

"What are you begging for? Do you think you deserve my hands on you?"

I shook my head. Even though I knew I'd broken the rules, I didn't care. I couldn't stand this. Too worked up to even string a sentence together. I didn't recognise myself lying there at Dante's mercy. I was completely undone.

"Please…"

I felt the heat of his body above mine leave as he straightened. He kicked my legs open wider, exposing me to him completely. I should be embarrassed, but I wasn't any longer. He wanted me. Dante thought I was beautiful. He'd wanted me since the moment he saw me. And I had to stop lying to myself. I wanted Dante too.

"Dante… I'm sorry. I promised I'd be good and I wasn't, but I meant what I said. I don't want to share you."

When he didn't say anything, I dared look behind me. He wasn't there. I whipped my head around and found him standing next to the bedside table. He picked something up and brought it back around before kneeling behind me. A moment later, I felt the soothing cream on my skin and his warm hand as he gently applied it.

"I know you don't," he told me. "And you won't. I don't claim to be a good guy, but even I'm not that much of a bastard. Do you really believe I'd fuck another girl when I have you?"

"No… I guess not."

His touch soothed my aching skin but did nothing to end the raging inferno inside me.

"Good because I wouldn't. I've told you enough times, I only want you. You're mine."

My heart soared and my chest felt tight. I tried to hold back the things I needed to say, but it came out as verbal diarrhoea anyway.

"I want you too. So much. I'm aching. I don't know why you hurting me turns me on, but it does. I'm so done with this game we're playing. I'm tired of lying to myself. I'm tired of pretending I don't want to sleep with you. I do. I really, really do. I want you. I want you so much it hurts."

I turned my face into the sheets. I didn't have it in me to look at him any longer. Not after I'd just blurted all that shit out. His hands stilled. For a moment, nothing happened, then I felt his fingers trailing up my inner thigh until they met my pussy. And there was his confirmation my words were true.

He leant his forehead against my sore behind.

"Fuck," he whispered against my skin. "You have no idea how long I've waited to hear you say that."

I didn't dare move, unsure of what he'd do next.

"You can't have a reward tonight, Liora. You know that and yet... you're offering yourself to me anyway."

Whether or not I deserved a reward was inconsequential. Dante wanted to fuck me and I wanted to fuck him. Didn't that surpass the stupid rules? Couldn't he just cast them aside for one damn night and let this thing between us take over?

He moved away from me. My heart cracked. I finally looked at him. He shucked his trousers and took a step towards me. His hands went to my waist and he flipped me over, pushing me up onto the bed properly. I barely felt the pain from the covers pressing into my skin.

Dante crawled over me and I could hardly breathe.

"Are you on anything?" he asked.

It took a second for me to comprehend his meaning.

"Oh… Um, no. I should've told you before. I just…"

"You didn't expect to want it."

I nodded. No point hiding the truth from him any longer.

"Do you want me to have my doctor come and discuss options with you?"

If I was going to be sleeping with him regularly, then it made sense. There was no kidding myself into believing this would only happen once. And he was asking me rather than demanding it.

"Yes, I do."

"I'll have Brent call him tomorrow."

His eyes roamed down my body. His gaze burning into my already heated skin.

"You're so fucking beautiful. I've pictured this moment so many times, but nothing compares to having you here beneath me."

I wanted to touch him. My fingers itched to be on his skin. I wanted to see Dante. I needed it.

"Dante… I want…"

"You want what?"

"I want to see all of you."

He gave me a strange look which cleared after a moment. He sat up on his knees.

"I have a stipulation about that."

I frowned.

"Yes?"

"I don't like having my chest or back touched. At least not skin on skin. If you can promise to keep your hands away, then I'll show you."

153

So many questions entered my mind. I squashed them all down immediately. If Dante had reasons for it and he wasn't ready to share those with me, I'd have to suck it up.

"I promise. Where can I touch you?"

"My arms, my shoulders, my face, my neck and below the belt."

"Okay."

His fingers went to the hem of his t-shirt. He tossed it aside. All my senses tingled at the sight of him bare chested.

Holy fuck, he's so beautiful.

Even though I wanted to run my fingers across his abs, I resisted the urge. I promised him and I intended to keep to my word. But he said I was allowed to touch him in other places.

I half sat up, reached over and hooked my fingers in the waistband of his boxers. I'd never been forward like this before, but with Dante, everything was different. I looked up to find him with a mischievous smile on his face.

I decided to be a little braver. I sat up properly and tugged them down, freeing his cock which slapped against his stomach. He kicked them away. Seeing him with nothing on made my heart thump uncontrollably in my chest.

I ran my fingers down his shaft. He shuddered, leaning into my touch. He was already rock hard and pulsating against my hand. I knew the spanking he gave me turned him on just as it had done me.

"Dante… please… please fuck me."

He took my hands and pinned me down on the bed. His lips brushed over my jaw.

"Beg me, Liora. Make it impossible for me to resist you."

154

His lips trailed lower, brushing down my chest until he met my breasts.

"Please, I want you so much."

"More."

His teeth grazed over my nipple before he bit down.

"Ahh, please. I'm so wet for you."

He kept my hands on the bed as he licked, sucked and bit my nipples. I writhed beneath him, desperate to feel him.

"Please, please. I want you. Fuck. I want your cock in me."

I'd never told a man I wanted such a thing before.

"Please fuck me, Dante. I can't take it anymore."

He raised his head, staring at me with lust filled eyes. He let go of my hands, leant over to the side and pulled open the bedside drawer.

"Tell me what you want," he said, pulling out a small foil packet.

"You."

He tore it open and sat up.

"Me? What part of me?"

"I want… I want your body against mine and…"

He paused, waiting for me to continue.

"I…"

"Say it again, Liora. Say it to my face or I won't fuck you."

I felt about ready to combust. How could I not?

"I want your cock inside me."

He rolled the condom on, gripped my legs, forcing them open wider and settled in between them. He ran the length of himself up and down my thoroughly wet pussy whilst I squirmed beneath him.

"I'm going to fuck you hard and make you come on my cock."

"I've never come with anyone before," I whispered.

He raised an eyebrow, cocking his head to the side.

"No? I'll make sure you come so hard, you'll lose yourself to me over and over again. Only with me for the rest of our lives. You know why?"

I shook my head.

"You're mine forever."

I couldn't string a sentence together with the way he was looking at me. Time felt like it slowed down. It was just me and Dante and none of the bullshit surrounding us. I never wanted the moment to end. I reached up and cupped his cheek. He turned his face into my hand, kissing my palm. He leant down and captured my mouth. My fingers curled into the hair at the back of his head. It wasn't full of fire and passion, but gentle and sweet. He began to press his cock inside me. I gasped into his mouth. He felt so good even though he was taking it slow and allowing me to adjust to him.

He released my mouth and rested his forehead against mine, staring at me intently as he thrust deeper. Reaching up, he held my face with one hand. The other was planted next to me, holding him steady above me so he didn't squish me. I could feel his chest brushing against mine and I wondered if that was okay with him after what he said.

"Fuck... Liora," he whispered. "You're so fucking perfect."

His words completely unravelled me. The raging inferno wanted more. It needed more. I couldn't stop this rapid descent into madness with him.

"Please, please don't stop."

He inched further inside me. I stretched to accommodate him, each movement stoking the flames burning inside me. My other hand fell on his shoulder, holding onto him like he was the only thing keeping me afloat. And perhaps he was.

He pulled back and started to settle into a steady rhythm. I felt as though I was in the clouds whilst simultaneously drowning in the sensations he elicited. I kept my eyes open, staring into his blue ones. The connection between us clear as day to me.

Was I meant to be his?

Is that why this felt so right?

"Shit, you're so fucking tight," he grunted.

He let go of my face and gripped my hip, anchoring me to him. His thrusts intensified, pressing harder and deeper inside me. I moaned, unable to keep the sound back. His mouth met mine, drowning out the sound. There was no gentleness any longer. Dante commanded me with his mouth and his cock. And I fell deeper into the abyss.

I was his.

I knew it deep down.

I held onto him as he fucked me with reckless abandon. His movements growing erratic as we became completely undone with each other.

"Liora… Liora," he murmured against my mouth. "Say my name."

"Dante."

"Again."

"Dante… I'm yours."

He kissed me, tongues clashing together as if we were battling each other for dominance. Except it was clear who was in control. Who had all the power.

"That's right. Mine. Don't forget it."

I don't think I ever could. I was so intoxicated by the man inside me. Even if he saw me as his pet. Even if my father had given me to him for some unknown reason. I stopped caring about any of those things. They no longer mattered when it was clear as day. Dante was the person I longed for. The person who haunted my dreams. His blue eyes. His midnight black hair. The way the tenor of his voice rippled over me like a caress.

No matter how much we argued or provoked each other. No matter how much I hated the way he treated me like I was his property. I still craved this man with every breath I took.

"Harder, please, fuck me harder."

A sheen of sweat covered both of us as Dante took me higher. Nothing and no one felt like this. I wanted his domination. I needed it. I wanted to obey his commands. To do everything he said. I wanted to relinquish control. Except I wouldn't voice any of that out loud. Dante might command my body, but I couldn't let him in my mind.

You're kidding yourself if you think he hasn't found a way in already.

I quashed down all those thoughts raging inside me, focusing instead on the physical pleasure I felt with him. He said he was going to make me come, but I wasn't sure I could let go enough, no matter how much I craved the release.

"Dante," I whispered. "I don't know if I can…"

He didn't slow in pace, but his eyes searched mine.

"You're thinking too much. Concentrate on me. Don't think, Liora. Just feel."

I tried. I closed my eyes and focused on his movements. On the way his body rubbed against mine. How his cock felt inside me. The sensations each thrust elicited. I tried so hard, but my mind kept whirling with thoughts about how I couldn't come. I couldn't let go.

"Look at me," he said.

I opened my eyes, staring up into his blue ones. His gaze was so intense, it almost burned me to a crisp.

"You're going to come because I said so. You know who I am. I want you to say it."

If I said what he wanted me to, there would be no going back. He knew that. It's why I shouldn't say it.

"Master," I whispered.

"And what does your Master want?"

I swallowed.

"For me to come all over his cock."

He shifted, gripping my legs and pressing them upwards. He thrust deeper and the angle had him brushing up against my clit. It sent my pulse skittering and my insides coiled.

"You will let go. Do you understand?"

"Yes, Master."

What the fuck had come over me?

Calling him Master again?

Absolutely crazy.

"Please, Master. Make me come."

I couldn't stop. All of it too much. The tension inside me overflowed. And the next moment caught me completely off guard.

I was staring at Dante when it all exploded at once. The intense rush of sensations drove through me at an alarming pace. My fingers dug into his shoulders. My body felt like it'd been transported to another place. I didn't know what the hell was up or down. I saw spots in my vision. And I cried out his name because I couldn't hold it back.

I barely registered him continuing to fuck me with long, hard strokes, drawing out every inch of my climax well beyond what I'd ever experienced by myself. If this is what sex with someone who consumed you felt like, I never wanted it to stop. I needed to experience this level of bliss over and over again.

I shut my eyes, panting as my head lolled on the bed. My whole body felt like jelly. The deep-seated satisfaction melted my bones. I loosened my grip on him. I felt his lips on my jaw, trailing down until he nibbled my ear.

"You came so beautifully," he whispered.

"Did I please you, Master?"

Hell if I knew why I'd said that, but today was full of surprises.

"Mmm, yes, you did."

I turned my face upwards, opening my eyes. His shone with lust before he kissed me. I melted into him. He gripped my face, holding me still before he raised his head and stared down at me. His pounding knocked the air from my lungs. I couldn't help but be enraptured by his expression. The darkness in his eyes. A lone wolf. And I was trapped in his den, completely at his mercy.

I felt him pulsate inside me when he let go. He grunted, riding out his own climax without missing a beat.

"Fuck. Fuck, Liora. Fuck."

He all but collapsed on top of me, panting. I didn't object. Seeing him come undone like that was unexpected. He looked so blissfully happy. As if he'd finally broken free of the shackles he kept on himself. I wanted to make him feel that way again. I wanted Dante free to be himself around me without the need for masks and disguises.

I couldn't help but feel remnants of the terror from earlier when his father threatened me. I'd made up my mind now I knew what it felt like to really be with Dante physically. I wanted to stay even if it meant being his pet. Even if it meant him taking all my control away from me.

"Dante," I whispered. "Please don't let your father take me away from you. I want to stay here. I want you."

He kissed my shoulder, trailing his fingers up my side.

"I won't let him take you."

I wanted to wrap my arms around him and hold him close, but I knew that was off-limits.

"Thank you."

He hauled himself up off me and walked towards the bathroom. It wasn't long before he was back. He pulled the covers out from under me and got into bed. He tucked them around us and pulled me against his chest. I froze, unsure where the hell to put my hands. Normally, I would've curled them around his back, but that wasn't an option.

I wriggled against him, trying to work out what I should do.

"What's wrong?" he asked.

"I don't know what to do with myself."

He stared down at me, amusement in his eyes.

161

"Turn around."

I did as he asked. He pulled me against him, tucking my head under his chin. My back was flush with his chest. I felt the rise and fall of it.

"Is this okay?"

"If it wasn't, I would've put a t-shirt on. It's… complicated."

I tucked one of my hands into his, finding my eyes drooping. The events of the day had worn me out and the sex was the icing on the cake.

"I don't want to do anything wrong."

"You haven't. You were perfect."

I yawned, closing my eyes.

"I didn't know sex could be so intense," I murmured.

"That's just the start. When I put you up on the cross, you'll understand what you've been missing."

"Show me soon then."

And just before I fell away into oblivion, he kissed the top of my head.

"Don't worry, I'll show you everything."

Chapter Twelve

DANTE

Liora was fast asleep tucked up against my chest with her hand curled around my waist when I woke up. I froze, expecting the usual skin crawling reaction to having someone touch me skin on skin. It didn't come. I looked down at her, unsure of how to react.

Last night constituted the first time I'd ever had sex without a t-shirt on. Liora wanted to see me and I couldn't say no to her. The way she looked at me when I'd been bare before her gave me fucking heart palpitations. Her forest green eyes shone with awe as if seeing me was something to be savoured.

I'd been half surprised she'd got so wet from her punishment. A part of me knew she'd enjoy the same things I did, but I wasn't sure she'd ever let herself go enough to admit it. And holy fucking hell, sex with her had been amazing.

Liora was the most responsive girl I'd ever been with despite me needing to fall into my dominant persona to make sure she came. Her skin lit up when I spanked her. She'd looked so fucking beautiful bent over the bed with a red raw behind. The way her nipples hardened and darkened when I'd bitten them. Her pussy so hot, wet and tight. And when she'd fucking called me, Master, I'd almost blown my damn load. It was only the knowledge she needed me to stay the course so she'd come which kept my own climax at bay.

After the events of last night, I really shouldn't have given in and had sex with her. I couldn't help myself. She wanted me. She said yes. She'd begged when I told her to. I'd been completely incapable of holding back. And this morning, I wanted her again.

I cupped her face, turning it up to me. Her breathing was steady and even, her eyes closed. I leant towards her and pressed my lips to hers. She shifted a little but didn't wake up. I kissed her jaw, trailing my lips down her neck.

"Dante," she murmured, arching into my touch, her hand tightening on my waist.

Again, the skin crawling reaction didn't come. I honestly didn't know how to deal with this little fact or if I wanted to test it further.

"Wake up, Liora. I want you," I whispered against her skin.

I nibbled her earlobe, grazing my teeth over the sensitive skin. I was so fucking hard already. A combination of morning wood and having her naked in my arms. One night inside her sweet, slick heat and I was already abandoning all my normal rules. Sex was supposed to be her reward for good behaviour. My need for her overrode that.

I kissed her jaw again. When I looked at her, her eyes fluttered open. She looked half asleep. I held her face and kissed her. She responded this time, letting me taste her thoroughly. Fuck. I wanted to taste every inch of her. Mostly, I wanted my tongue between her legs.

"Come with me," I told her, pulling away.

I threw off the covers and picked her up out of the bed. I took her into the bathroom and set her down. Walking into the shower, I flipped it on before tugging her in with me. The water cascaded down both of us.

I held her face and kissed her. Whilst she kissed me back, her hands stayed at her sides as if she was scared to touch me. I dropped mine from her face and grasped hers, pulling her closer. I rested both her hands on my shoulders and held her body against mine. Her nipples grazed my chest, causing my cock to twitch.

Seriously, why the fuck is her touching me okay?

I couldn't understand it. I didn't want to question it, but this was a fucking revelation I had no idea how to handle. So I didn't. I backed her up against the wall of the shower, still under the stream of the water and pressed kisses down her neck.

I pulled away so I could kiss her breasts, running my fingers over her soft, wet skin. She gasped, her hands tightening on my shoulders. And then I got on my knees for her, running my tongue down her stomach.

She looked at me, green eyes wide. I spread her legs a little more and ran my fingers up her inner thighs before they met her pussy. Before she could say a word, I pressed my face to her, running my tongue up her entrance. She bucked against me and cried out when my tongue met her clit. Hell, she tasted so good.

I flicked my tongue over her clit, sliding two fingers into her. Her hands curled into my hair.

"Dante, oh… Oh shit."

I was getting water in my fucking eyes, but I didn't care. I closed them and continued pleasuring her. Her fingers dug into my head. I could feel her body shaking and bucking. This time, she'd have no trouble letting go. I'd make sure of it. I curled my fingers up, finding just the right spot as I fucked her with them. Her moans and pants got louder.

"Please, oh fuck. Please don't stop. Fuck, I'm going to…"

She cried out my name over and over again. Her body spasmed, her pussy clenched around my fingers and I tasted her all over my face. It was everything and fucking more. The way she came apart made me harder. I needed to fuck her.

I pulled away and stood up. I grabbed her face and kissed her, not caring her arousal was still all over my tongue. I pinned her to the wall, grinding into her stomach. My hands went to her hips. I picked her up so she had to wrap her legs around me to stay upright.

"Dante, you can't… not without…" she said, her eyes wide as she stared at me.

I'd completely forgotten. Too wrapped up in my need to have her.

"For fuck's sake."

I set her back down on her feet. I wanted to punch the wall. Why the hell had I never talked to her about birth control before last night? I should've fucking sorted this shit out long before now.

You know why. You didn't want to force her.

I ran a hand through my hair before shutting the shower off and taking her by the hand. I walked her over to the bath and made her bend over it. Her hands gripped the other side.

"Stay there."

I grabbed a towel and dried my hands before walking out into the bedroom. I pulled my phone off the bedside table.

ME: Call my doctor and tell him he needs to come over today to see Liora. I won't take no for an answer.

BRENT: No problem. Does this mean you two... ;) ;)

ME: Fuck off.

BRENT: I'll take that as a yes.

ME: Again, fuck off.

BRENT: Face it, D, you needed to get laid.

I was going to punch his stupid face in when I saw him. I dropped my phone back on the desk and pulled open my bedside drawer, fishing out a condom. Ripping open the packet, I rolled it on and threw the foil in the bin on my way back to the bathroom.

She hadn't moved, but she looked back at me. Her behind was marked with faint bruises from my spanking yesterday. My pulse spiked at the sight of them. Fuck. She was so beautiful.

I gripped one of her hips and lined myself up before sinking into her pussy. I grunted, feeling her clench around me. This would be hard and fast because I was so damn turned on by having her come all over my face and seeing her bent over the bath for me.

I held onto her other hip and pressed deeper until she'd taken most of me. I couldn't hold back. I gripped her tight with both hands and fucked her. It wasn't remotely gentle. I took her with brutal thrusts, feeling her contract each time. She moaned. I could see her knuckles going white from her hold on the bath.

"Do you like this? Do you want me to fuck you harder?"

"Yes, please, Dante, please."

My name on her lips had me slamming into her harder. I was so close. All the blood rushed to my head. I couldn't fucking stop. I needed to blow my load in this girl. She was the fucking universe.

"Fuck. Take it. Fuck."

I felt the familiar tingling in my stomach before I erupted. I grunted her name, continuing to fuck her with no mercy as the waves of pleasure rushed over me. Fuck. She drove me crazy.

When the last pulses faded, I leant over her and wrapped my arms around her, kissing her shoulder.

"Thank you," she whispered.

"For what?"

"Showing me how to let go."

I hadn't expected her to appreciate it enough to thank me for it. Liora continued to surprise me. I kissed her shoulder again. I'd show her as many times as she needed if it meant she continued to want me.

Liora was digging her way into the parts of me I didn't allow anyone access to. She made my heart race. I desired her more and more each day. Especially now I could actually fuck her.

I had to face it.

I needed her.

I just wasn't sure if she needed me too.

And that thought soured my mood completely.

The days which followed were almost blissful. Liora saw my doctor and in a couple more days, I could have her without worrying about condoms anymore. And I really fucking wanted her without having to stop to remember them. I was waiting until we were sure before I took her in the playroom.

It didn't stop her bending over my knee and letting me spank her. It turned her on just as much as it did me. She told me it was almost like a sexual awakening for her. We were provoking each other in a completely different way. One that led to passionate, heated exchanges. And everything about it was fucking wonderful. I'd known she'd be my match in the bedroom, but this far exceeded anything I expected.

I strolled into the kitchen. The staff weren't here as it was a Sunday, but Brent was pottering around upstairs. She'd promised me dinner later. Just the two of us. I'd scrapped most of the rules. She was allowed around the house without needing an escort. She wanted to be here with me.

Liora stood by the conservatory doors, staring out at the small garden with a cup of tea held in both hands. Her blonde hair caught the afternoon light, making her look almost ethereal. I didn't want to disturb her when she looked so peaceful. I stood in the doorway, smiling. It was if we were a whole new set of people now we'd found a way to communicate. Sex brought us together.

"I know you're there," she said.

I walked in and leant against the table. She turned to me, smiling.

"I have something for you."

It wasn't a reward for anything she'd done. I just wanted to make her happy. I'd told her she was allowed to use the bedroom I'd decorated for her, but she preferred to stay with me. She said she'd gotten used to having me there next to her. And truthfully, I couldn't imagine not having her curled up in my arms at night and it wasn't just because it gave me easy access if I wanted to fuck her.

"You do?"

She walked over and set her mug down.

"Mmmhmm."

I pulled out the envelope from my back pocket and handed it to her. She looked down at it, her eyes going wide. She fished out the documents and put her hand to her mouth. It wasn't exactly much, but I'd bought the two of us joint membership for ZSL, the Zoological Society of London, so I could take her to the zoo whenever she wanted to go. I knew how much she loved animals.

"That's not all, we can go on one of those Keeper for a Day experiences too when you're ready."

"Dante... you didn't have to do this."

I took the papers from her hands and placed them on the table. I tugged her towards me, staring down into her forest green eyes.

"I know you wanted to work at a zoo, so I'm trying to give you the next best thing."

I heard the doorbell go, but I ignored it. Brent could answer it.

"I've not been to London Zoo since I was a kid."

I cupped her face. This fucking girl. The way her eyes shone with happiness almost killed me. We both knew she wasn't my pet any longer. Liora was so much more. We hadn't spoken about my father or his threats yet, but we would. What the fuck would he think now if he saw us acting like a couple?

Whilst there were so many things we hadn't said and things we didn't know about each other, the deep pull couldn't be contained. I'd calmed down considerably now I had a part of her to hold onto. Her body was mine completely. I'd made sure of that.

"We can go during the week if you want."

She grinned, wrapping her arms around my neck. She brought her lips to mine, kissing me, pouring all her appreciation into it. I loved how affectionate she'd become towards me since we'd started fucking. My fingers tangled in her hair, the other hand running down her back, pressing her closer.

"Get your hands off my sister, you fuckin' prick."

Liora pulled back, staring up at me with wide eyes before she looked to the side. Her face drained of all colour. What the actual fuck was her brother doing here? And why the hell had Brent not stopped him? I looked over at the door. Brent

171

was hovering behind Liora's brother and another person. I immediately recognised him.

"Declan... Harrison... What are you doing here?" Liora said.

Her ex-boyfriend. Just what I needed. He looked exactly as he had in the photos Angus sent me. I had no idea what she ever saw in him.

"What am I doing here?" Declan seethed. "Getting you the fuck away from this fucker."

Liora's hands dropped from my neck. I watched her carefully. Would she want to go with Declan? Her brother looked like her, just older and male. My heart felt tight all of a sudden. I wouldn't let Declan take her, but I wanted her to stay willingly.

"Why?"

"Why? Why the fuck do you think? You're not some piece of fuckin' property Da can sell off to the highest fuckin' bidder."

I had no idea what Angus told them, but that wasn't the reason he'd given Liora to me.

"I wasn't up for auction, Declan."

I looked at Brent. His expression was pained, indicating Declan with his hands. I could understand why he'd had trouble keeping her brother out of my house. He was like a pitbull, his face contorted with rage.

"I don't give a fuckin' shit. You aren't staying here. I'm taking you home."

Liora looked up at me. I could see the conflict in her eyes. I wasn't going to tell her what to do. She reached out, took my hand and levelled her gaze back on her brother.

"No, you don't get to tell me what to do. I'm staying here with Dante."

Declan's eyes widened. Her ex-boyfriend just looked pitifully sad. And I wanted to wrap my arms around her and kiss her senseless.

"You what?"

"You heard me."

I took a step towards her brother, pulling Liora behind me.

"I'd like you to leave," I said.

"Oh, of course you fuckin' do. Don't want your dirty little secrets getting out."

I looked at Brent again. If Declan proved to be troublesome, it would take both of us to get rid of him.

"Look, I don't know how you found out where I live nor what Angus told you, but this has nothing to do with you."

Declan stepped towards me, fists clenched.

"He told me nothing. Our Ma sent me."

That made much more sense. Heather didn't know anything about this. I doubted Angus told her the whole truth.

"It doesn't really matter either way. Liora isn't leaving with you. She belongs with me."

"Belongs with you? Like fuck she does. You took her against her will."

Harrison put his hand on Declan's arm. Her brother looked back at him.

"Maybe we should go," Harrison said.

"Like fuck we are."

Liora came out from behind me, tucking herself under my arm and wrapping hers around my waist. Shit. I really didn't think she'd actually take my side over her brother's.

"I'm not going with you, Declan. You should leave. I don't know why you brought H here either. This has nothing to do with him."

Declan stared at her, his eyes bugging out as if he couldn't comprehend her words.

"What the fuck is this?" He pointed at her. "Have you got some kind of fuckin' Stockholm Syndrome? Is that why you won't leave him?"

She stiffened. This wasn't Stockholm Syndrome. I knew the way she felt about me was genuine because I felt it too. I just hoped she realised that.

"And I fuckin' brought him because he's your lad."

She looked over at Harrison. Her eyes were sad, but they also held a hint of irritation.

"He's not."

"What the fuck did you just say?"

"I said, he's not." She looked up at me. "Dante is."

Fuck me.

Of all the things I thought she'd say, that was not it. I saw it in her eyes. The stark honesty there disarmed me. I needed her brother out of my house because I needed a conversation with her.

"You're fuckin' kidding, right? Liora, don't be so fuckin' stupid."

She pulled away from me and took a step towards her brother.

"Go fuck yourself, Declan. You don't give a shit about me. You never have. You're only here because Mum fed you some bullshit story and you're her fucking golden boy. I'm not going with you. End of fucking discussion so you can leave and take

174

H with you. And I suggest you go now before Brent and Dante make you."

Declan stared at her as if she'd grown two heads. I'd been on the receiving end of Liora's diatribes before. Despite her small stature, she sure didn't pull any punches. Harrison looked at her as if seeing the girl he'd spent two years with for the first time. I guessed Liora was normally quite quiet and reserved. She certainly hadn't been that way with me.

Declan looked between us then he pointed.

"This isn't fuckin' over. I'm going to find out what the fuck is going on here and then I'm going to fuckin' take you down. You hear me?"

I rolled my eyes. He could certainly try. He really had no idea what he was up against when it came to my family, especially not my father.

"Just go. I don't want you here."

Without another word, Declan turned around and stormed out of my house. Harrison gave Liora one last significant look before he too turned and left. Brent followed them to make sure they were really leaving.

Liora rubbed her temples. I took her hands and pulled her into me, wrapping my arms around her back.

"I'm sorry," she whispered.

"You have nothing to be sorry for."

She looked up at me.

"I don't?"

"No, especially not after you told them to get out. I'm curious though… Why were you so adamant about staying?"

Her eyes darted away and she stiffened.

"If I'd gone, it'd piss your father off and I doubt he'd let you keep me after that." Her eyes met mine again. "I don't want to go. I want to be with you. Even if how I got here was really fucked up and I still don't understand any of it."

I swear my heart stopped in my chest. In a few short weeks, Liora changed everything. I knew now more than ever I'd made the right decision in making my father call in Angus' debt. Liora belonged with me.

"Don't… don't you feel what I feel? Tell me it's not just me. That I'm not being delusional."

I cupped one of her cheeks, brushing my thumb across it.

"You're not delusional. You're my girl, Liora. Haven't you realised that by now?"

I was so fucked. So, so, so fucking fucked. If Zach knew what was happening. If he ever suspected I felt things for Liora. Everything would go to fucking shit.

She went up on tiptoes and kissed me. Her mouth was desperate on mine. She pressed me back into the table, her hands running down my chest. I knew she loved to touch me even if she didn't voice it. I saw the longing in her eyes when we were naked together. I couldn't though. Not yet. Not until I was sure I wouldn't freak out on her.

She was out of breath when she pulled back.

"We have to pretend this isn't happening for Zach, don't we?"

"Yes."

"Okay. I can do that. Just… don't stop, Dante. I want to know you. And I know you want that from me too. Truth is, I've already let you in. So please, please don't let him ruin it."

My heart snapped at her words. As if I'd let my father fuck this up. She didn't know how much I despised him nor how much I wished he was dead. It was nothing less than he deserved for all the shit he'd put me, James, the twins and our mother, when she was alive, through. I almost shuddered at the thought of her. I couldn't. Not right now. Not with Liora looking at me as if I could break her if I said the wrong thing.

"Zach can go to fucking hell as far as I'm concerned. You and I aren't going to let him ruin anything."

The relief in her eyes was everything. I held onto her, pressing her face in my chest.

"I promise, Liora. I promise I'll do everything in my power to keep him from breaking apart you and me."

I just wasn't quite sure if it was a promise I could keep.

But I'd try.

I'd really fucking try my hardest.

I'd do it.

I had to.

For her.

Chapter Thirteen

LIORA

Standing just inside the zoo grounds with Dante's hand clasped tightly in mine, I felt like I was on cloud nine. Today was the day we could finally have sex without condoms. I knew it was driving him crazy having to remember every time. And there'd been a lot of times after the night of the gala.

I quashed those thoughts down. Tonight would be special. How he and I had gone from arguing and punishment to sex and spanking was beyond me. I knew our connection to each other was intense, but this was an entirely new level of insanity. Insatiable desire leading to explosive and mind-blowing sex. Every. Single. Time.

It wasn't just the sex. Something changed between us. Dante started opening up to me. In small ways, but it was still significant to me. It felt like we were at the beginning of the journey to get to know each other. The walls between us were tumbling down. His masks slipping away one by one. And the glimpse I had of the man underneath made my heart thump.

"Where do you want to go first?" he asked.

I looked down at the zoo map in my free hand.

"Why don't we go under the bridge and see that side first? I want to see the lemurs."

He smiled as I stuffed the map in my coat pocket.

"The lemurs, huh?"

"You can go in the enclosure with them, so yes, the lemurs."

He leant down and kissed the top of my head before tugging me away towards the tunnel. I'd been bouncing off the walls this morning much to his amusement. I didn't think he understood my obsession with animals, but I'd show him.

We stood in the lemur enclosure ten minutes later after we'd gone to see the giraffes and zebras. Dante was watching one of them climb up onto a post nearby. I adored their long ringtails and how cute they were.

"How can you not fall in love with their little faces? They're so inquisitive."

"I suppose they have a certain charm."

I looked up at him. He was grinning.

"Okay, fine, they're pretty cute. Happy now?"

"Very. Just wait until we go see the lions and tigers. Big cats are my favourites."

I squeezed his hand. He was doing this for me, but I could see he was happy here too. This was the first time we'd been out of the house together. Just the two of us. It almost felt like a date.

Is this a date?

After he'd called me his girl when my brother and Harrison turned up unannounced, my heart went into overdrive. I wasn't his pet any longer. I was something more.

As we walked towards the otters twenty minutes later after I'd got excited over seeing the sloths, I looked up at Dante. I couldn't help but wonder what exactly I was to him now. I'd been trying to work up the courage to ask him.

"So… Have you ever taken a girl to the zoo before?"

He eyed me for a moment.

"No. I haven't been to one since before my mum died."

I winced. I hadn't meant for him to bring that up.

"I've never really done the whole taking girls out thing."

I was sort of glad he'd chosen to glaze over the part about his mother.

"Does that mean you consider this a date?"

I put my hand to my mouth, stifling a smile. We stopped by the otter enclosure. A couple of them were swimming and the others were up on a rock. He raised an eyebrow.

"A date? Is that what we're doing? Dating?"

"Well, I don't know. I mean, I know I'm not allowed to leave your family, but it doesn't feel like I'm being held against my will any more."

He caught me by the waist and dragged me closer, leaning down so our noses were almost touching.

"Are you trying to ask me if we're in a relationship, Liora?"

I shifted in his grasp. Sometimes he read me all too well.

"No…"

"Oh, I think you are. It's written all over your face."

He captured my face in his hand and kissed me. It wasn't the sort of kiss he should be giving me in public. I felt as though he was devouring me whole. My face burnt. What if people saw us? So mortifying.

When he pulled away, his eyes were full of mischief. His thumb curved over my bottom lip.

"I don't think you've been listening to what I've been telling you from the start. You're mine forever."

"What if I want that to go both ways?" I whispered.

Why the hell did I just say that? I was seriously being idiotic now. How could he ever be mine too? I was his family's property, so that meant he would never be mine because you couldn't own someone who owned you. Could you?

"It already does."

My heart stopped. The whole damn world stopped. I stared at him for the longest time.

"Does that answer your question?" he said.

I nodded slowly.

"Good." He released me, turning to the otter enclosure. "Oh look, they're all cuddled up together."

I couldn't look at the otters, still reeling from his confession.

"Even I have to admit those little squeaking noises they make are cute."

He looked over at me.

"Liora?"

"Do you mean that?" I whispered.

His blue eyes grew darker.

"Would I have said it if I didn't?"

I shook myself. No. Dante never really said anything he didn't mean. I couldn't help the way my heart pounded in my ears, all the blood rushing to my head.

"Hey, are you going to faint on me? You look really pale."

He put an arm around me.

"If I thought you were going to get all weird on me, I wouldn't have told you."

I reached out, clutching his coat in a tight hold. What was wrong with me? Except I knew why I was reacting like this. What he'd admitted was monumental to me.

"Tell me truthfully. I've never really been a pet to you, have I? This was what you wanted all along. Just me and you."

He loosened the hold I had on his coat, taking my hand and placing a soft kiss to my knuckles. His blue eyes blazed with affection.

"I'm surprised it took you this long to work it out."

He didn't make it easy for me to see past his masks and the truth which lay behind them. He knew that. He was teasing me.

"Funny man."

He grinned, running his thumb across the back of my hand.

"Come on, I thought you wanted to see animals. We can talk about us later."

He was right. We'd come out to do something I loved. I turned to the otters. They were all huddled together, making squeaking noises. It made my heart sing.

"They are the cutest little things. Look, those ones are still young. They must've had babies recently."

"I'm sure you know all about otter mating habits."

I nudged him with my shoulder.

"Behave."

"Didn't they teach you? It's only natural."

I took him by the hand.

"Okay, we're going to see something else if you're going to start on that."

I dragged him away from the otters towards the tunnel so we could go back to the main part of the zoo.

"What? I wasn't trying to be crude."

"Yes, okay. Try telling that to those kids over there."

"I'm not sure their parents would approve."

"See? You've got such a dirty mind."

"Can you blame me? I mean look at you."

I rolled my eyes, continuing to lead him away into the main part of the zoo. He really did have a one track mind when it came to me. And I couldn't hide the fact that I loved it either.

Dante in the bedroom made my toes curl.

Literally.

The rest of the day was almost a blur. I hadn't felt so happy and free in such a long time. I even got Dante to admit he liked watching the lions and tigers. There was just something so majestic about them. He told me I got all gooey eyed and misty when I was around animals and it was 'cute as fuck'. His exact words.

He'd let me get several items in the gift shop and taken so many selfies of us with the animals, I was surprised his phone memory wasn't full. I was going to look at them all later. It'd remind me of how much fun we'd had together. How it'd felt so real between us. Because it was real. Me and Dante. We were something. We meant something. And I couldn't be without him.

We were laughing as we got through the front door. I almost didn't notice Brent hovering, a concerned look on his face. Dante frowned when he saw him.

"What's wrong?"

"Zach is here. He's been waiting for half an hour. He's not happy with you. I had to lie about where the two of you were and why you weren't answering your phone," Brent hissed.

Dante swore under his breath.

"Go upstairs," he said to me, his voice low. "Stay in my room and hide this stuff."

He pushed me towards the stairs. I looked back at him. He gave me a tight smile. This wasn't good. It wasn't good at all.

"What did you tell him?"

"That you'd taken her to a doctor's appointment," Brent said.

"Okay. Where is he?"

I started up the stairs, watching the two of them over my shoulder. I didn't want to see Zach.

"Dining room."

Dante sighed, running a hand through his hair. He nodded at Brent and strode towards the room he'd only shown me once. It was a formal dining area, but he never used it.

I hurried up the stairs and the second flight. When I got in his room, I stuffed my gift bags from the zoo in the wardrobe, kicked off my trainers and pulled off my coat. I sat on the bed, unsure what to do with myself.

We'd had the most amazing day together and now, Zach could possibly ruin everything. My heart went out to Dante having to deal with it. I worried. All his walls would go right back up. Everything we'd shared hidden under a carefully constructed mask. One I would have to wear too.

Having Zach here was a painful and stark reminder. I was their prisoner even if I didn't feel that way about being with Dante any longer. All of this could go wrong and it probably would. Who were we kidding? I still had no idea what was really going on. What my father had given me to Dante for.

I put my head in my hands. What a complete fucking mess. I couldn't afford to forget the sinister side of this relationship between the two of us. How I'd come here. How he'd told me I was their property. My heart cracked, fracturing into tiny pieces.

I tried to stop the tidal wave of doubt threatening to burst through. What if Dante was lying to me about how he felt? What if all these moments we'd shared meant nothing to him? What if today was part of his elaborate plan to destroy me completely by making me fall for him?

None of that seemed logical or rational. I knew the truth. I'd seen it in his eyes. In the way he touched me. Held me. The freedom we found together when we had sex. The moments of pure ecstasy and bliss.

I wrapped my arms around my chest. What Dante and I had surpassed anything else I'd ever felt about another person. I needed to remember that. Needed to focus on how he made me feel. I couldn't let Zach being here ruin it. I had to be strong. Dante would need that from me. I was determined to be exactly what he required.

Provoked

The door opened. I looked up as Brent walked in. His face was grave, his eyes betraying his inner turmoil.

"You're wanted downstairs for dinner. I suggest you put on something appropriate for it. I'll wait outside."

"Brent... Why is Zach here?"

"I honestly don't know, but you should be prepared. D said you'd know what to do."

I nodded and he left, closing the door behind him. I got up and went to the wardrobe. Searching through the rack, I found a rather demure black dress. I pulled off my clothes and put it on before slipping on a pair of black ballet flats. I brushed my hair and looked at myself in the mirror. The dress fell just above my knees. The long sleeves were sheer black lace.

Time to face the music.

I walked out of the room. Brent nodded at me. We walked down the stairs in silence. I felt sick to my stomach. Nerves coiled inside me. Sitting through a dinner with just me, Dante and Zach filled me with dread.

"It'll be okay," Brent said to me in a low voice when we stood outside the dining room door.

He opened it and I stepped in. There were three places set. Zach sat at the head of the table, Dante was to his left and the last plate was on his right. I walked around the table and sat down.

"Good evening, Liora," Zach said.

"Good evening, Zach."

I looked down at my place setting. Looking at Dante would kill me right now so I didn't.

"Dante tells me you had a check-up today. You're not unwell, are you?"

"I'm quite well."

What the hell else did I say? What kind of shit did Dante expect me to make up? I wished we'd had time to talk. I clenched my fist under the table, digging my nails into my palm. I had a part to play. He'd explained the rules to me. I'd do this for him. I had to.

"Sir wanted me to have a full health check amongst other things."

I dared glance at Zach. His smile chilled me to the bone.

"I see." He turned to Dante. "She's a little less… defiant."

"We've had words, Zach. She knows how to behave, don't you, pet?"

Nausea coiled in my stomach.

"Yes, sir."

This was just us playing our parts. No matter how much I wanted to run from the room and hide upstairs, I couldn't. I had to see this through.

Two of the staff came in with the first course. It was a cold dish of an assortment of beetroot, tomatoes and burrata cheese with micro herbs. Dante and Zach started, but I waited. This felt stupid. Zach looked at me, his eyes narrowing.

"Aren't you going to start?"

"Sir has not given me permission," I replied.

He looked back at Dante who shrugged and sat back. I finally looked directly at him. The mask was there. The sight of it almost crippled me. His blue eyes were sharp and cold. His whole posture was off. It made me feel incredibly alone.

"Come here and bring your plate with you," he said.

I stood up, picked up my plate and walked around the table, coming to a standstill next to him.

"Why don't we show Zach exactly how obedient you are, hmm?"

"Yes, sir."

He pointed at the floor.

"Kneel and put your plate on the floor."

I held back a retort. What the hell had gone on between him and Zach before I came down? I couldn't think of any other reason he'd be doing this.

I lowered myself down onto the floor and knelt at his side, placing the plate down in front of me. He gave me an approving nod. I stared up at him, trying not to betray the horror I felt at what I thought he was going to ask me to do next.

"Pets kneel at their master's feet. Have you forgotten that?"

"No, sir."

"What else do pets do?"

My tongue stuck to the roof of my mouth.

No. Please don't make me say that, Dante. Please.

"I'm waiting."

"They eat off the floor, sir."

He indicated the plate with his head. I died a little inside.

"Good girls get rewards, pet. Now be a good girl and eat for your master."

"Yes, sir."

I lowered my hands to the floor. The humiliation burnt into my skin. This went far beyond anything Dante told me I might have to do. Having to eat like an animal on the floor. Like his dog. An obedient bitch for her master. All of it was mortifying. And the very worst part of it all? Because it was Dante doing it. Because he was telling me what to do. Because I'd given him power and control over me. My body responded to it in a way I was not comfortable with. Especially not with Zach being there. Was I really that enamoured with Dante even this would provoke a reaction?

I pressed my knees closer together, trying to ignore what my body was doing. Tears pricked at my eyes. And I lowered my head towards the plate and ate. I ate everything on that plate like I was a dog whilst Dante and Zach continued on with a mundane conversation above me.

I probably had beetroot juice all over my face amongst other things. Raising myself back up on my knees, I waited patiently. When they finished, Dante finally looked down at me. He handed me his napkin. I took it, wiping my face before folding it up and placing it in my lap.

"Good girl."

"Thank you, sir."

He reached over and stroked my hair.

"You may eat the rest of the meal at the table."

"Thank you very much, sir."

"Take your plate and go back to your seat."

"Yes, sir."

I picked up the plate, held the napkin in my hand and got off my knees. I walked around the table and sat down, placing the plate in front of me. I held the napkin under the table between my fingers, pulling it this way and that in agitation.

"Give him your napkin, girl," Zach grunted.

I almost jumped. I hurriedly picked up my own napkin and slid it across the table to Dante.

"Yes, sorry, sir. I apologise."

Dante nodded, taking it and unfolding it across his lap. The staff came back in and took our plates. I kept my eyes on my lap. The shame I felt at being aroused by Dante telling me to eat food off the floor almost tore me in half. Why the fuck did that turn me on? It was awful. Never had I felt so degraded in my entire life. Not even when I realised my father had basically given me up to a man who was keeping me like I was his property.

No matter how I felt about Dante, none of this was right. I couldn't feel this way. I couldn't understand why my body would react like that. Did I desire Dante's dominance so much even that would get me going? What kind of sick joke was this? I'd been betrayed by my own body.

The rest of the meal passed without incident. Neither Zach nor Dante engaged me in conversation. I was allowed to eat in peace. By the time we'd finished dessert, I was exhausted and wanted to be far away from this room.

"Pet, you're dismissed," Dante said.

I looked up at him. His blue eyes held just a tiny hint of an apology in them. It made my heart sink. Could I even forgive him for putting me through this?

"Yes, sir. Thank you, sir."

I rose from the table.

"It was nice to see you, Zach. I hope to see you again soon."

"Goodnight Liora."

I gave him a smile before I gave them both a little curtsey and walked out of the room. Brent was in the hallway. I felt like shit and I needed something to make it all go away.

"Will you walk upstairs with me?" I asked.

"If you want."

We walked up the first flight of stairs in silence. Then I couldn't hold back tears any longer. They flowed down my face. I tried not to make a sound, but it was useless. Brent looked over at me, frowning when he realised I was crying. I ignored him, walking up the second flight of stairs until we stood outside Dante's bedroom door together.

"Liora…"

"Can… can I have… please, I need… something," I sobbed.

"What happened?"

"I can't… don't make me say it."

He fidgeted, rocking back and forth on his heels.

"Fuck it."

He stepped towards me and tugged me into his chest. I stood there with his arms around me, crying on his shirt.

"Whatever happened, I'm sure it'll be okay."

"It… it won't."

He rubbed my back.

"It will. D will make it better for you."

I stiffened. The mention of Dante was like a knife to the chest. He was the reason I was crying. What he'd made me do. How it'd made me feel. How it'd made me face the fact that I craved Dante dominating me on every level. I hated it all. I hated everything about this situation.

I stepped away from Brent and his arms dropped. I looked at our feet.

"No… he won't. Goodnight Brent."

I turned away, opened the bedroom door and closed it behind me. I couldn't face being around anyone. I tore off the dress and kicked off my shoes. Stripping off my bra, I pulled out a long t-shirt and tugged it over my head. Turning out the overhead light, I crawled into bed and sobbed into the pillow.

I was done with this. I'd had enough. I didn't want to want Dante any longer. How could I want a man like him? One who got off on dishing out pain. And how could I be a woman who allowed a man to hurt her because it aroused her? None of it made sense any more. This wasn't normal, was it? How could it be? I knew people enjoyed BDSM, but that wasn't me.

That's a lie and you know it. You want Dante's control. You love it when he hurts and fucks you. You crave him telling you what to do.

I sobbed harder, trying to drown out the voice in my head. It was no use. That voice was right. I did enjoy every part of it. And it brought me nothing but shame for ever feeling that way.

The door to the bedroom swung open. I saw him silhouetted by the light from the hallway. He shut the door behind him, plunging us back into darkness.

"Brent said you were crying."

I didn't answer him. How could I? I heard him move towards the bed before it dipped from his weight. He reached out, his hands finding me. Ripping back the covers, he tugged me against his chest.

"I'm sorry. You know I'm sorry I had to do that to you."

I cried harder, racking sobs escaping my mouth. Sickened with myself for finding solace in his arms around me. Hating myself for wanting his comfort.

"Shh, I'm sorry. Don't cry."

"It… it… humiliating."

He stroked my hair, kissing the top of my head before he leant his cheek against it.

"I know. I'm so, so sorry. He was such a fucking arsehole to me. Please understand. Please know it was so he'd believe me. Believe us. I never wanted to make you do that, Liora. That's not how we work and you know it."

I pulled myself out of his grasp. He didn't know what I was actually upset about. He didn't understand. How could he? I'd never told him how ashamed I felt.

"No… I'm… I'm not upset… Dante," I sobbed. "I'm not upset about that."

He tried to pull me back into his arms, but I shoved him away from me.

"What are you upset about, then? What did I do wrong?"

I wrapped my arms around myself and took a shuddering breath. I had to be honest with myself and him. Be honest about what was really going on. If I didn't tell him how I felt, then he'd never understand.

"I'm upset with myself and you."

"Why?"

"Even… even though it was humiliating… even though I should've hated you making me eat off the floor like a dog… I… I…"

"You what, Liora?"

"You telling me what to do... It... it made me wet," I whispered. "I hated it. I feel so ashamed of myself."

I looked at my hands.

"I've never been more degraded or humiliated in my life and the worst part is I feel betrayed by my own body. Don't you understand? How could I feel that way with him right there? How could I still want you when he was staring at me, making me feel like I'm some kind of animal?"

Chapter Fourteen

DANTE

Having Zach here this evening made my blood boil. He'd fucked up our perfect day together. Ruined it completely. And now she was crying. Crying and telling me how humiliated she was about finding me ordering her around a turn on. How she'd hated it because he was there.

I didn't know what the fuck to do, think or say. I thought she'd be upset about the dinner, about what I'd made her do. This was not at all what I'd been expecting to find when I came upstairs after seeing Zach out.

He'd told me in no uncertain terms before dinner if he didn't see progress this evening, he'd take her away and I'd never see her again. The thought of that damn near fucking killed me. So I did what I had to. I never wanted to make her eat off the floor like an animal. I'd seen Zach do worse things to women, but I couldn't subject Liora to his methods.

He'd slapped me on the back when she left the room and told me I'd become the perfect son. That made my skin crawl.

His hand on me. The words which left his mouth. All of it caused my stomach to rebel against me. I'd had to bite back my disgust and need to be sick. I was thankful he left quickly rather than forcing me to be in his company any further.

And then Brent told me she'd cried on his shoulder. I literally couldn't get up the stairs fast enough. Seeing her huddled under the covers, the awful sobs coming from the bed. That almost decimated me.

I had to say something to her. Break this silence between us. I had to acknowledge what she'd told me. I knew what I had to do. How to fix it for her. How to make her feel better. To help her understand she shouldn't be ashamed of her desires.

I reached over and turned on the lamp. Her tear streaked face and bloodshot eyes made my heart fracture, but I had to do this. I pulled out some tissues from the box on the bedside table and took her face in my hand. I gently wiped away her tears. She stared at me, green eyes wide with self-loathing.

"I want you to come with me," I said.

"Why? Didn't you hear what I just said."

"I did. Let me help you understand yourself better. Let me make it okay, Liora. You don't need to be ashamed of how you feel. Of what you desire. I know it feels awful because he was there, but please let me give you what you need."

"How can it ever be normal for me to want any of this?"

She looked at me like I could break her. So fragile. Christ, I really needed to help her.

"It has nothing to do with being normal. Let me help you."

"You're going to take me in… there, aren't you?"

I nodded. It was the only way. I had to show her what she wanted wasn't shameful.

"Okay," she whispered.

I helped her off the bed and we walked out the bedroom and along the corridor to the playroom hand in hand. I could tell she was nervous by the way her fingers tightened in mine. I unlocked the door, flipped the light on and walked in with her. I shut the door firmly behind us, locking it and leaving the key on top of the drawers.

She put her arms up whilst I pulled off her t-shirt and stepped out of her underwear. I left them on top of the drawers too, neatly folded. She didn't try to cover herself. She stood there waiting for me.

"In this room you will address me as Master. You will do exactly as I say without hesitation and you will thank me for everything I give you. If at any point you're uncomfortable or it's too much, then you will say the word tiger and we will stop. Do you understand?"

"Yes, Master."

The way she said it made my cock twitch. Fuck. This was going to drive me insane. I was not going to fuck her. I couldn't. Not like this.

I took a step towards her, cupping her face with one hand. Such a beautiful girl. I knew if this went wrong, I could seriously fuck her up. I leant down and kissed her forehead.

"I promise I'll make this okay for you, Liora. Do you trust me?" I whispered across her skin.

"Yes, Dante, I trust you."

I let the fact that she'd called me by name slide because this was me asking her for permission to do what was necessary.

I pulled away and walked over to the drawers. Pulling open the second from bottom one, I selected four leather cuffs. I took them out and closed the drawer.

"Go and stand in front of the cross with your back to me."

"Yes, Master."

She walked over and waited. I could see her hands shaking, but she didn't voice her fears. I walked over and stood next to her. I attached each cuff to her wrists and ankles. Taking one hand, I secured it to the loop on the cross above her head, followed by the other. I knelt down and secured her ankles.

I stepped back. Fuck. She looked so damn beautiful up there. Spread wide, awaiting my command. Liora had no idea what this did to me. I went over to where the whips were hung up. I selected a riding crop and a braided leather whip. Since this was the first time, I wouldn't be too rough with her. I set both down on the chest of drawers.

"Are you ready?" I asked.

She looked back at me. Her eyes were full of hesitation.

"Yes, Master." Her voice quivered on the words.

I picked up the whip first. It wasn't long, but it would hurt. I took a deep breath as I walked towards her, stopping far enough away to give me room to strike her. I uncurled the whip and it hung by my side.

It was time to show her exactly what pleasure from pain meant. To show her what she wanted from me wasn't wrong. To help her understand her desires weren't something to be ashamed of.

I flicked my wrist, the whip striking out across her back, just below her shoulders. It wasn't hard, but it left a faint red line. She whimpered but didn't cry out. She would be before the end.

I struck again and again, the red lines stark across the white skin of her back. She looked so beautiful. So, so beautiful up there. And she took each one without saying the safe word. She cried out as the lashes got harder, but I never took it too far. I wouldn't hurt her too much. Just enough to get her to let go of her fears and shame.

When I began to feel sweat beading at the back of my neck from the exertion, I stopped. She looked back at me, her green eyes wide.

"Th…thank you, Master," she choked out.

Fuck. Fuck me.

Too damn perfect. My jeans suddenly felt far too tight. This was not about sex. It was about teaching her to let go. I chanted that to myself over and over again in my head.

I placed the whip down and unbuttoned my shirt. I was getting far too warm. I stripped it off and folded it, placing it on top of her clothes. I picked up the crop. I'd marked her back and now it was time to mark her in other places. I stepped towards her.

"Do you think you deserve to be let go yet?"

"No, Master. I've been a bad girl."

"Bad girls get punished, don't they?"

"Yes, please punish me, Master, please."

Her forest green eyes screamed at me to hurt her. She wanted the pain. She needed it. Had she let go? Did she understand yet? I wasn't quite sure she did.

The crop made a slapping sound across her behind. She jerked in the cuffs, crying out. I hit her again. I could see tears welling in her eyes.

Slap.

"Please, it hurts, Master."

"I know it does. You wanted this, remember that."

Four more strikes. Tears fell down her cheeks. She whimpered with each one. If she wanted me to stop, she knew what to say. I trusted her to tell me it was enough. She had to trust herself. To know that this wasn't wrong.

I struck her further, noting how red her skin looked. How much she was suffering.

Damn it, Liora. Tell me to stop if you don't want this.

I wasn't sure how much longer I could hurt her without talking to her. Without her telling me it was okay. That this was what she needed. As much as I loved this aspect of our relationship, my heart was fracturing inside. She had no fucking idea how much it killed me. This whole thing. I had to be stronger for her.

"Have you had enough?"

"No," she whimpered. "Please, please don't stop."

"Liora—"

"Please, Master, please. I need you to continue. Please. I need it."

So I did. I hit her over and over until I was done. I was so fucking done. Her arse was red raw and the tops of her thighs too. As much as the sight of her almost had me abandoning all pretence that this had nothing to do with sex, I just couldn't.

I stood there, panting. Sweat dripped off my forehead and covered my chest. Fuck.

"Thank you for my punishment, Master," she whispered.

I threw the crop down and fumbled with the drawer, pulling out more cream to damn well rub into her skin because I couldn't stand it. What the hell had I done to her? Why had I thought this was a good idea?

I walked towards her and undid the cuffs on her wrists then her ankles. She stepped back, a little unsteady on her feet. I led her over to the bed and made her lie down whilst I applied cream to all of the lashes across her back and everywhere her skin was red. She hissed, but didn't complain.

I had to take her out of here. We had to talk because I had to fucking apologise for being such a dick to her. Why did I think this would help her? I said I wouldn't take her in here until she was ready. How could she be ready? And yet she'd begged me not to stop. I didn't know what the hell to think any more.

I helped her to her feet, grabbed our clothes off the dresser and the key. Unlocking the door, I tugged her out, not bothering to lock it behind me. No one would come up here this evening so it didn't matter.

When we were in the bedroom, I put the clothes down and strode into the bathroom. I splashed water all over my face and around my neck, trying to calm down the raging storm of emotions inside me.

"Dante…?"

I looked up. She was standing in the doorway, still completely bare. She took a step towards me.

"Let me help you."

"What? No. I don't need you to do that," I said.

"Why not? I know you don't like being touched, but that doesn't mean I can't help you."

I wasn't ready for this. To have her be concerned about me whilst I was fucking freaking out over everything.

"Liora, go back in the bedroom. We'll talk about it in a minute, okay?"

Her face fell.

Well shit. I'm really fucking this all up now.

I closed the distance between us before she could retreat, taking her face in both my hands.

"You shouldn't be concerned about me, Liora. Are you okay?"

"It hurts, but I'm okay. I feel... a little better."

My heart stopped.

"You do?"

She nodded, taking my hands away from her face and holding them in her own.

"I'm not going to lie. Having him here tonight was horrible, Dante. I hated it. You know he terrifies me. I wanted it to just be you and me and then he was there. You made me do something humiliating. It hurt me, knowing he was watching with the two sides of me warring with each other. One wanted you to tell me what to do and the other felt ashamed of it."

She squeezed my hands, looking away.

"I didn't know how to feel. How to react to it. I barely even recognised myself. You hurting me helped me focus. It calmed me down enough to think clearly. And I'm really not okay with this. Any of it. I don't know if I want this with you."

She dropped my hands, taking a step back from me. I couldn't move. I couldn't fucking speak. What she'd just said tore my insides to shreds.

You've fucked up. You've well and truly fucked up.

"How can I ever reconcile the fact that you act one way when we're alone together and another when he's here? I don't like that version of you. I hate it. You were so cold to me. I felt so alone at that table. You weren't on my side, Dante. You were on his and it hurt me. It really, really hurt me. Do you know what that was like for me? To see you look at me without any hint of the feelings I know we have for each other. Do you understand how much it broke something inside me? I can't deal with it."

She put a hand to her chest.

"It physically hurts. Right here."

My hands trembled at my sides. If her heart hurt, mine did too. What was she really trying to tell me? Was this the fucking end? Had we really come this far only to fall this hard at the first hurdle? If she thought this was the worst of it with my father, she was wrong. So very wrong. If she couldn't handle this, then how would she ever handle the truth of why she was given to me? The thought of it filled me with unending dread.

"What are you saying?" I asked.

I almost winced at the fear I heard in my own voice.

"I'm saying I think I should sleep in my own room tonight. I'm sorry, Dante, but I just can't. I need to be alone."

My stomach dropped out from me. The world fucking crashed down. I almost stumbled backwards. My heart burnt. My whole body burnt. Everything felt wrong. So, so wrong.

"Please, please don't look at me like that."

"Like what?"

"Like I'm hurting you. Please, Dante, please understand. Please let me have this. If I don't… I'm going to break and I can't. Not when there are so many things I still have to face."

"Then go."

Her face fell. I couldn't do this. I couldn't fucking breathe. She stepped towards me again. I wanted to back away, but I couldn't. She went up on her tiptoes before pulling my face towards her because she couldn't quite reach. She kissed my cheek, lingering there. Her mouth hovered over mine. I daren't move a muscle.

Her lips brushed against mine and she kissed me. My body went haywire. The knowledge she wanted to spend the night apart yet she was kissing me confusing me on every single level. She wrapped her arms around my neck, pressing her naked body against my bare chest. I almost lost it.

"Dante," she whispered against my lips. "Please kiss me back, please."

"I can't."

She pulled away, looking into my eyes.

"Why?"

"I won't be able to stop at just kissing. Do you realise how difficult it was for me to whip you without wanting more? I know this has been tough for you, but it's hard for me too. I don't want to put you through all this shit with Zach. I never have. For fuck's sake, Liora, all I care about is you. Can't you see that?"

Her small frame pressed against me trembled. I wanted so desperately to touch her. To hold her, but that would make it almost impossible for me to hold back.

"I've been so selfish. It's my fault you're here."

She shook her head.

"No, don't say that."

"But it is, Liora. I asked my father for you. He wouldn't have called in your father's debt if I hadn't wanted you."

Her eyes got watery. I felt like the world's biggest fucking arsehole. I'd done this to her. I'd made her feel like this. I saw it so clearly now. I'd sunk so damn low in my own estimation.

"Please, please, no. You're making it sound like you regret ever having me here."

"What? No, of course I don't regret being with you. Christ, you're the best fucking thing to happen to me, but that doesn't make any of this okay."

"Then what?"

What was I even saying? I hated the fact that I'd hurt her. Made her feel alone because I had to act like a complete prick to her in front of my father.

"I never meant to hurt you. I'm sorry I did."

It wasn't about the pain I'd dished out physically, but the emotional pain I'd caused her. The kind I couldn't take back or fix. Her body would heal. The marks I'd made on her back would fade, but the hurt she felt inside? That wouldn't go away. It wouldn't disappear so easily.

"Dante…"

"Just stop, Liora. Let go of me and go to bed before one of us says something we don't mean."

She dropped her arms from around my neck and stepped back. Her eyes shone with unshed tears. It ripped my already shattered heart into smaller pieces. She turned away and walked out of the room. I heard the bedroom door close quietly behind her when she left.

I backed away until my legs met the edge of the bath. Sitting down heavily, I put my head in my hands. I felt broken, battered and bruised on the inside. This was worse than the physical abuse I'd received at the hands of my father. Those scars healed, but the memories remained. Emotional scars running deep in my soul.

And Liora had just successfully torn my heart out and stamped all over it. I thought she was my perfect match. The girl who'd accept me for who I am. I'd hoped she'd understand when I told her the truth. Now I was worried she'd never get it if I did.

Zach would fucking kill me if he knew I'd even considered telling her the truth of what he'd done. How he'd completely torn our family apart and ruined my relationship with my siblings irrevocably. How he'd beaten me to within an inch of my life on several occasions and made me hate the touch of others. How he'd forced me to watch him hurt them over and over again. Forced me to watch him hurt her. Her. My heart burnt. I squashed the memories down.

Would Liora understand? Would she accept the broken man I was inside because of it? If I told her the truth, would she stay with me?

I was fucking terrified of losing her. If she left, Zach would find her and take her. And there was no way in hell I was ever letting that happen. Not when I knew what he'd do to her. The ways he'd hurt her far worse than I ever could.

Provoked

I'd done this. I'd fucking done this. Zach would've left her alone if it hadn't been for my idiotic need to have her. One look at Liora and I knew. She was it. No other girl would do.

I hadn't told her in the three years I waited to have her, I'd only been with one woman. I didn't really desire sex with anyone but Liora. And she'd probably think it was sick that I'd paid Gia to let me whip her on a regular basis and fuck her on a rare occasion. It wasn't as if she didn't enjoy it too. I hadn't seen her in six months nor did I plan to ever again. She wasn't Liora.

I got up, stripped off the rest of my clothes and stepped into the shower, washing away the dried sweat on my skin. Exhaustion set into my bones. The minefield of emotions I'd been through today left me tired and pissed off.

My perfect date with Liora?

Ruined.

The day I'd planned to worship every inch of her because it was supposed to be special?

Destroyed.

I flipped off the shower and dried myself before pulling on a clean pair of boxers and getting into bed. I turned out the light, laying on my back. Staring at the ceiling, my world continued to crash down around me.

What if she wanted to stay in her room longer than just tonight?

How would I cope if she told me she wanted to leave?

How could I convince her to stay with me?

How would I survive knowing she was in the next room and not right here with me?

Fuck.

My heart.

It burnt.

And I couldn't stand it.

I had to fix this. Had to make it right.

Because a life without Liora would be no life worth living at all.

Chapter Fifteen

LIORA

The bed felt strange and empty. Even though I was in pain, laying there on my stomach with the covers resting over me, it didn't matter much at all. Not when all I could think about was him.

There were so many things I hadn't known about myself before I came here. Hadn't recognised or wanted to acknowledge. The parts of me too dark to ever be normal. But he'd seen them in me. He'd known. In a strange sort of way, he'd made it okay. And now I'd fucked it up between us.

I couldn't stop thinking about what happened in the Den of Sin. I'd begged him to hurt me. Begged because of all the shame I felt at being the girl who wanted pain from someone she didn't understand. I wanted to. Desperately. I needed context to this messed up situation. I wasn't going to get that from hiding away from him but talking now would only make it worse. I hadn't articulated myself properly to him. So I'd wait until dawn broke. That's if I could even sleep.

The pain radiating from my back wasn't the issue. The pain in my soul was. The pain of knowing I didn't understand myself. Of forgetting I had a life I was going to lead until they'd taken me. The pain of my father giving me up and how it'd broken me seeing my mum fall apart. And having to witness the truth that I'd essentially strung Harrison along for two years.

I didn't much care about Declan and what he'd said to me when he came here. He was self-involved. If he ever cared about me, he had a fucked up way of showing it. When the other kids picked on me at school for being a nerd, he'd laughed along with them. He never looked out for me. He'd tease me about my love of animals, saying I was clearly into bestiality because I preferred our cats to humans. I'd lost count of the number of times I'd cried, so ashamed of being accused of wanting to have sex with animals. I didn't. I just understood them more than humans. I understood their motivations. Their needs. Their drive. Humans were a minefield of complications in comparison.

Was this why I'd gotten so worked up over having desires I didn't understand?

Had Declan really got inside my head that much and wrecked my own self-image?

He was such a prick. I could see his face now, telling me I was sick in the head for wanting a man to dominate me. Wanting pain because it brought me pleasure. Nausea coiled in my stomach.

I threw off the covers, scrambling out of bed. Every movement sent pain radiating down my back. I cried out before slapping a hand over my mouth. Then I ran, tearing open the door and sprinting across the hallway. I slammed into the bathroom door, fell to my knees in front of the loo and promptly threw up my dinner. I threw up everything in my stomach, the violence of it burning my throat.

Tears streamed down my face, spit and bile mixing in with them across my cheeks. I lay on the floor; the tiles cool on my heated skin and I sobbed.

I was messed up.

So fucked up.

"Liora?"

Light filtered through from the hallway.

"Christ, you're naked, right… Um… let me just uh… put this towel over you."

I recognised that voice. It wasn't Dante.

"Brent?" I croaked, my throat raw.

"What the fuck? Did D do that to you?"

He'd seen the lashes across my back. I felt something warm and fluffy cover me up.

"Are you okay?"

Was I? I didn't think I could answer that question right then.

"What are you doing here?"

"I had a rather frantic phone call from D saying he heard you crashing about and throwing up. He said you probably didn't want his help."

I'd be less embarrassed right now if it had been Dante seeing me like this. I ached inside at the thought. I wanted him, not Brent.

"Wow, it looks like a massacre in here."

I heard the toilet flush.

"Here, can you sit up? Let me help you."

I clutched the towel to me as he knelt down and pulled me into sitting position. My backside stung from pressing into the tiles.

"No offense but you look like something the cat dragged in."

He stood up and went over to the sink. I heard it running for a moment before he came back with a washcloth. He crouched down and mopped up my face with it gently.

"Thank you," I whispered.

"No need. You've obviously had a tough night. You know, he won't be happy I saw you naked."

That got a smile out of me. No, Dante would be pissed. Brent straightened, going back over to the sink. He brought back a small glass of water for me which I took and drank. It helped soothe my aching throat a little. He gave me a cap of mouthwash. I gargled and spat it in the cup.

"Right, now you look a little more presentable, do you want to tell me why you're naked, throwing up in the guest bathroom with lash marks all over your back?"

I looked away from him, feeling my face burning.

"We had a fight... sort of."

"Don't tell me he hurt you in anger?"

"What? No. That's not... he was trying to show me it was okay to want..." I looked up at Brent. "You do know what he likes, right?"

He rubbed the back of his neck.

"Well yes, I have seen the inside of his playroom. I helped him install everything."

"It doesn't freak you out?"

214

He gave me a long searching look.

"You're asking me because it bothers you that you like it too."

I looked down at my hands. Was I really that transparent?

"Look, what you and he enjoy together isn't wrong, Liora. Niche perhaps, but not wrong. You're both adults. If you've never done anything like this before then it's only natural to be scared or afraid. D is a good person deep down, okay? He's had a tough life and having you around… well… all I can say is he seems happier, less burdened."

"What did Zach do to him?"

He gave me a sad smile.

"You need to ask him that question."

I fiddled with the towel. What Brent said made sense. We were adults. And all I'd done was behave like a child. Running away from my problems and not wanting to face my new reality.

I wanted Dante. I wanted his domination. I wanted his pain. I wanted it all. What I didn't want was Zach and his threats in our lives.

"Do you think he'd want to see me now?"

"Considering how frantic he sounded on the phone…"

"Can… can you tell him I'm okay? I don't want him to worry."

"Do you want me to get him for you?"

I wasn't sure I did.

"Just tell him I'm okay."

"Are you? I mean really. Are you really okay?"

I shook my head. I wouldn't be okay whilst there was still this distance between Dante and me with all these unresolved issues.

"You're going to have to talk this out with him. Maybe not now because you've both had a long day and I'm sure you're exhausted, but you need to tell him how you really feel. He'll understand. He's probably the only one who will."

"I know… thank you, Brent."

"Don't forget what I said. It's perfectly okay to want the things you want with D."

I nodded. Hearing another person say that eased my troubled mind a little more. If Brent wasn't judging me then why was I judging myself so harshly? It's not as if I saw Dante as wrong for having what were essentially sadistic tendencies. I never really thought of him as being disturbed for needing to inflict pain. I just saw it as a part of him. A part I wanted to understand.

How could I judge myself as being sick and twisted and not him? Were we not the same? I wanted pain and he wanted to give it to me.

Brent walked out of the room. I heard him knock at Dante's bedroom door. It opened and their voices filtered through.

"Is she okay? She didn't hurt herself, did she?" Dante asked.

I could hear the worry and concern in his voice. It made my heart snap.

"She threw up her dinner, but otherwise, no extra injuries."

"What do you mean extra injuries?"

"Well… D… she wasn't exactly dressed for company."

216

I winced. Why did he have to tell him?

"For fuck's sake… you saw then."

"Oh yes. Was that you going easy because it didn't look like it from where I was standing?"

Had he gone easy on me? It hadn't felt like it at the time. Then again, it also felt right so what did I know.

"Don't start with me. You know I'd never go too far."

"She wanted you to know she's okay."

I wondered why Brent hadn't commented further on what Dante said. Did he have limits to the amount of pain he'd give another person?

"She did? I hope that means I haven't fucked up completely and lost her forever."

That felt like a kick to the stomach. Had I really made him think I'd leave him? At this point, I wasn't staying because of Zach's threats. I was here because of how I felt about Dante. He hadn't fucked up. I had. Or maybe, just maybe, we both had.

I got to my feet and walked over to the bathroom door. Both of them froze when they saw me. The look in Dante's eyes broke my heart in two. Scared, lost and alone.

"I'll say goodnight then," Brent said before making a hasty retreat downstairs.

For a very long moment, neither of us moved or said anything. The distance and the ache in my chest felt like a chasm, fracturing me in half. The towel fell from my hands and I strode towards him. I wrapped my arms around him, pressing my face against his bare chest. A part of me knew this was a bold move considering his aversion to being touched.

"I'm sorry," I whispered.

I felt the steady rise and fall of his breath and heard his heart beating double time against his chest. He didn't stop me or pry me off. Slowly, he brought up his arms and held me.

"I'm sorry too."

I lost track of how long we stayed like that before he pulled away. Taking my hand, he drew me towards my bedroom, away from his. Inside, he settled me back in bed, pulling the covers over me. He leant down and kissed my forehead.

I was struck with the sudden need not to be alone. I couldn't stand the ache and loneliness.

"Don't go," I whispered.

He sat down on the edge of the bed. Reaching out, he stroked my hair from my face. He didn't speak, just took one of my hands and held it in his own.

"I shouldn't have hugged you. I know how uncomfortable touching makes you."

I didn't know why I had to fill the silence. I wasn't ready to sleep. My mind was too full even though my body was running on empty.

"With you... it's different."

"What do you mean?"

"With everyone else who has ever put their hands on me, it makes my skin crawl. That doesn't happen with you."

I stared at him, trying to unpack what it meant. How could I be the only one he could stand touching him? Was this a part of our connection to each other? It wasn't as though I believed in destinies or fate.

I let go of his hand. He watched my hand as I reached out towards him until it landed directly on his chest. I felt him shudder beneath my fingertips and let out a long breath. I was about to pull away when he placed his hand on top of mine.

"Don't… don't move," he whispered.

He dragged my hand down the length of his chest and across his stomach. I could feel every ridge of his muscles. How soft his skin felt against mine. I'd wanted to touch him for weeks. I couldn't believe he was letting me.

"Is it okay?" I asked.

His eyes met mine as he let go of my hand. All I could see was the relief in them.

"Yes."

I twisted around and sat up, facing him. I brushed my fingertips across his chest, watching his expression for any hint of discomfort. When I found none, I continued my tentative exploration lower, brushing across his abs.

I took a deep breath, trying to steel myself. Brent told me to tell Dante the truth. Even though our evening had been emotionally charged, I felt calmer. Being able to touch him gave me a sense of grounding.

"Declan used to make fun of me all the time, making out like I had some kind of sick perversion about animals because I liked them more than humans. He started this rumour at school and it got out of hand. I tried to ignore the looks and the taunts. He never got in trouble, but I knew he'd done it."

I licked my bottom lip, trying to work out how to explain things properly.

"I cried at night, ashamed of the accusations. To me it made no sense. My love of animals isn't something shameful and he made out like it was. I feel like that's maybe why I've reacted so badly to this whole situation between us. Because I felt that level of shame all over again."

I pulled my hands back, settling them in my lap as I looked down at them.

"All of this has been confusing for me, but what Brent said to me is right. What I want with you isn't wrong. I don't judge you for wanting it. So I've been asking myself why I'm judging me. Why do I look at myself like I'm some kind of freak for wanting your dominance? The truth is, I don't really know. I don't know who I am anymore. And that terrifies me."

He was silent for a long time. I looked up at him when I couldn't stand the silence any longer. His eyes were assessing, taking in the parts of me I'd laid bare to him.

"Your brother is a dick."

"He hasn't gotten any better as an adult."

"No, can't say first impressions endeared me to him."

"Having him here felt like my old life collided with my new one."

He reached out and took one of my hands.

"You're not a freak or any other terrible things Declan might have said about you. It's okay to be scared. You just need to tell me, okay? Tell me what's wrong rather than pushing me away. I know I really fucked up this evening with Zach and I didn't make it easy for you to talk to me. I'm not blaming you for any of it."

The situation between us was all kinds of messed up but placing blame on each other was pointless. I knew that.

"This is only going to get harder, Liora. It's going to get worse with him. I understand if you can't handle it, but I need you to. Not for my sake. For your own. Tonight… before you came down, he told me if he didn't see improvement right then, he'd have taken you with him."

Dread filled me instantly. My skin prickled at the thought of Zach tearing me away from Dante. No wonder he'd been so cold and distant towards me. His behaviour made more sense in that context. At least to me, it did. All Dante had done was try to protect me and keep Zach from taking me. Even if it'd hurt me, he'd done it for the right reasons. If there were any right reasons in this fucked up mess.

"I hate your father," I whispered.

"Join the club."

"Why do you do it? Why do you put up with him?"

He looked away from me, his expression growing dark.

"I don't have any other choice. It's the only way I can keep them and you safe."

"Them?"

"Jen, Fi and James."

Wait, what? Protect his siblings from Zach? What does he mean?

"Why do they hate you if you're protecting them?"

"They think I'm like him. I had to do that in order to fool Zach too. They don't know the truth. They can't. It's for their own good. So even if they hate me, it's worth it to keep them safe from him. I couldn't sit back and watch him hurt them any longer. So I did what I had to… it's a lot to explain and now isn't the time but know that I'm not my father. I'm not a monster like him."

My heart broke for him. I read between the lines. Zach abused them all. I could see it in his eyes. Physical and emotional abuse. I didn't want to press him. I couldn't imagine it was easy to talk about.

Was that why he had an aversion to touch? Had his father really hurt him that much?

The whole thing made me ill. I didn't think I could hate Zach any more than I already did. I was wrong. He was a monster like Dante said.

"I won't lie, you did behave like a dick to me in the beginning. It's different now."

He smiled at me. A smile which made my heart thump.

"Not that I'm excusing your behaviour or anything, but I didn't make it any easier."

"I think we're both at fault for different reasons. I'd like to try and put this behind us so we can move forward… together."

"Together?"

He took my other hand in his.

"Yes, you and me. Us. Together. No matter what I ask you to do, it's to protect you from him. To keep you safe. I meant what I said at the zoo. This goes both ways. I am yours and you are mine."

My hands tightened in his before I let them go and shifted closer to him. He wrapped his arms around me and held me close to his chest with a gentle touch so as not to aggravate my back any further.

"Will… will you stay here with me?"

"Didn't you want space?"

"Not any more. I just want you."

He shifted back a little, lowering his face and brushing his nose against mine. His hand curled around my waist, thumb brushing over my stomach. His breath dusted across my lips.

"Liora," he whispered.

My name on his lips sent my pulse skittering out of control. "Dante."

His mouth met mine in a gentle kiss. Pulling away, he shifted up onto the bed and tugged me onto his lap. I cupped his face with one hand and the other ran down his chest. He shuddered, letting out a groan. We kissed again. It wasn't passion. It was desperation. We needed each other. Needed the connection. Craved it with every breath we took.

His fingers tangled in my hair, gripping the strands. I pressed closer, my nipples brushing against his chest, sending sparks across my skin.

"I want you," he murmured against my mouth. "I want you so much."

I fumbled with his boxers. He shifted enough for me to pull them down. His fingers were between my legs, stroking me. My body felt tight, my back hurt, but I didn't care. I reached down and grabbed his cock. He shifted his hand up onto my thigh and I sunk down on him. I held his face in both hands, kissing him. He gripped both my hips, encouraging me to rise and fall on him. He felt so good. The events of the night melted away, leaving just me and him.

He sat up straighter, hands running up my sides before his fingers tangled in my hair. His other hand splayed out across my back. Whilst it stung a little, the pain kept me grounded. It helped me focus. Each lash mark reminded me I'd enjoyed every moment of his punishment. I'd let go of so many things in that room with him. So many burdens I didn't realise I still held onto.

I wrapped my arms around his neck, releasing his mouth as I rested my forehead against his. We were both breathing heavily, staring into each other's eyes. There were so many unspoken words between us.

Don't leave me.

Stay.

Be in this with me.

We can face this together.

I am yours.

You are mine.

I couldn't leave him. Not because of Zach. My feelings ran too deep. I'd have to cut them out by the root if I was ever to be free of Dante. I had no desire for freedom. He'd ensnared me. I was his. And Dante? He was mine too.

I rode him harder, feeling the now very familiar sensations building inside me. I ran a hand down his chest and my fingers found their way between my legs. As if he knew exactly what I needed, he gripped my hip and thrust up inside me whilst I stroked myself. It sent ripples across my skin. Wave after wave of intense bliss pulsated through me. I moaned, shuddering and clenching around him. He continued to thrust into me, grunting as he met his own end.

He collapsed back against the headboard, taking me with him. My head lolled on his shoulder with his fingers still stroking through my hair. There weren't any words, so neither of us spoke.

After catching my breath, I pulled away, grabbing the tissue box off the bedside table before I slid off him. I cleaned up. Sex without condoms was a little messy, but I didn't care. It'd been exactly what we needed.

We curled up under the covers together with me pressed up against his chest and my hand curled loosely around his waist. My eyes grew heavy. I listened to the sound of his breathing and the steady thump of his heart against my fingertips.

I hoped we could put this evening behind us. Hoped we could learn from this and move forward.

I should've known this was only the beginning of the horrors awaiting us.

I should've known Dante and I weren't safe.

Not whilst Zach still lived and breathed.

And not whilst his threats loomed over both our heads.

Chapter Sixteen

DANTE

I watched her sleeping for the longest time, tracing my fingertips down the lash marks covering her back, careful to be gentle so she wouldn't stir. Liora was the most beautiful girl I'd ever known and seeing the marks I'd made on her back, marring her perfect skin made me so fucking hard. I wasn't about to wake her up for sex though. She'd been through enough. Christ, we'd both been through enough fucking shit yesterday.

I shook myself inwardly. Now wasn't the time to think about my father and his threats. He'd fucked things up between Liora and me last night and I wasn't about to forgive him for it. At least I knew why she was so upset. I was fucking pissed as fuck at her brother for ever making her feel like she was a freak. She could never be a freak to me. Liora was like a breath of fucking fresh air. And I was done denying I needed everything about her.

"What are you doing to me?" I whispered. "How do you make me feel so vulnerable when I'm around you?"

It was as if she could strip everything back with a single glance. I never let her know that's what she did, but it was the truth. The way her forest green eyes seared into my soul was unnerving at times. Did she know she was doing it? Did she realise she had that much power over me?

I leant down, pressing a kiss to each mark on her back in turn. She uttered a soft sigh, but her breathing didn't change. She was still dead to the world. Such a fucking beautiful sight she was. So innocent with her blonde hair a mess on the pillow. That halo she always wore. Fuck. I didn't want her to change it. Her hair suited her the way it was. When we'd first met, it'd been longer, but now, it framed her face perfectly.

"Christ, Liora, you make me feel things I've never felt for anyone," I murmured against her skin. "I hated seeing you in so much pain last night."

I didn't want her to wake up and hear me confessing this shit to her. I wasn't ready to face up to the reality of how I felt about this girl. How she was the only thing keeping me fucking sane in this mess.

I shifted away, snagging my boxers from the floor and pulling them on before I stood up. I left her in the room I'd designed for her whilst I prowled to my bedroom and pulled on a t-shirt and shorts.

It was Saturday, so the staff weren't here. I took the stairs two at a time and strolled into the kitchen. I noticed the cafetière had been used. Brent was up then. At least he wasn't in here. I wasn't in the mood to discuss what happened last night. Not when he knew I'd taken Liora in the playroom. I'd seen his disapproving expression when he told me he'd seen her back. It wasn't like he didn't know what happened in there. It was for her, not for me. I didn't have to explain that to Brent though. It was none of his fucking business.

I set about pulling various things out of the cupboards deciding she deserved breakfast in bed. I wanted to make shit up to her. Make sure she understood I cared about her. Wanted to make her happy even if it cost us everything. Liora was worth that. She was worth everything I'd gone through.

I was just mixing up pancake batter when I heard the front door slam. I frowned. Had Brent gone out? He usually told me if he was. Except it wasn't Brent at all. I heard footsteps down the hall until they stopped at the kitchen door. There were only a few people who had the keys to my house.

"Hello, James," I said without turning around. "What brings you here?"

The twins never came here so it could only be him. I knew what Brent's footfall sounded like. He lumbered around like a fucking beast.

Why the fuck was my brother here? He almost never came around willingly even though I'd told him enough times he was welcome here whenever. I suppose it didn't help that he hated me and that was entirely my fault.

"Is Liora here?" he asked.

"She's sleeping. Why?"

"I need to talk to you."

I turned, setting the whisk down in the bowl. He was leaning against the doorframe, his arms crossed over his chest. He did not look happy.

"About what?"

Of course he hadn't come here wanting to actually see me. Not for the first time I felt like the world's worst fucking sibling. Even though this was for his own good, it still didn't sit right with me. It never had.

"What is really going on?"

"You're going to have to elaborate."

"You might be able to fool the twins into thinking she's your girlfriend, but not me."

I raised an eyebrow. Is that what this was about?

"She is my girlfriend."

She was now, at least. I hoped I'd made that clear enough to her yesterday. She wasn't my pet or my gift. She was just mine full stop.

"I don't fucking believe you. You and Dad are involved in something and she has everything to do with it. Tell me the truth."

"The truth? What truth would you like, James?"

He huffed, looking even more put out than before. His brow furrowed.

"I thought it was all in my head, that what I heard didn't amount to anything, but then you show up with her."

I stiffened.

"Heard what exactly?"

"You and Dad last year, you were talking about her, weren't you? Arrangements and stuff and then that time where Dad almost ripped me to shreds and you pulled him off me, I heard the name Stewart. Drop the act and tell me the truth. What is she to you and Dad?"

I took a step towards him.

"Like eavesdropping on us, do you?"

230

"Don't look at me like that. I'm not an idiot, I'm your fucking brother and I deserve to know what the hell you and Dad are involved in."

I wasn't going to tell him anything. I'd been careful to keep him out of this. Keep him and the twins safe.

"I'm not involved in anything with Zach and Liora is my girlfriend."

He sighed, uncrossing his arms from his chest and straightening.

"I knew this was a bad idea. Fucking Avery meddling in shit. You know, she told me to give you a chance. Seems to think there's something good still lurking underneath all that fucking bravado you put on, but she's wrong, isn't she? You're just like him."

I clenched my fists. I wasn't like Zach at all.

"You have no fucking idea what you're saying."

"Don't I?"

"You wouldn't understand even if I did tell you the truth. Just leave it alone, James. It's better that you stay as far away from this shit as possible."

His eyes widened a fraction.

"What do you mean?"

"I just told you to leave it alone."

He stepped towards me.

"No, what do you mean?"

I ran a hand through my hair, stepping backwards until I hit the counter.

"Did you ever stop to think why I took you and the twins away from Zach in the first place?"

He eyed me for a long moment.

"No."

"Then perhaps you might want to consider that before you start accusing me of being like him. You might want to remember what he did to all five of us."

His face crumbled. I knew the exact words to hit him with.

"Don't bring her up."

"Then don't toss around accusations. I protected you. Think about that next time you want to come around here and have a go at me."

"Dante…"

"What? What do you want me to say, James? I'm fucking tired of this."

He looked like a little lost puppy, staring up at me like I'd just stamped all over him. I couldn't fucking take it. I was exhausted. Putting up these walls between us. Trying to protect him. It'd taken a toll on me.

"I'm sorry."

My heart almost stopped in my chest. What the hell was he apologising for? If anyone needed to do that it was me for treating him like shit for too long. It didn't matter why I'd done it; I knew I'd hurt him.

Before I could reply, Liora walked in. Her hair was tousled and she was only wearing a robe, her bare legs on show. And fuck if it didn't do things to me seeing her like that. My heart slammed against my ribcage and my cock stirred in my shorts.

James turned at the sound of her footsteps, eyes widening.

"Oh… hello," she said.

I wanted to reach out to her and hold her to me, but I stayed where I was, watching the two of them silently. James shifted on his feet.

"Hey… um… I should go."

"You don't have to," I said without thinking.

"No, I really should."

"James…"

I made to take a step towards him but he put his hand up.

"I need time, Dante, just… leave it."

He nodded at Liora before walking out. Her green eyes met mine as she teetered on her tiptoes. Christ, she was so damn cute, it almost killed me. We both heard the front door slam.

"Are you okay?" she asked.

"You were supposed to stay in bed."

If she noticed I'd avoided her question, she didn't comment on it.

"I wondered where you'd gone."

I indicated the bowl behind me.

"I was making you breakfast until James turned up."

"Why was he here?"

I shook my head. I really didn't feel like rehashing that conversation. Especially not with her. I'd already said enough last night.

"Dante—"

"Come here."

She frowned but took a step towards me. I reached out, snagging a hand around her waist and pulling her into me. She hissed at the contact with the lashes on her back. I felt shit momentarily before my mouth descended on hers. She clutched my t-shirt, a small mewl of surprise emitting from her throat. Warmth spread through me. She tasted so sweet. She always fucking did.

She flattened her palms on my chest and pushed me back. Her lips were red and glistening. I picked her up and planted her on the counter next to the bowl and continued preparing breakfast. I was very tempted to untie her robe to see if she was wearing anything else underneath it, but I resisted the urge.

"Why was he here?"

"Just leave it alone."

She put a hand on my arm.

"What's going on?"

I sighed.

"He wanted to know the truth about you, but obviously I can't tell him that. Zach would kill me."

Literally. He wouldn't tolerate me revealing his dirty fucking secrets to James. No matter how much I wanted to heal the rift between us. And we'd been this fucking close to having a genuine conversation without any of the bullshit before she walked in. It didn't matter. All of it was better left unsaid right now. Better for James because if Zach found out he'd come here and demanded to know the truth, he wouldn't hesitate to teach James a lesson. With his fists. He didn't give a shit that his son was a twenty two year old grown ass fucking man.

I looked at her. Her eyes held the compassion I knew I'd see but didn't deserve in the slightest.

"I'm sorry," she whispered.

I shrugged her hand off and went back to making her breakfast. I set the pan on the stove and let it heat up.

"Dante… don't do that."

"Do what?"

234

"Just shut me out like that. Didn't you tell me we're in this together?"

I had, but this was different. Shit. Why did she see through me? Why did she have this much damn power over me? I needed to regain some semblance of control over this shit. I needed her to stop trying to get in my head.

"Do I look like I want you to play therapist for me right now?"

She flinched, her eyes betraying how my words cut her.

"Why are you acting like this?"

"Just sit there quietly and let me make fucking breakfast for you. Can you do that one thing for me or are you content with pushing me further? I'm warning you, I'm not in the fucking mood."

She stared at me, but kept her mouth shut. The myriad of emotions flashing across her face killed me. I'd upset her. I knew that, but I couldn't fucking help it. James being here had messed with my head and now her pressing me was making it worse. Why the fuck couldn't I just be normal for once?

I continued with what I was doing. Keeping my hands busy would stop me lashing out at her any further. She didn't need that from me at all. Hell, she really didn't need any of this shit from me. I'd put her through far too much last night. What with making her eat like a dog in front of Zach and then putting her up on the cross and whipping her delicate skin. I didn't deserve her being nice to me or trying to help me.

I pulled out plates and mugs, setting the table in the conservatory before I sliced up fresh fruit. I cooked the pancakes, making sure to turn them at the right time until there was a nice stack of them for both of us. I made tea and set everything out on the table.

She sat on the counter, waiting for me with her hands in her lap. I stepped towards her, nudging her legs open as I cupped her face.

"Don't be upset with me."

She didn't answer.

"Liora…"

Her green eyes were pools of pain and her fists clenched in her lap. I dropped my hands to them, placing them at her sides. I undid the belt of her robe and sucked in a breath when I pushed the sides back, revealing she was wearing nothing underneath.

"I'm such a bastard to you," I whispered, dropping to my knees in front of her.

I closed the distance between my face and her pussy, keeping her legs open with my hands banded around her thighs.

"Dante… what are you—"

My tongue met her clit and she bucked against me.

"Oh, oh… but they'll get cold. Oh, sweet… fuck…"

I no longer cared about breakfast. All I cared about was my face between her legs, bringing her to the brink. Her fingers tangled in my hair, tugging at the strands.

"Oh fuck, don't stop, please. Dante, please."

Her breathy moans of pleasure drove me crazy and the way she said my name set me on fire.

"That's it, Liora, come on my tongue," I told her.

I nipped and sucked on her clit as she ground her hips into my face.

"Oh fuck. Oh god."

"I'm not your god," I growled.

"No," she moaned. "No, you're not. You're my Master."

I just about lost it. My tongue lashed against her clit harder, feeling her shake and tremble in my hands. I couldn't help it. Whenever she called me that, it made me feel like I was her everything. I was the only man she looked at like she was drowning in me. Like she couldn't get enough.

She cried out, her fingers digging into my scalp as she came all over my tongue. Hell, she was the sweetest damn thing I ever tasted. I loved being the only one who gave her this. The only one who brought her to the brink and sent her over the edge. No one else could have that from her. Just me.

Leaning back, I looked up at her flushed face and her chest heaving as she tried to steady her breathing. Such a beautiful sight.

"Was that your way of apologising to me?" she whispered, her voice all breathy.

I smiled. Maybe it was or maybe I just needed to have her come all over my tongue. Either way, it didn't matter. She was talking to me again.

I pulled myself up off the floor, tied the belt on her robe and plucked her off the counter. She had to wrap her legs around my waist as I carried her into the conservatory and set her down on a chair. I pointed at the plate.

"Eat."

I sat down opposite her and poured out the tea whilst she picked up her knife and fork.

"You've never made me breakfast before."

"I don't make a habit of cooking for anyone else."

She smiled as she dug in, like it was special that I'd actually made the effort for her. I had shit to make up to her after last night. Plus, I was pretty sure she wouldn't want to deal with a 'Brent Special' consisting of orange juice and cornflakes. Fuck knows why he enjoyed eating it.

"Thank you," she whispered before sticking a fork full of pancakes and fruit in her mouth.

She groaned, the sound vibrating right through me.

"This is so good."

"Even though it's cold?" I replied eyebrow raised.

"Worth it."

I bit my lip. Fuck yes, it'd been worth it. Getting to hear her call me Master was worth anything. I wanted her to call me that again when I fuck her against the cross. I'd promised her that. Whipping her until she begged and then fucking her until she came. Her back had to heal first. Then I'd take her back in there and show her what it could be like between us. Show her that what we'd had was just a taster of how much pleasure I could give her. I doubted Liora would be the same after I was finished with her. And I was fucking hard just thinking about it.

I finished off my own plate in record time, watching her over the top of my mug of tea. She fidgeted under my gaze as she ate.

"Dante…"

"Hmm?"

"Quit staring at me."

"I want to look at you. You're beautiful."

She averted her eyes as her face blossomed red. Shit that was always so cute. Her getting flustered over me. She set her knife and fork down, pushing her plate away.

"Come here," I said.

She looked up at me, cocking her head to the side. When I didn't say anything else, she sighed and stood up, coming around the table to stand next to me. I twisted the chair around so I was facing her.

"I like it when you obey me."

"Don't get used to it," she retorted, but I could see from her eyes she wasn't being serious.

"There's something you need to take care of."

I leant back, deliberately looking down at where my dick was straining against my shorts. Her eyes followed mine. She bit her lip.

"How would you like me to do so?"

"You can return the favour or you can sit on me, the choice is yours."

Liora hadn't yet gone down on me, which was fine, but I was curious of whether she'd choose to do so or fuck me. She shook her head.

"I want… no… I need you to tell me which one you want… Master," she said, her voice just above a whisper.

Holy fuck.

"Get down on your knees and suck my cock."

To her credit, she didn't miss a beat. She dropped to her knees and reached for me, curling her fingers into my shorts and boxers and tugging at them. I shifted so she could pull them off me. She wrapped her hand around the base of my cock, stroking it slightly. I stifled a groan.

"Now, Liora. I want your lips wrapped around me."

"Yes, Master."

She leant over me and took the crown of my cock in her mouth, using her tongue to swirl around the tip. I almost fucking died. Shit, her mouth felt so good.

"Fuck," I grunted.

She took more of me, using her tongue to lavish the underside of my cock. I was in heaven. How the fuck did she get so good at this? Actually, I really didn't want that question answered. Thinking about anyone else having their hands on Liora or her pleasuring them made me sick to my stomach. I knew she'd only been with two people before, but it didn't make me feel any less irritated by it. She was meant to be mine three years ago and instead she'd had a fucking relationship with another guy.

I had to reign this in. Three years was the agreement so she could finish her degree. I didn't want to pull her away from the things she loved. Not really. It didn't mean I had to like that she'd been with another guy for two of those years.

I wound my hand into her hair, gripping it as I shoved her down further on my cock. She gagged a little, pushing against my thigh with her free hand. I didn't let her up for a long moment, savouring the way her mouth felt around my cock.

She took a gulping breath of air when she pulled back, staring up at me with those insanely intelligent green eyes of hers. Her hand was still wrapped around me, squeezing gently.

"You're good at that," I told her.

"I want to please you, Master."

Fuck me.

Something shifted within her last night. I could see it now. The way she was looking at me spoke volumes. She needed this. Needed me to tell her what I wanted her to do and when. Right now I was her master and she was my pet.

"You are."

Her smile made my heart stop. It was if my praise was the only thing she needed.

Fuck Liora.

How the hell could I have ever lived without her? This girl was like a drug and I was addicted to her smiles. Addicted to the way she tasted. Completely addicted to the feelings running through my veins when she was around me.

Her sweet mouth was on my dick again and I couldn't stifle a groan. Fuck she really did know how to drive me crazy.

"Hey, D… oh, oh holy fuck, what the…"

I looked up. Brent was standing in the doorway, eyes wide before he slapped a hand over them, turning away. I'd been so wrapped up in having my dick attended to I hadn't noticed him coming in.

Liora tried to pull away, but I kept a hand on her head, forcing her to stay.

"I need to talk to you, but I'll come back later."

"No, don't… Hold on one sec," I said.

When I was sure he wasn't going to leave, I leant down towards Liora, my lips brushing over the shell of her ear.

"I didn't say you could stop," I told her, my voice low. "I told you to take care of my cock and you're going to unless you want me to bend you over my knee and spank you in front of Brent as punishment for displeasing me."

Sarah Bailey

I probably shouldn't have fucking said that. I probably should've let her go given what happened last night in front of Zach, but I didn't care. Her lips around my cock felt too good.

She shifted on her knees, pulling my cock out her mouth to respond to me.

"Yes, Master," she whispered.

"I'm going to come down your throat and I want you to swallow every last drop for me."

"I want your cum, Master."

Fuck. How on earth could I even think straight when she said shit like that? She took me in her mouth again and started sucking me in earnest. I could feel her trembling, but she didn't stop.

"Good girl."

I leant back and looked up at Brent. He was still averting his eyes and his face was a little flushed. He'd worked for me for years and not once had he ever walked in on me before. Though, honestly, I'd never had a girl on her knees for me in my conservatory. Usually I kept that strictly in the playroom.

"What do you want?" I asked.

"Really, D? I can come back."

He looked so fucking uncomfortable.

"Just spit it out."

"I… For fuck's sake, okay… I need to go deal with some shit next week with my family so I won't be around. Sorry I didn't say anything earlier, but you know what my sister is like."

I'd never met any of his family, but I knew his sister was a pain in the arse.

"How long will you be gone?"

"A couple of days."

That meant I had to be here to make sure Liora was safe. No real hardship, but I just fucking hoped Zach wouldn't start any shit with me.

"Fine. Is that all?"

"Yes... Yeah..."

He shifted on his feet for a moment.

"Fuck, okay, I'm going. I really didn't want to see this shit," he muttered turning away and walking out of the room.

I smiled, turning my attention back to Liora who was still sucking my cock like it was the tastiest thing she'd ever had in her mouth. She looked so fucking hot with her lips stretched around it, taking as much as she could without gagging.

"Faster," I told her, my fingers digging into her scalp.

I was so close, wound up so fucking tight.

"Fuck, Liora, more... please."

I hadn't meant to sound like I was pleading with her, but my voice was all fucking high pitched and needy.

"Fuck, fuck," I grunted as hot streams of cum erupted from my cock, coating her mouth and the back of her throat.

Ecstasy didn't quite cut it. Coming in her mouth was utter fucking bliss. I felt her struggle to swallow as I jammed my dick further in her mouth just to prolong the damn fucking insanely delicious sensation of her lips wrapped around me.

When I finally let her go, she used her tongue to clean my cock, making sure she got every last drop. Then she pulled my boxers and shorts back up, tucking me away before she looked up at me. I was almost too spent to say anything.

"You're such a good girl," I murmured.

I put a hand out to her. She shifted off her knees and crawled into my lap, curling her arms around my neck. I captured her chin and kissed her, not caring I could taste myself on her lips. I needed that connection, craved it.

"Thank you, Master," she whispered as she lay her head on my shoulder when I released her mouth.

I was fucking done. She was perfect. So fucking perfect. I couldn't live without Liora. Not when she embraced what was between us. Not when she submitted herself to me entirely just by doing everything I said.

I kissed the top of her head.

"Let's go take care of your back, hmm?"

I picked her up and carried her upstairs so I could take care of her.

And I'd keep taking care of her if it was the last fucking thing I did.

Liora was mine.

And I was fucked because I was hers too.

Chapter Seventeen

LIORA

Watching Dante pace back and forth in front of me, gesticulating with his free hand whilst he was on the phone to Zach had me on edge. The irritation in his voice made the hairs on the back of my neck stand up. Whatever Zach was saying had well and truly set Dante off.

"No… I'm not fucking bringing her to that shit so you can think again… What? No. I don't give a shit, Zach. This was not part of the deal."

I wanted to reach out and hold him, but I knew Dante wouldn't welcome that type of affection right now. It was hard enough to get him to accept any affection when he was in a mood. It was on his terms. Honestly, most things were on his terms and I was beginning to be okay with that. After our conversation about Declan things had changed significantly for me. I'd been trying to let go of my fears. Let myself be Dante's girl. His pet. His sex toy. The submissive girl who got off on the pain he wrought. All the roles he needed me to play.

It didn't stop me wanting to reach out to him and make sure he was okay. Hell, I was so bloody enamoured with the man in front of me it was borderline pathetic. I craved Dante every moment of the day. I wanted his attention. His affection. His pain. I wanted all of him, but he wasn't so keen on me getting inside his head. He was mine, but I still wanted more. Sometimes he was so open and others, he had his guard up and hid behind all his masks.

"You don't have to fucking remind me… I'm not being fucking precious. She is mine. I don't recall what I do with her being any of your fucking business… What the hell is that supposed to mean?"

My fingers itched. I stared up at him, wondering what Zach wanted and why Dante was so against it. I mean, it was Zach so likely it was nothing good, but Dante always seemed to defer to his father. He said it was to protect me, but I was beginning to suspect there was more to it. Like him having feelings for me. Ones he'd never voiced aloud, but I knew deep down were there anyway. Just like I had feelings for him. Feelings I'd never really wanted to have.

"You're going to pull that card? Fuck… Fine, but you tell your friends no one is to touch her. I don't share my toys and I don't want their fucking hands on her. Do you hear me? She is out of bounds… Fine. I'll see you tomorrow."

He hung up the phone and threw it on the bed, storming away to the window where he slammed his hand down on the wall.

"Fuck."

I wasn't sure what to say. Whatever he'd agreed to clearly had been under duress.

"I'm going to kill him, fuck," he muttered.

"Dante… Is everything okay?" I ventured.

His back stiffened. I knew very well everything was not okay, but what else could I say to him? I just wanted him to come here so I could wrap my arms around him and tell him we'd get through whatever it was Zach wanted us to do. Even though I wasn't sure exactly what it was.

"No, everything is not fucking okay. Fuck, he's fucking everything up again."

I stood up, taking a step towards him.

"Will you let me…" I faltered.

"Let you what?" he barked, causing me to flinch.

"Hold you?" I whispered.

My heart ached seeing him like this. The sensation burnt in my chest. I needed to be close to him. To feel his heart pounding against his ribcage. I needed the reminder I was more to him than just a girl he liked to punish and fuck.

When he said nothing, I crept towards him and came to a halt inches from his back. He knew I was there. I was still the only person who was allowed to really touch him so I decided to take my chances. I closed the distance, pressing myself into his back as my hands drifted under his t-shirt and came to rest on his stomach. He took a long shuddering breath before he somewhat relaxed into my hold.

"I've got you," I whispered.

And I did. No matter what, I wasn't about to run from this. This man who captured my attention on a fundamental level and was digging his way into my very being. My soul.

His hand dropped from the wall and he leant back against me, a deep sigh emitting from his throat. He curled both hands around mine, holding me to him.

"I wanted to take you in the playroom later, but now I can't."

"Why not?"

We'd discussed it a few times. He wanted my back to heal first, which it had. The marks had faded because he'd been careful in his approach to whipping me. He knew exactly how much to dish out for my first time. I desperately wanted that feeling back. The pain of his lashes set my body on fire. And this time, I knew he'd have me begging for his touch. Begging him to fuck me because his pain brought me pleasure. I'd stopped beating myself up for wanting that with him.

"I can't take you to this fucking party tomorrow with marks all over you. I want to, fuck do I want to. I need it, Liora. I need to hurt you and that's really fucked up, but it is what it is."

"What party?"

I wasn't going to comment on the fact he wanted to hurt me because I already knew that's what he needed. And I liked it.

"Zach holds these parties for his friends where they… share their toys."

I stiffened. That's what he meant by telling Zach his friends weren't allowed to touch me.

"Have you been to one before?"

"Yes, but I didn't get involved. They're all willing participants. Doesn't make it any less fucked up. I wish I didn't fucking have to take you there, but Zach wouldn't take no for an answer."

Zach had some kind of power over Dante, but I didn't ask him what that was because I was pretty sure he wouldn't answer me.

"Why does he want us to go?"

"Apparently I still have things to prove to him. Like doing his bidding and keeping his secrets isn't enough."

My heart broke for him. He'd told me he was doing all of this to protect me and his siblings, but I could feel how much it weighed on him. I wanted to help him. Take away his pain. And I knew how to do that. It was just a question of whether he'd let me.

"Dante…"

"Hmm?"

"Won't marking me show them I'm yours?"

"I can't… it's part of the deal. Girls must be clear of all evidence of their masters. Zach would fucking kill me."

I ran my fingers over his stomach. He tensed. He still wasn't entirely comfortable with being touched. I hated pushing him, but he told me he had to get used to it. He wasn't going to let his aversion to touch rule his life any longer.

"How can I give you what you need if you're not allowed to mark me?"

He was silent for a long moment before he ripped my hands off his stomach and spun around. Holding my shoulders, he backed me towards the bed and pressed me down on it, covering me with his body. His blue eyes blazed with frustration.

"Do you have any idea what you do to me? Christ, I can't take it, Liora. I need you so much." He leant down, burying his face in my neck and breathing in. "Say my name."

"Dante."

He groaned, moving his hands up to pin mine on the bed below him.

"Again."

"Dante."

"Fuck."

I could feel his cock hardening against my thigh.

"Fuck me, Dante," I whispered.

He groaned again, his teeth nipping at my neck. Using sex to distract him might not have been the best idea, but I knew it's what he needed. An outlet for his frustration and pain.

"Please... Master."

And that simple word was his complete undoing.

I thought I'd never really have a use for all the skimpy underwear Dante had bought me, but I certainly had a reason this evening. I'd let him dress me up in a black and red corset, garter belt attached to stockings, see-through black underwear and eye-wateringly high heels I could barely walk in. I wasn't particularly pleased to have myself on show like this, but I refrained from commenting. This evening was hard enough for him without me adding to it.

I wrapped the coat tighter around me as we walked into the large townhouse I recognised. This was the place I'd come with my father. Dante told me it was where he'd grown up and he hated being here. We carried on up the first flight of stairs and along the corridor until we reached a set of double doors at the end.

He stopped me going in. He turned me around and slid my coat off my shoulders before hanging it up on a coat rack which stood outside.

"Ready?" he whispered in my ear.

I nodded even though I wasn't. He stepped up next to me and the doors opened.

The room beyond was large with dark red leather sofas. On the walls there were shelves with various sex toys and whips. There were men milling about with scantily clad girls. All of them had collars on. And all eyes were on me and Dante. The whole thing made me very uneasy, but I kept a straight face.

Dante led me towards the end of the room, ignoring the pointed stares until we reached Zach. He turned at the sound of our approach.

"Liora, it is nice to see you," he said with a deadly smile. "You're looking exquisite."

I inwardly shivered. His blue eyes roamed across me in a distinctly predatory way. I hated it. Hated that Zach was sizing me up like I was on display for his enjoyment. He turned to Dante, his eyes narrowing.

"Why is she not collared?"

I watched Dante pull something out of his pocket. It wasn't like the collars the other women were wearing. They were all uniformly white with little dog tags on them. This one was black and red leather with a little silver heart in the middle. I couldn't read what the inscription said.

He shifted behind me and wrapped it around my neck, securing it. It wasn't too tight, but I hated it all the same. Dante and I didn't need this to show I belonged to him.

Zach's eyes were still narrowed.

"Are you trying to cause problems for me?" he hissed.

"She's mine and she's collared. End of discussion."

There was a tense moment of silence before Zach's expression cleared and he nodded. I almost breathed a sigh of relief, but I didn't dare do anything untoward in front of Zach.

"Enjoy the party."

Dante took my arm and tugged me away to the corner of the room. I looked back at Zach who was giving me daggers. I wasn't quite sure why he hated me so much. It's not like I'd really done anything but have the misfortune of being Angus Stewart's daughter. Did he suspect that I wasn't really Dante's pet? That his son had feelings for me just as I had feelings for him?

Dante sat down in an armchair and indicated his lap with his hand. I sat down on his knee, both my legs in between his. He wrapped a hand around my waist and the other lay on my thigh. He was making a statement. I was his. I could feel it in the possessive way he held me and his eyes as he scanned the room.

He looked absolutely gorgeous this evening, dressed in a blue shirt which brought out his eyes. His midnight black hair perfectly styled. My fingers itched to run through it. That had always been a problem. Dante was far too easy on the eyes.

It'd made him seem less monstrous and more human. And I knew he had a heart beneath all those masks he liked to wear. I'd had the privilege of seeing him without them.

He hooked his thumb under the top of my stocking, running circles around my skin. I tried not to shift in his grasp, but his touch did things to me even in front of all these people. He'd promised me he wouldn't fuck me with an audience, but everything else was fair play.

I should've hated him making me continue to suck his cock in front of Brent last week. The thing is whenever Dante told me to do something, I couldn't say no. I had an innate urge to please him. And somehow it didn't matter anymore that someone else was in the room. All that mattered was him. Giving him pleasure. Making him come.

I could withstand this evening as long as Dante was next to me. As long as he was the one dishing out the commands. The pleasure. The pain.

"Stop wriggling," he whispered, his mouth close to my ear.

"Sorry," I murmured.

I tried to stay still but his touch set my skin on fire.

"They're watching us because I almost never attend these things and they're wondering why I've made you off-limits."

"You didn't tell me about the collars."

His hand around my waist shifted up, skimming across my side before he fiddled with the collar at my neck.

"Pets get collared."

"Why have you never done it to me if I was meant to be your pet?"

I turned my head slightly so his face was in my eyeline. His mouth curved up at the side in a smirk.

"You and I know you've never really been that."

His fingers trailed across my collarbone, sending shivers up my spine. I dug my nails into my palm. The gesture was hidden as my hand was resting on his thigh, dangerously close to his crotch.

"You're mine without it." His teeth grazed along my earlobe. "My girl."

My heart pounded against my ribcage. I wanted to rub my thighs together to relieve the ache building between them. The pressure of his thumb on my leg increased. His fingertips trailed across my shoulder.

I looked out over the party to distract myself. There was soft music playing under the background noise from the guests. Several girls were on their knees next to the men who'd brought them. Some of them had leads attached to their collars like they really were dogs. I inwardly shuddered. I was glad Dante had no real interest in treating me like that.

On the sofa nearby, one girl already had her master's cock out and was going to town on it and the man next to him was watching with a gleam in his eye as he cupped the girl's breasts. I wasn't sure how to feel about it. It wasn't like I'd never seen porn, but seeing people engage in sexual acts in front of your eyes was entirely different. Maybe this is what Brent had felt like.

I looked away, finding another girl bent over a chair with a ball gag in her mouth. One man was rubbing his cock over her face and the other was spanking her with a large paddle. Dante had warned me what happened at these parties but seeing it with my own eyes made me feel a little uncomfortable.

"Not to your liking?" he murmured.

I shook my head slightly.

"Can't say I enjoy watching a bunch of rich pricks get their kicks either."

"Would you ever make me wear one of those?"

I inclined my head towards the girl with the ball gag.

"No, never. I want to hear you when you moan. Hear you cry out and beg. Your accent is such a fucking turn on."

His grip on me tightened. I glanced at him. His face was impassive but I could see the restraint in his eyes. I wasn't supposed to say his name this evening. I could only call him, Sir, but the urge to make him unravel before my eyes pulsed in my veins.

"Do you prefer it when I call you, Master or... Dante?" I whispered.

"Liora..." His tone was laced with warning.

"Tell me."

"Now, in front of all these people is when you want to have this conversation?"

I nodded. I did because he couldn't avoid it. His hand on my leg shifted, fingers moving towards my inner thigh. I couldn't help trembling under his touch.

"Fine. The truth... it should be hearing you say Master but listening to you say my name is addictive. I'm like a fucking drug addict when it comes to hearing you say Dante."

My heart soared. I hadn't been holding out any hope for that answer, but deep down, it's what I wanted to hear.

I didn't get a chance to respond to him because a man with dirty blonde hair walked up to us with a deadly gleam in his light green eyes.

"Hello, Dante."

I felt Dante stiffen beneath me.

"Marcus," he ground out.

"Is this who I think it is?"

Marcus indicated me with his head. I was already uncomfortable with this guy's gaze, but his words sent a chill down my spine.

"What's it to you?"

"She's pretty, I'll grant you that."

He reached out as if to touch me, but Dante was faster, slapping Marcus' hand away. The man didn't even blink. He just smirked instead.

"My, my, don't like to share your toys."

Dante practically growled in response.

"Didn't you get the memo? She's off-limits."

Marcus put his hands up.

"No need to get your knickers in a twist."

He looked me up and down again.

"Send Angus my regards."

He strolled away, whistling. Dante practically vibrated with irritation. I could feel it in the way his fingers tightened around me and the tension in his body.

"How does he know who I am?" I whispered.

Dante didn't answer me. I risked a glance at his face. His blue eyes were dark. He wasn't looking at me. I followed his gaze to Zach who was staring at us with narrowed eyes.

"Get up," Dante said, his voice low.

I complied immediately, but my mind was whirling with the implications of what Marcus had said. Did everyone here know Angus was my father? Did that mean they knew what he gave me to the Bensons for?

Dante got up and took me by the arm, tugging me towards another set of double doors. In the next room, I almost faltered. There were several racks which a few women were cuffed to. A couple were being whipped and one woman was on her front with a man either end.

Dante took me over to the wall where there were a set of cuffs on chains.

"Arms up," he told me.

He pressed me to the wall, not waiting for me to obey. Grabbing one hand, he wrapped the cuff around it followed by the other.

"Dante…"

"What was that?"

"S… Sir…"

He leant into me, his breath hot on my ear.

"I think you need to be taught your place again, pet."

I shuddered at his tone. What the fuck? This wasn't part of the deal. He said he'd touch me up a little but cuffing me to the wall? I didn't want it. Not in a room full of people I didn't know, some of whom were fucking.

"Dante, please don't do this," I whispered.

"Trust me," he whispered before pulling away.

I stared at the wall in front of me unable to comprehend what exactly was going on. On one hand, he was disregarding everything he told me before and on the other, he told me to trust him. Even though I wanted him to tell me what to do, when it came to being in this environment, I was completely out of my comfort zone.

257

I took a steadying breath, trying to relax my tense muscles.

Trust Dante. Concentrate on him. Let him do what he needs. He's keeping us safe.

His hands curled around my waist, pulling me back from the wall until the chains no longer had any slack.

"Tell me… how do pets get punished for disobeying their masters?"

"They get whipped, spanked or paddled, Sir," I replied although my voice trembled on the words.

"You'd like it if I punished you like that, wouldn't you?"

"Yes, Sir."

Even in front of these people, I knew I would.

"What did you do wrong?"

"I called you by your given name."

"And what else?"

What the hell did Dante want me to make up? I could've sworn I hadn't done anything else. His fingers tightened around my waist making the corset boning dig into my skin. I stifled a whimper.

"N… Nothing, Sir."

I didn't care if it was the wrong thing to say. This game we were playing had rules I still didn't understand. Was he doing this because Zach had been looking at us or because of Marcus, whoever the hell he was?

"Bad girls beg for their punishment, pet. Do you want to pay for disobedience?"

"Yes, Sir. Please punish me."

Please don't, Dante. I won't forgive you if you hurt me in front of these people. I won't forgive you if you make me want you even though they're watching. Please don't do this.

I wasn't sure if he realised this was a step too far for me. That even though I'd sucked his dick in front of Brent, I wasn't prepared to let him whip me in front of Zach's friends. I could feel my limbs trembling, shaking as I tried to stay in control of my reaction to his words.

I hated this. I hated it, but I didn't hate him.

I was pretty damn sure I was falling in love with Dante even if I hadn't ever wanted to admit it to myself. Falling in love with his words, his touch, his body, his mind and most of all, his heart.

How could I ever love a man who did this to me?

How had I fallen this far?

How?

Chapter Eighteen

DANTE

This was just about the most fucked up I'd gotten into with Liora and that was saying something. The urges I kept at bay were clawing at their cages. The need to hurt her pulsed in my veins. I didn't even care that Zach could see us. That his friends were watching me. But she did. She was shaking like a leaf. And the part of me which cared about Liora knew I couldn't go through with this even if it proved to Zach once and for all that I was his perfect son. That I'd embraced the role he'd carved out for me.

Fuck.

I'd made a fucking promise to her. That I wouldn't fuck her or force her to do anything she wasn't on board with at this stupid party. Why had I agreed to come to it? Why had I given in?

I knew why. Zach had pulled his trump card yet again. Warning me that he wouldn't hesitate to take her and bury me in the process if I didn't bring her. And that he'd take it out on my siblings too. I couldn't allow that. I just fucking couldn't. The four of them were the most important people in my life and if Zach hurt any of them again, I wouldn't forgive myself. Liora was mine and my siblings didn't deserve any more pain.

There was only one way I could damn well show Zach I had Liora under my control whilst keeping my promise to her. I just hoped she trusted me enough. I'd told her to, but there was always a part of her that held back. I could feel it. Whatever reason she had for not letting go entirely, I was sure she wasn't ready to tell me. I could be patient with her. She'd given me so much already.

My hands skimmed down her waist to her hips. I tugged her against me, her form moulding to mine.

"Too bad I don't feel like punishing you," I told her.

I felt some of the tension leave her body as she almost sagged into me. She was mostly hidden from view so I didn't tell her off for it. Instead, I walked her towards the wall and flattened her against it. I bit down on her earlobe as I moved one hand to cup her pussy.

"Are you wet for me, my little pet?"

"Y… Yes, Sir."

"Always ready, just like I taught you."

I slipped my fingers inside her underwear, stroking her curls but moving no further.

"I promised you I wouldn't fuck you here," I whispered. "I need you to pretend for me."

I hoped this was convincing enough because otherwise we were both utterly fucked. Reaching for my belt, I undid it along with my button and fly. I pulled away slightly and turned her around. The chains were crossed over above her, but there was enough slack that she didn't have to cross her arms. Her green eyes were wide, but her expression was otherwise neutral.

Somehow, I managed to pick her up and she wrapped her legs around my waist. I balanced her on my hips, wedging her between me and the wall. I put my hand in between us, making it look like I was sticking my cock in her, but in reality, I hadn't done anything.

"Oh god," she groaned.

"Did I tell you to speak?"

"No, Sir, sorry."

I smiled at her. Mostly because no one could see my face, but also because I wanted her to know I was happy with her acting. Showing me she trusted me enough to get us out of this situation without breaking my promise.

"Scream for me, pet. Show them all how much you love it."

"Yes, Sir."

I started to move, making it look like I was fucking my girl whilst her head lolled back against the wall and she moaned. I held onto her tightly, making sure she stayed in position. We could not afford for this to go wrong.

"Tell me, pet, does it make you feel dirty that we're being watched?"

"It makes me feel so dirty. Please fuck me harder, Sir."

Even though this was meant to be pretend, having her against me, her pussy rubbing up and down my cock drove me crazy. I wanted her despite our audience. And I knew she wanted me too. She was wet and it'd soaked through her underwear.

"You like this, don't you? Having all eyes on you whilst I fuck you."

"I do, Sir. It feels so good."

I didn't relish taunting her like this. If I hadn't made that promise, I would be fucking her right now and I wouldn't give a shit about who saw. I respected Liora enough not to push her though. She was still getting used to this relationship between us. Her need for pain. My need to inflict it.

"You're going to come all over my cock, pet. No one fucks you as good as I do."

"No, Sir, no one else fucks me like you do."

I buried my face in her neck, breathing in her scent of lavender and heather.

"Come for me," I whispered. "Then I'll take you out of here. Fuck what Zach thinks."

I pulled away and watched her face. Her lips were parted, her breath coming fast. I knew she wasn't remotely close to being done because I knew the signs. The way her body tensed up. The little noises she made. The glazed over look she got in her eyes. And the way she always called my name out in the heat of the moment. That was why I could never make her come for real in front of them because she wouldn't be able to control her reaction.

She cried out, bucking against me as she 'came'. I bit my lip to keep from laughing because it was so fucking utterly ridiculous. I never thought I'd ever have to fake sex with a girl, but for Liora, I'd do just about anything. I hoped this was convincing enough for Zach.

She winked at me as she panted, coming down from her supposed high.

"You've been a good girl, pet."

"Thank you, Sir. I just want to please you."

I made a show of 'pulling out' of her, readjusting her clothing and mine. I set her back on the ground and zipped up, buckling my belt. I didn't give a shit what they thought about me not finishing. The only way that was happening is if my cock was really thrusting in and out of her hot, slick pussy. Something I'd need to do at the earliest fucking opportunity.

I reached up and uncuffed her. Liora sagged against me. I knew her arms must hurt after being kept up in that position for so long. Hell, mine ached from holding her in place. After a moment, she straightened, staring up at me with unconcealed desire simmering in her forest green eyes. Christ, she was just as affected as I was by that little show.

I indicated with my head she should follow me. Dutifully, she walked back through the room with me, avoiding the gazes of the other men and women. Some of them were staring. There was only one person I really cared about. Zach's expression was neutral. I saluted him before we went into the other room. I could've sworn his eyes darkened a fraction, but who gave a shit? I'd given them enough to talk about.

Putting my hand to her lower back, I guided her out of the second room into the hallway. I plucked her coat from the rack and slipped it around her shoulders. I really fucking hated this house with a passion. Everything had happened here and the reminders tore at me.

I pulled my phone out of my pocket and fired off a text to my driver.

We were both silent as we walked down the stairs. In the lobby, one of Zach's men was waiting. I didn't try to engage him in conversation. I was done with being here. Hearing footsteps on the stairs behind me, I stiffened.

"Dante," Zach's voice rang in my ears.

"Yes?" I replied without turning around.

"Family dinner next week. Attendance is non-negotiable."

I almost breathed a sigh of relief.

"Just let Brent know when it is and we'll be there."

There was a long pause.

"Make no mistake, son, I'm watching you."

I heard his footsteps retreating just as there was a knock at the front door. Zach's man opened it. My driver stood on the threshold. I hurried Liora down the steps and into the car, wanting to be away from here and Zach's threats. He was always watching me.

Liora sat ramrod straight with her hands settled in her lap as the car pulled away. I wondered for a moment what was wrong, but then I had just made her fake sex with me in front of Zach's friends.

"Liora, I—"

Her sudden movement cut me off. She unclipped her seatbelt, throwing the coat off her shoulders before she grabbed hold of my face and planted her mouth on mine. I was too startled to respond. She shoved her tongue in my mouth, kissing me with reckless abandon.

My hands wound their way into her hair, tugging her closer as I kissed her right back. She tasted like heaven. She shifted up on her knees, moving to straddle me without ever breaking contact with my mouth. Having her body against mine made me lose all my restraint. My hand fell to her hip as I ground her into my cock.

"Dante, please, I need you," she whimpered against my mouth.

Had I ever actually fucked a girl in the back of a car before? No, but her plea was far too much for me to take. I put my hands on her shoulders and pushed her back a little.

"Hold on," I said reaching over to the intercom button. "Voss, just keep driving until I tell you to return us home."

"Yes, Mr Benson," my driver responded a moment later.

I released the button and then my hands were on her, unhooking the corset she was wearing at the front until I could get my hands on her breasts. My thumb flicked over her nipple and she arched into me, moaning.

"Did that turn you on, huh?" I asked, my voice low.

"Yes," she hissed.

"Need me to give you a release?"

"Please, I can't take it. I want you."

Christ, she wasn't the only one desperate to come.

"Unzip me."

She didn't hesitate, reaching between us to unbuckle my belt and tear down the zip of my trousers. I shifted so she could tug them down enough to allow my cock to spring free. I unhooked the rest of the hooks on her corset before dispensing with it. My mouth was on her nipple, biting down. She cried out, her hands grasping my forearms.

"Dante, please."

I reached down and shoved her underwear aside before gripping my cock and guiding her down onto it. Both of us moaned as I sunk into her tight, slick heat. Exactly what I needed. To feel her on me.

I pulled her against me, rocking deeper into her as my fingers found their way into her hair.

"Do you hate me for it?" I whispered.

"No… I…"

The hesitation in her eyes and her voice made my heart thump against my chest. Her hands rested on my shoulders, gripping lightly.

"I could never hate you."

That wasn't what she was going to say. We both knew it. There was something else here neither of us were remotely prepared for. As I stared up into her forest green eyes, I knew what it was.

Love.

An emotion, sensation, feeling I never thought I'd ever experience outside of the familial bond. To be honest, I wasn't sure I was capable of it after what I'd been through with Zach. And yet here it was. Clear as day.

"You don't need to say it." The words were out of my mouth before I could stop them.

"Say what?"

"You know what."

"Dante…"

"Don't lie to me. You don't have to admit it, but don't lie to me."

She shifted, resting her forehead against mine.

"Do you feel the same?" she whispered.

"Yes."

"I'm not ready to say it."

I nodded, bringing a hand up to cup her cheek, running my thumb across it.

"Then kiss me instead and let me make you come for real this time."

She smiled, bringing her lips to mine. My other hand gripped her hip, encouraging her to rise and fall on me. Christ, she felt so good. The way her pussy pulsed as she rode me was blissful.

I let go of her face, running my hand down her back. I lifted it away and slapped her behind. She groaned into my mouth so I did it again. It made her pull away.

"Fuck, please, more. Hurt me."

I wasn't one to deny her when she begged like that. I struck her again and again. Each time she moaned and arched into me, her pussy clamping down on my cock. Hell, I didn't even need her to start calling me, Master. This was enough. It kept my burning needs at bay. Satisfied the cravings. This high was so much sweeter than anything I'd experienced before. Mostly because Liora really did want it too. She craved it as much as I did. The pleasure from pain.

I wasn't ashamed to admit I'd paid women to let me whip them. Now I'd met my match. A girl I didn't have to pretend with. A girl who got off on letting me take control of her. Telling her what to do and when. Her need called to mine. We sated each other's cravings.

She cried out my name, her pussy clenching wildly around my cock, her head thrown back and an expression of utter bliss painted her features. My hand stilled as I watched her come apart. I hadn't been expecting it. Hadn't realised she was so close to detonating on me.

She was so beautiful. Every time I looked at her, I was struck by it. Liora really had the most perfect elfin features. Her little blonde halo of hair never ceased to stir my senses.

I was pathetically enamoured with her.

No.

It was high time I admitted the truth.

I was in love with her.

Her laugh. Her smile. Her voice. The sharp intelligence radiating behind those forest green eyes.

I had to find a way to end this shit with Zach. End it so I could have Liora all to myself without his bullshit threats. That meant going against him. It meant risking everything to fight against the hold he had over me. The thing he had used to manipulate me for years. The very thing I promised him I'd never reveal in exchange for Liora. The thing I'd seen him do that still haunted me to this day. That's the only thing I had left to stop him.

Liora opened her eyes and smiled at me. The sight of it made my heart thump wildly in my chest.

"I want to take care of you," she whispered as she moved again.

Having watched her come apart on my cock, I was close to finding oblivion myself. Even with all the fucked up thoughts racing round my head. I pushed them down, concentrating on her riding me, her movements and pace increasing. I gripped both her hips and thrust back against her, pressing deeper inside her slick heat. She leant towards me, capturing my earlobe between her teeth.

"I want you to come inside me," she told me. "I want to feel you let go."

I grunted, feeling it building as my muscles tensed in anticipation.

"I need it, Dante."

My name on her lips was the catalyst.

"Say it again."

"Dante, come inside me."

"Fuck."

I couldn't hold back. I erupted, my cock pulsing inside her. Giving her exactly what she wanted. I let go. The waves of bliss crashed over me. My fingers dug harder into her hips, anchoring her to me. Because really, Liora was the only thing keeping me afloat. Keeping me from sinking further into the hell that was my existence. The hell which kept me from being free.

When I opened my eyes, her smile greeted me. My eyes went to the collar around her neck. The sight of it made my gut clench. I reached up and unbuckled it, tossing it away like it burnt my skin. I hated the thing.

She wasn't my pet. She was my girl. My everything.

She reached up and cupped my face with both hands.

"When your masks are gone, you have the most expressive eyes of anyone I've ever met," she told me. "I see everything you feel. I feel it. Right here." She dropped one of her hands to her chest, pressing it against her heart. "I feel all of you. Sometimes it hurts because you've buried yourself so deep inside my soul. I don't think I can ever be free."

My heart was still beating wildly in my chest, but this just made it worse.

"I don't want to be free," she whispered, leaning into me, her lips brushing against mine. "Not now. Not ever. I need you right here. Don't hide from me. Let me in. Let me be your balm. Let me fill the void."

How could she see all of that? The dark parts I locked away. The emptiness threatening to consume my every fucking waking moment.

I was so close to the edge with her. So close to drowning. Her words. I had her fucking words. Her honesty cut into me. Carving out a huge hole in my chest and she was burying herself in it. And with her words, I had her mind.

Body. Mind. Soul.

Mine.

And the biggest mind fuck yet?

She had all of that from me too.

I was irrevocably hers. I'd fallen. I'd damned myself to a lifetime of being at the mercy of this girl. Her power over me. She had no idea what she wielded. How she'd taken the very essence of my being and made it her own.

Instead of clamming up and disregarding everything she'd just said to me, I put my hand on top of where hers lay on her chest.

"You already are," I whispered against her lips. "You're everything to me."

I could feel her trembling, trying to hold back the emotions threatening to burst through. Her heartbeat thundered against my fingertips where they connected with her chest.

"Take me home and show me exactly how you feel for the rest of the night."

So I did. I laid her down on my bed when we got back and took her without mercy. I poured out my soul to her in each thrust. Made her aware of the depth of my affection for her with each kiss. Each touch proving I was hers if she wanted me. She could take it all if she was brave enough.

And I knew in those moments, I had to tell her the truth.

I had to trust her with my secrets. Tell her the real reason she was here with me.

The truth behind why the Stewarts owed the Bensons a blood debt.

I had to hope she wouldn't hate me after this. Hate me for what our parents had caused. And hate me for allowing myself to get sucked into their bullshit because I'd wanted her so much.

I really fucking hoped she still looked at me with that same adoring expression.

Because I wouldn't survive it if she turned from me now.

Liora was my life.

And she'd destroy it if she left me behind.

Chapter Nineteen

LIORA

"Wake up, my heart," a voice whispered across my skin.

I was halfway between consciousness and sleep. I recognised the voice. I knew the rich timbre of it deep within my soul. I wasn't sure it was real because the person it belonged to never called me, his heart.

I burrowed further into the chest I was pressed up against, savouring the warmth and safety I felt there. My hand splayed out across their bare back. Such soft skin with a contrast of hard muscle underneath.

"I know I tired you out, but I need you to wake up for me, my heart."

Those two words again. Why did they make mine thump in my chest?

"I'm sleepy," I murmured.

I felt lips on my forehead.

"I know, I'm sorry."

I cracked an eye open as he tipped my head back. Dante's face filled my vision. I blinked.

Dante just called me, his heart. What the hell is happening?

"What's wrong?" I whispered.

"James is here."

I blinked again. Why was his brother here? And what did that have to do with me? He didn't seem to want to talk to me about what they'd discussed last time James was here. I didn't get a chance to ask him because he kissed me. I melted, pressing closer to him. His touch seared into me, fire lacing my veins. Even in my hazy, sleep deprived state, he affected me.

His lazy smile when he pulled away was a glorious sight. Dante without masks. He was enthralling. Captivating. He held my attention like no other.

"Have I ever told you just how handsome you are?" I asked without thinking.

He raised an eyebrow.

"You did call me beautiful once."

I ran my hand down his bare chest. For once, he didn't tense up. If anything, he relaxed further.

"We might be opposites in looks. I'm the light to your dark, but I think you're perfect."

His smile widened, blue eyes twinkling with amusement.

"Do you now?"

"Mmmhmm."

What the hell was coming out of my mouth right now? I felt sort of giddy with happiness because of him calling me, his heart, and apparently my brain decided it was okay to just start telling him how attractive I thought he was. It was the truth, but he didn't need to know that. I wasn't one for stroking a man's ego and he really didn't need his stroked. He knew how much I desired him without me having to say anything. I'd sort of proven that yesterday when I'd thrown myself at him in the car.

He leant down towards me again, his mouth brushing against my ear.

"If I didn't suspect you were too sore right now, I'd have you on your back so I could bury my cock in your tight pussy again."

I shivered. He wasn't wrong. He'd spent all night making me come over and over again until I was so wrung out, I couldn't move. I wasn't sure if he was trying to make up for what happened at Zach's or it was because I told him to show me how he felt with actions rather than words. Either way, it had been deliciously wonderful. I'd never felt so satisfied and content as I did when I fell asleep in his arms, my face pressed against his solid chest.

"Don't tease," I whispered.

"I wasn't teasing. Why? Is the ache still there? Do you need me to relieve it for you?"

His hand skimmed my bare hip and dipped between my legs.

"Dante!"

His chuckle reverberated around my skull.

"Oh god," I groaned, unable to help myself as he stroked me.

I was sore, but his fingers were making a very different ache become prominent. The kind that only he could cure.

"I told you, I'm not your god."

No. He was my Dante. And he was driving me crazy at that moment.

"I think you're going to have me on my back anyway."

"You're right."

He shifted, pressing me down on to the bed and towering over me. I stared at him in all his naked glory, completely unabashed. I loved to look at him. To touch him. Every inch of him was stunning.

"What about James?" I asked, suddenly remembering that's why he'd woken me up.

He groaned, sitting up and rubbing his face.

"Fuck. We'll have to continue this later." He dropped his hand, a wicked smile appearing on his face. "By then you'll have recovered and I can fuck you as hard as I want."

I squirmed, feeling my face heat up. Perhaps our appetite for each other was insatiable but I stopped caring about that. My desire for him was like a raging inferno inside me and I wasn't about to put that fire out.

I didn't get a chance to say anything else because he scooped me up in his arms and took me into the shower. His touch was lingering as he washed me as if he was branding himself into every inch of my skin.

When we were finally dressed, we left the bedroom hand in hand and entered the conservatory a few minutes later. James was nursing a cup of tea at the table where there was breakfast laid out.

"Aren't you supposed to be working today?" Dante asked as he pulled out a chair for me.

James eyes flicked between us.

"Like you'd know anything about real work."

"Well?"

"Like anyone cares if I skip a day. Not everyone lives a life of idleness like you."

Dante raised an eyebrow as he sat down next to me. I poured myself a cup of tea and started on my usual fruit and yogurt the staff had prepared. I still wasn't sure why Dante wanted me here, but I wasn't going to interject. Clearly the two of them needed to have it out.

"Yes, because I just sit around all day doing fuck all."

James looked away. I'd never asked Dante what he did, but I figured he'd tell me when he was ready.

"I didn't come here to fight with you."

"Then why did you?"

His eyes flicked to me and narrowed.

"I was hoping we could continue our conversation from last week… in private."

Dante rested his arm across the back of my chair and wrapped his hand around my shoulder.

"Liora's part of this now so whatever you have to say, you can do it in front of her."

My heart soared and then abruptly came crashing back down to earth. Whilst I was glad Dante wanted to include me in whatever his family shit was, I was also aware I was still very much a pawn in this game. I might be in love with Dante, but that didn't change the fact that I had to stay here or Zach would take me and break me.

In love with Dante. Had I just admitted it to myself?

He'd captured my heart and I was pretty sure I'd caught his too.

279

"Well if you're going to be like that, then you can start by explaining what exactly is going on between the two of you."

I eyed Dante whose expression didn't change. He just stared at James with unnerving intensity.

"Her father owed Zach a debt. Liora was payment for it."

"What the fuck? You can't give up your child as a debt, that's insane."

"This is Zach we're talking about."

"Dad's crazy, but not that… that's fucked up." His eyes fell on me again. "Did you know this?"

I shook my head. I had no idea and I really wasn't sure how I felt about it either. Dante's hand on my shoulder tightened but he didn't look at me. I stared down at my bowl, trying to work out why, if I was the payment, Zach had given me to his son.

"You didn't even tell her the truth? What the fuck is wrong with you, Dante? Why would you go along with this? I get that you're in with Dad, but this is a whole new low, even for you."

That was the one thing I did know. He'd done it because he wanted me. Dante didn't speak but I saw his fist clench in his lap.

"Well, are you going to explain why her father was indebted to ours? Explain why the fuck you went along with it and fucked up her life because I'm pretty damn sure she wasn't on board with this shit if she didn't even know she was a debt."

Dante ignored his brother, instead he turned to me. His blue eyes were dark and full of anguish. My heart was in my mouth as he encouraged me to turn in my chair. He took both of my hands in his.

280

"I'm sorry," he whispered. "I'm so fucking sorry."

I couldn't open my mouth. I was sure whatever he said next would completely destroy me, but I couldn't move. I couldn't run away.

"Zach had a younger brother, Zander. He died in a shooting accident when he was twenty. Except it wasn't an accident at all. You see, your mother, Heather, she was his fiancée. Her, Angus and Zander knew each other from university. The way Zach tells it… they had all gone on a shooting party in the Highlands and well, Zach was pretty sure Angus had a thing for Heather even though Zander was his best friend. After Zander died, he discovered they were seeing each other behind Zander's back, which is a part of this."

I felt sick. If what Dante was telling me was right, then something really fucked up at happened.

"On this shooting party… your father, Angus, shot Zander in the back. He died shortly after; paramedics were unable to save his life. Angus claimed it was an accident, but Zach made him admit it wasn't and the truth about him and your mother. In exchange for not telling the police, Zach made him agree he would give up his first born child and he or she would become payment for what Zach saw as a blood debt. And Zach would give that child to his first born if he or she wanted them."

I wasn't my father's first born though. That was Declan. Except Dante wasn't finished. Not by a long shot.

"As it obviously transpired, both Declan and I are male and as I'm not interested in men, I refused when Zach told me about this. But then he said Angus had a daughter and that if I wanted her, he would force Angus to pay the debt that way. I didn't think anything of it. I wasn't going to go through with his idiotic shit because I thought he was crazy. Blood debts don't exist. We're not living in some medieval society where it's an eye for an eye."

Dante's hands tightened around mine.

"I was going to tell him to get fucked until I saw you. And that was it for me. I'd give up anything just to have you. Zach recognised I was instantly infatuated, so even though he agreed to call the debt in, he had stipulations and rules. I wanted you enough to agree to them. I'm not proud of it, but it's the truth. I'm sorry I pulled you into this mess. I'm sorry I put your life in danger. I'm just fucking sorry."

The sincerity in his voice and his eyes broke something inside me. My heart fractured in two. I'd always known he'd gone along with it because he wanted me, but this was a step too far. The fact that my father had killed his own best friend was one thing, but blood debts were another. My father had given me up just so he could stay out of prison. It made me ill. I felt so betrayed. He would rather save his own skin than keep his children out of his mess.

"I'm not sorry for how I feel about you, Liora. I'm not sorry for all those moments we've shared with each other."

"Why didn't you tell me?" I whispered, trying to hold back tears.

"I didn't want you to hate me."

I didn't. I don't think I ever could. I loved Dante, but it didn't negate what he'd done. It didn't change the fact that he'd kept this from me. That he'd gone along with it.

I pulled my hands out of his. I could see the agony in his expression, but I couldn't do this.

"Liora—"

"Don't, please, don't."

I stood up and backed away. I knew now why I'd held back from telling him about my feelings. From admitting them. Because of this. Because he hadn't been honest with me about why I was here. He began to stand but I put a hand up.

"Do not follow me."

I couldn't with him. I had to get out of this room. Away from the man who'd stolen my heart and destroyed me in the process. My heart fractured and the open wound bled. Dante was nothing but the instigator of my ruination. He'd dragged me into his world. Taught me to accept I had dark desires and that they were okay because he had them too. That what I desired, craved wasn't a sickness or something I should be ashamed of. He'd made me fall in love with him. Then he'd ripped the rug out from underneath me.

I turned and ran out of the room. I heard their voices as I tore through the kitchen.

"Well, you royally fucked that up," James said.

"Don't even start with me," Dante growled back.

I didn't want to hear anymore. I was out in the hall and running up the stairs, trying to stop the tears from falling. I ran face first into a solid chest on the first floor landing. Rubbing my head and taking a step back, I looked up.

"You're in a bit of a rush... Hey... are you okay?" Brent asked, his brow furrowing.

"No, no... I need... Brent, I need you to help me."

"Okay... What with?"

I gripped both of his arms, feeling panic rising in my chest.

"I need to get away from here. I can't... I can't be here. Not when... I need to just not be here. Please, Dante will kill me if I go out alone, so please, please take me somewhere, anywhere that's not here."

He tugged my hands off his forearms, his frown deepening.

"What did D do?"

"Please, Brent. I'm begging you. If I spend one more moment in this house, I'll break wide open. Please."

I could see the conflict in his eyes. He sighed, rubbing the back of his neck.

"Fine. D is going to kill me, but fine. You're going to tell me what happened though."

He took my arm and brought me back downstairs. He helped me into a coat and shoes before opening the front door and ushering me out. We walked up the street a little way before he turned to me.

"Where do you want to go?"

"I don't know."

I hadn't really thought about it. All I knew was that staying in Dante's house for one more minute would kill me inside. I needed to think clearly and get some space.

Brent tapped his foot for a moment before his eyes brightened.

"I know where I should take you."

Half an hour later, we were wandering through a big pet shop together. I couldn't help but smile. Brent knew I loved animals. We stopped where the rabbits were. I looked over the top of the enclosure, watching one of them chewing on a piece of lettuce.

"You going to tell me what happened?" Brent asked, leaning on some shelving.

"Dante told me why my dad gave me to him."

"I see."

"You knew, didn't you?"

"I like you, Liora, but my loyalty is to D and always will be. I keep his secrets and it really wasn't my place to say anything."

"I know. I'm not upset with you."

I sighed. I'd managed to keep it together in the car, but now, my heart was broken and I wasn't sure how it could be repaired. Dante had kept too many things from me. I should've stayed and been there for him whilst he had it out with his brother, but I couldn't. Not after that revelation.

"I keep asking myself how my dad could do such a thing, but I'm beginning to think I've never really known him at all."

"Sometimes people do questionable things when backed into a corner."

"I need answers Dante can't give me. Answers from my parents about what really happened. I don't completely trust what Zach said."

"You know D will kill me if I let you speak to your dad."

I nodded. I had to get permission first, which ridiculous because I was my own woman. Except Dante had control over me in ways I didn't realise possible. No matter how much it hurt right now, I was still his. I still wanted to please him. Make him happy. Do what he said.

And that made me completely fucked up.

"I didn't know you were back," I said, changing the subject.

He'd been away dealing with some stuff with his sister. It hadn't really occurred to me until now.

"I got in this morning. Look, I know this whole thing is really fucked up and I told D it would go to hell if he kept the truth from you, but he cares about you. He didn't want to hurt you. Zach wanted to take you straight away, but D gave you three years. He wanted you to finish your degree because Angus told him how important it was to you."

"I was there the day Dante decided he wanted me."

"I know, but they were aware you were at Uni before that. D knew everything about you, at least everything Angus was willing to tell him."

I wasn't sure if that made me feel any better or not. My degree was important to me, but now I was never going to be able to use it. Dante had taken that away from me. All I'd ever wanted to do was work with animals and now I was his prisoner instead. A willing prisoner, but a prisoner all the same.

"I don't want to go back to the house, Brent, but if Zach finds out I'm gone, he'll make Dante and me suffer for it."

I looked up at him. He rubbed the back of his neck.

"I have a second bedroom in the basement, you can stay with me tonight, okay?"

"You're going to tell him I'm there, aren't you?"

"I have to, but I won't let him down to see you. I get it. You need time. I think anyone would after finding that shit out about their parents."

"Thank you."

I wasn't sure what I'd do without Brent. He might be Dante's friend, but he was helping me all the same. For that I was grateful. He was the only person I had here other than Dante. There was no one else I could turn to.

"You ready to go?"

I shook my head.

"Can we go look at the fish?"

He grinned.

"Of course, just let me call him, okay?"

I nodded, knowing it'd be worse for the both of us if he didn't.

I hoped I could get past this revelation because my life without Dante would be bleak. Not only had he opened up my eyes to who I really was, he'd shown me compassion and, dare I say it… love. Not the love you felt for your family or your friends, but all consuming love which tears your heart to pieces and drowns you.

That's what my desire for him had grown into.

Love.

I needed that love. I craved it. That connection. That spark.

I couldn't deny it any longer.

I wanted him. I needed him. I loved Dante.

And I couldn't live without him.

Chapter Twenty

DANTE

I knew everything was going to fall apart the moment I told her, but I didn't imagine it would hurt this much to have her walk out on me. My heart felt like it had been ripped into tiny little pieces and scattered at my feet. And James telling me I'd fucked up wasn't helping. I knew that. The look in Liora's eyes was like shards of glass slicing into my skin. She trusted me and I'd betrayed that.

"I'm just saying," James said.

"Well don't."

"Hey, don't take it out on me. I'm not the one who went along with Dad's fucked up plans."

I turned to him.

"You really have no fucking clue. Did you think I wanted to go along with it?"

He raised an eyebrow.

"Are you really telling me she was worth it?"

"Yes. She's worth everything. For fuck's sake, James, I'm in love with her."

His eyes widened as I heard the front door slam. I was on my feet immediately. What the fuck? Was she leaving me? She couldn't. Not with Zach still on our case. I took one step towards the door when James' voice brought me up short.

"I might not know Liora, but she told you not to follow her. I think you should listen."

He was right, but she was in danger if she'd just walked out on me.

"You don't understand. If she leaves me and Zach finds out, he'll take her and he'll ruin her completely."

"Does she know that?"

"Yes."

"Then she won't have left you."

"How do you know?"

"She values her life. If she didn't, she would've walked out the second you took her and never looked back."

I clenched my fists. Again, he was right. I hated it. All I wanted was to go after her. Beg for her forgiveness. Tell her how much she meant to me. How much I cared for her. How much I goddamn loved her. And that I'd destroy my own father just so she could be free if that's what she really wanted. If she wanted to be free of me, when I'd dealt with Zach, I'd let her go no matter how much it hurt.

I'd lost myself completely to her. My head. My heart. My body. My fucking soul. All of it was Liora's. It should terrify me that a single girl brought me completely to my knees, but it didn't any longer. Last night hadn't been about sex. Liora and I made love, over and over again. Proving how deeply we were bound to each other.

I sat down, placing my hands on the table. Liora wanted space. Needed to process what I'd told her. And I needed to concentrate on having things out with James.

"You wanted to continue our conversation from last time," I said.

Everything inside me screamed, raged, ranted, but I kept a lid on it. I took a steadying breath. I had to trust she would eventually understand why I'd kept it from her.

"How come Dad never told me or the twins we had an uncle?"

I looked up at James.

"Zach might be a heartless piece of shit, but I think Zander was the only person he cared about. At least the way he talked about him made it seem that way. There was only a couple of years between them."

"I've never understood why you don't call him, Dad."

I flinched. He didn't deserve it.

"Why would I call a man who terrorised me as a child that? He's not been a father to any of us. Fuck, James, he still does it. Uses everything to keep me in line."

The truth was spilling out and I couldn't stop it. The need to unburden myself pulsed in my veins. To make James understand everything I'd done was because I cared too fucking much.

"You think I wanted to ruin our relationship with each other? Do you really think I hate you? I don't. Fuck. You're my brother. I never wanted any of this, but you have no idea what Zach is capable of. You didn't suffer the worst of it and you know why that is? Because I protected you. I made sure he took out his shit on me and not on you and the girls. When he realised how much I cared about the three of you, he hurt you to get back at me. Me and her."

Our mother. She suffered the worst of it. The brunt of his abuse until she died.

James' eyes widened, but he didn't speak.

"You want to know the truth? Are you sure you're prepared for it? I won't be able to take it back. It can't be unsaid."

It had destroyed me, so I knew it would hurt him too. There was one thing I couldn't tell him. Not yet. But the rest? I'd share it with him if he was willing to listen. Willing to try to understand.

"Tell me," he whispered.

"You know he beat her? Beat her until she was a bloody mess and couldn't go out for weeks. You didn't understand because you were too young, but I did. I saw. He forced me to watch. It only started after you were born. He used to come home in such a rage and he took it out on her. Then he started taking it out on me too. He did it because he thought she loved me more than him. Loved all of us more than him."

I looked down at my hands, unable to meet his gaze any longer. The memories flooded my mind. His taunts. His fists. The bruises. The blood.

"He beat me so brutally I couldn't stand to have anyone touch me. Not even Mum. When she cleaned me up afterwards, I'd wince and hiss, trying to get away from her. What type of man does that to his own son? Makes him hate the touch of others?"

I shook my head. A fucked up, worthless piece of shit. That's what our father was.

"It lessened when I got older, but I still can't stand anyone touching my back and chest, skin on skin... except Liora. I haven't told her why I hate it, but I think she knows."

I sighed, running a hand through my hair. Telling her my own father had beat the crap out of me as a kid was never going to be easy for me. Hell, it was hard enough telling James the truth. I'd never really spoken about it. Not after she died. I kept it all inside where it'd festered, destroying me from the inside out. Twisting me into someone I didn't recognise any longer.

My need to inflict pain was so intrinsically tied to my father. It was a part of him I carried inside myself. Except what I practised wasn't abuse. It was about pleasure. It was about testing limits and finding freedom with in it. Pleasure from the good kind of pain. And it was consensual. I might not have had Liora's agreement the first time I spanked her, but after that, she learnt to trust me not to go too far. I never would. I never lost control with anyone. Going so far as to learn how to whip someone without inflicting lasting damage at BDSM clubs. Practising it safely was important to me.

Zach, on the other hand, got some sick satisfaction from hurting other people. It fed the monster inside him. He relished in it. When he hurt my mother, I could see it in his eyes. How he craved having a person at his feet. At his mercy. He loved the way each bruise formed. Each welt. Each time he hit so hard, she bled for him. I know because he told me.

"After she died, he hurt me worse and then he started hurting the twins and finally, you. It fucking killed me. I was still too young to do anything about it. She made me promise to take the three of you away when I was eighteen and the money she'd left me came through. That's how I was able to buy this place."

I finally looked up at him. There was sympathy and compassion in his expression as well as abject horror.

"I had no idea," he said quietly. "If I'd known…"

"It's okay. It was better for you to grow up not knowing these things. Not having to take on that burden. I wanted to save you from it. Save you and the twins, but even when I forced Zach to let me take you, he still found a way to hurt me all over again."

James frowned.

"How did you convince him to let us go?"

"He signed over custody to me after I told him I'd go to social services and tell them about the abuse."

That wasn't the whole truth, but the other thing I couldn't tell him. I had to stay silent until the time was right. It was the only real leverage I had against Zach now.

"What did he do to hurt you?"

"You don't want to hear this, James. It'll be too much."

He shook his head.

"You've already told me things that make me sick and hate him even more, what could possibly be worse?"

He had no idea. This was one of the worst things Zach ever did. I couldn't look at him the same way after he told me.

"Trust me."

I wasn't sure I could tell him. Reliving that day was hell and the aftermath, torture.

"Dante, I want the truth. That means facing everything even if it's awful."

I saw the sincerity in his eyes. I sighed again, dropping my eyes to the table.

"The girls hadn't quite turned sixteen yet when we moved here. It was a week before their birthday and a few days before we moved. I'd had an argument with him. He couldn't beat me any longer because I wouldn't let him. I wouldn't take it. I was done. After I tell you this, you'll understand how fucked up and insane our father is. How far he'll go to get back at anyone who crosses him and I just crossed him in the worst way possible. By taking you and the girls away. By depriving him of the outlet for his temper."

I shifted in my seat, already uncomfortable. Nothing about this conversation was comfortable, but this was the worst of it. Almost the worst of it. The things I couldn't tell him ate me up inside.

"The girls came to me. They'd been crying, but they wouldn't tell me what was wrong. They asked if we could leave sooner. If the two of them could go to the house because they couldn't stay there any longer. I said yes because I couldn't stand to see them like that. I brought them here even though I'd not stocked the house with food or anything, but they didn't seem to care. They both just sat in the living room staring at the wall with haunted looks in their eyes."

My heart fractured in my chest. I remembered how the twins looked like they could break at any moment. I hadn't wanted to leave them there, but I was determined to find out what happened to them.

"I went back to Zach's and cornered him in his office. I asked him what the fuck he'd done to Jen and Fi. He had the audacity to laugh in my face. Then he proceeded to give me a detailed account of exactly what he'd done to them."

I clenched my fists, trying not to let my emotions get the better of me.

"He raped them, James. He took their virginity. He started with Fi, forcing Jen to watch and then he took Jen too. That's why they were mute for months. Because their own father deprived them of their innocence at fifteen years old. I was incensed. He'd done it to get back at me for taking you and the girls away. So I turned my fists on him. I beat him until he was almost unconscious and all he did was smile at me. He promised me one day I'd come crawling back and he'd welcome me with open arms. I spat in his face and left, taking you with me."

Tears welled behind my eyes because I hated everything about that day. I hated everything about Zach. I hated that he was right.

"That night, I ordered pizza in and we all sat in my bedroom and ate it on the floor. I put you to bed and the girls didn't want to be alone. So I let them stay with me. I held them all night whilst they cried on my chest. They told me in their own words what happened. It fucking broke my heart. I told them I'd never let him hurt them again. That they were safe with me now."

When I heard a choking noise, I looked up at James. Tears rolled down his cheeks and he was holding back from sobbing. I stood up, walked around the table, tugged him up off the chair and hugged him, not caring it wasn't something men did. My brother needed me and I wasn't too proud to admit I needed him too.

"He didn't touch them again. They would've told me. I know they act like they don't care about anything and they treat Zach like he's done nothing wrong, but they're good at hiding their feelings. Their connection to each other helps. They still talk to me sometimes when it gets too much. They'll call me and cry down the phone after they've seen him. Those memories will haunt them for life. I'm the only one who knows. And now so do you."

I let my brother cry on my shoulder. I might not get along with my sisters, but this was different. They knew they could come to me at any time if they were suffering. Fi called me the night of the Gala. Liora had fallen asleep so I slipped out of bed and spoke to my sister. Jen had the worst flashbacks. I think it was because she had to watch Fi go through it first before Zach took her.

Liora was none the wiser about me leaving her for half an hour whilst I calmed them down and told them not to see Zach. Every time they did, it brought on the memories and whilst they never let on in front of him, they were haunted by that day all the same.

I wasn't sure how much time had passed, but my phone ringing startled both of us. I dug it out my pocket and looked at who it was.

"I need to take this, are you going to be okay?" I asked.

He pulled away and nodded, wiping his eyes. I gave his shoulder a squeeze before answering.

"Brent."

"She's with me, so you don't need to worry. I took her to a pet shop and she's looking at the fish."

The relief I felt sucker punched me in the gut. Liora was safe.

"Is she okay?"

"No, D, she's really not."

"Fuck. Thank you for taking her."

"She begged me. Told me if she stayed at the house, she'd break. You've really fucked with her head, you know that, right?"

I sighed.

"Yes. I do."

I hadn't meant to. None of this was meant to happen. She was never meant to know, but not telling her ate me up inside. How could she ever trust me fully if I was keeping secrets from her?

"You're not going to like this but I told her she could stay with me tonight."

"You what?"

What the fuck?

"She's hurting, D. She needs time and space."

"She has her own room here."

"Are you really telling me you'd leave her alone? You and I both know you wouldn't be able to stay away from her."

I paced away, running my hand through my hair. I wanted her so fucking much. The need burnt in my veins.

"Does she really not want to see me?"

"No."

I almost shoved my fist through the glass door of the conservatory.

"Fuck. Fuck. How can I fix this? How do I make it right?"

"You can't fix everything, D. Sometimes you have to let people come around on their own. This isn't her leaving you, okay? So don't start thinking like that."

It's exactly what I was thinking. She didn't even want to see me. It was stupid of me to jump to that conclusion. Only I wasn't entirely rational when it came to Liora. And she had something of mine. My heart. I'd been calling her that this morning when I woke her up. That's what she was. My fucking heart.

"I can't do this without her. Fuck, you know how I feel about her. You probably knew before I did."

He chuckled. The sound irritated me, but I didn't say anything.

"Yeah, I do. Seriously though, she just needs a bit of time. You owe her that much. And you owe her something else too."

"What?"

"You need to let her talk to her father."

My chest tightened. I didn't want her talking to him because I knew it would hurt her. And I knew Brent was right.

"I'll think about it."

"D…"

"I know, Brent. Okay? Just let me think about it."

"I should go before she asks me to buy her the whole store on your behalf or something."

I wanted to smile but I couldn't. I wanted to get her a pet, but if I did that now, she'd think I was trying to bribe her.

"You know you can if she asks."

"Yeah like you'd want a menagerie of animals in the house."

"I would if it made her happy."

"You're going soft in your old age, man."

"Fuck off, you're older than me."

He chuckled again.

"I'll see you at home."

He hung up and I slipped my phone back in my pocket, leaning my hand against the doorframe and staring out at the garden.

"Is she okay?" James asked.

"No, but there's not much I can do about it."

"I'm sorry."

"Not as sorry as I am about this entire fucking mess."

"Will you tell me the rest?"

He wanted to know why I'd gone back to Zach. Why I'd turned into such a fucking arsehole. Except I couldn't tell him that because it would destroy him.

"I did it... all of it for you, Jen and Fi. That's all you need to know. I'm doing all of this to protect you. It's because I love the three of you so much."

I turned to him.

"Make no mistake, one day I will tell you what hold he has over me, but right now, I can't. Right now, I need you to trust me and know I will stop him. I'll take him down and make sure he can't hurt any of us again. Can you do that for me? Can you wait and pretend like you don't know a thing? Go back to hating me in front of him?"

He stared at me for the longest time, not saying a word. I saw so much of myself in him. I wanted more for my brother.

He deserved so much fucking more than our piece of shit father and our shitty mess of a family.

"I can... but, Dante, I don't want to go back to not having a relationship with you."

"You won't. You know you're welcome here at any time. I promise. Just please, please, trust me and let me do this for all of us."

He nodded.

"Even though all of this is really fucked up and what you did wasn't right, I hope she forgives you. I like her. She's good for you."

I smiled. She was more than good for me. She forced me to do better. Be better.

"I hope so too."

"You really love her?"

I nodded, rubbing the back of my neck. I hadn't even admitted it to her yet, but I would. She just had to start talking to me again. She had to come back to me.

"I do. Even though going along with Zach was fucked up and I regret it, I can't regret her. I can't change how I feel."

I shook my head. I sounded like a lovesick fool. And I was one. Liora really was everything to me.

"Anyway, since you're skiving work and I need a distraction, why don't we watch a bunch of shit films and critique them like we used to?"

James gave me a half-smile and nodded. It'd been a weekly thing the four of us had done as a family until Jen and Fi moved out and it was just me and James. Brent had joined in sometimes. I missed those days. Honestly, I just missed my family and I wanted to make Liora a part of it.

As I followed James upstairs, I just hoped she would let me apologise to her. Even if she never came back to me, I wanted to say sorry properly. I wanted to tell her how I felt and that no matter what, I'd always be there for her if she needed me.

I loved that girl.

And deep down, I knew she loved me too.

Chapter Twenty One

LIORA

I spent the entire night tossing and turning, unable to sleep. For as long as I'd been here, I'd spent every night next to Dante. Even when he came to bed after I'd fallen asleep and left early, I'd instinctively known he was there. I'd fought against the urge to text him and tell him how much I missed him. How I needed him there.

Brent had been great. After we'd got back to the house, he took me straight to his basement flat and locked the door behind him. He'd spent the rest of the day with me, trying to cheer me up and making sure I had dinner and lunch. He didn't mention Dante or try to get me to talk about things further. Then he'd tucked me up in bed and told me I'd feel better in the morning.

The problem was. I didn't feel better. Not at all. If anything, I felt worse.

My chest ached. My heart was broken. And I missed Dante with a force which threatened to tear me apart. I longed for his presence. Even though he'd hurt me and kept things from me. I knew I should be upset with him, but I wasn't. I understood. At least now I'd had a chance to calm down, I did. He hadn't wanted to hurt me. He was trying to protect me. All Dante did was try to protect those he cared about even if he had a skewed and fucked up way of going about it.

He had really messed up though. Going along with this ridiculous blood debt business. I didn't care how much he wanted me. He could've got my attention another way. Honestly, if he'd just made the effort to speak to me and get to know me over that three year period after the first day we'd seen each other, maybe I would've been more open to this. Then again, this was purely speculation on my part. And it was stupid to think like that.

I rolled out of bed. Brent had brought me some clothes down so I got dressed and went through into his kitchen, which he told me he rarely used. I made myself some tea and cereal and sat down at the table, drumming my fingers on it. I wondered where he was. Had he gone upstairs to speak to Dante?

Sighing, I dug into my food and tried to forget about everything. It was impossible. All I could think about was him. Dante. I wanted to see him. Hold him. Kiss him. Most of all, I wanted that connection between us. I craved it. My heart burnt with longing.

Brent lumbered into the kitchen holding a laptop which he set down in front of me.

"Dante said you can speak to your dad."

"Good morning to you too."

He smiled, indicating the laptop.

"He's awaiting your call when you're ready."

I stared at the screen. Skype was up with my dad's name waiting there for me to click call. My heart pounded and my palms felt sweaty. Talking to my dad after all this time would be strange. I hadn't seen him since the Gala and even then, I hadn't said a word to him. I knew he was sorry, but it didn't stop me feeling resentment towards him.

I shook my head. Something inside me cracked wide open and bled. I wasn't sure I could sit and listen to my dad tell me what really happened. There were so many questions I wanted to ask, but they whirled around my head like I was on a carousel.

"I can't," I whispered.

Brent frowned.

"You can't? You wanted to speak to him."

I didn't want to do it alone. There was only one person I wanted there with me. Holding my hand.

"I need... I need... I need him."

"Who? D?"

I nodded. Brent sighed, giving me the once over before he picked up the laptop and put his hand out.

"You two need to sort your shit out, you know that, right?"

"I know."

I got up and took his hand. He gave it a squeeze before taking me upstairs.

"I can't help it. How I feel I mean," I said when I couldn't stand the silence.

"Hey, I'm not judging. Personally think you and him just need to admit how you feel to each other and work it out."

I looked up at him as we went up to the first floor. Brent was the only person who I felt comfortable talking about pretty much anything with. Well, the only person other than Dante himself. Maybe it was because Brent understood Dante and what I had to deal with when it came to him. Or maybe it was just because I liked Brent. He was straight forward and didn't beat around the bush.

"How do you know we've not?"

"Because I know D and I'm starting to understand you too."

"I wish things were different."

"I'm sure he does too, but you're stuck with what you've got so I suggest you make the best of a shit situation."

I snorted. It was a shit situation, but the only saving grace was that I had finally found love even if it was with a complicated man. Brent was right yet again. I just needed to tell Dante the truth. We needed to put this stuff behind us because I was pretty sure Dante and I didn't want to let each other go.

Brent left me in the living room with the laptop sitting on the coffee table and went in search of my errant boyfriend. Was he even my boyfriend? I mean he'd said we were in a relationship, but I didn't want to make assumptions. I was being an idiot yet again. I was going to go with yes, Dante was my boyfriend and if he wasn't on board with it, then tough shit. He'd made me fall in love with him.

I felt it the moment he entered the room. Looking up, I found him standing just inside the doorway, his blue eyes cautious. He looked so good dressed in jeans and a black t-shirt which hugged his muscular chest. I'd missed him even though we'd only spent a day apart.

I was on my feet before I could stop myself and walking towards him. He watched me approach him. I could've sworn he was about to say something but I didn't let him. I pressed myself against his chest, wrapping my arms around his back and breathing in his familiar scent of citrus and sandalwood. He hugged me back, leaning his cheek against the top of my head.

"I'm sorry," he whispered.

"I missed you." Tears welled in my eyes. "Don't allow me to run off and spend the night away from you again. I don't care how angry I am."

"Do you mean that?"

"Yes, I can't sleep without you. Promise me."

He kissed the top of my head.

"I promise."

I pulled away enough to look up at him. My anger was gone. All I saw was Dante. His blue eyes twinkling. His beautiful face. The face I loved so much. All his lines and contours. They were etched into my mind. Every inch of him.

Maybe it was stupid of me to forgive him for everything he'd done, but I was over beating myself up over the way I felt about him. I was done denying it. Done trying to run away from what was between us. I was in this with him for the long run.

"Brent said you couldn't call your dad without me."

"I need you to hold my hand."

He gave me a lopsided smile.

"But you have to sit far enough away that my dad doesn't know you're here, okay? I want him to tell me the truth and I don't know if he'll do that if he suspects I'm not alone."

"Okay… Can I kiss you?"

I nodded. He reached up, cupping my cheek before his mouth was on mine. Everything else faded away. It was just me and him. I shifted, moving my hands up so I could wrap one around his neck and the other tangled in his hair. The kiss deepened, tongues melding together as we pressed against one another.

It felt right. Being with him just felt right. He was it for me. The one. Even though we'd only really known each other properly for a few months, I was sure. Deep in my heart, in my soul, I felt it. Dante was the right one and I'd tell him just as soon as I'd got this conversation with my father over.

I pulled away, staring up at him. The words were on the tip of my tongue but I held them back. I didn't want the shit with my dad hanging over me. I took his hand instead, pulling him over to the sofa. He sat far enough away from me that he wouldn't be picked up by the camera.

I clicked on the call icon and waited as the camera blinked on and I could see my face on screen. I reached over, taking Dante's hand. My dad answered the call and appeared on the screen a minute later.

"Lass," he said.

"Dad."

"How have you been?"

"Okay, I guess. How's Mum?"

"Still mad at me, but she's doing well."

I was silent. Where did I even start? He shifted in his seat. I could see he looked tense through the screen.

"Dante told me, Dad. He told me why you gave me to him."

His face fell further. There was no point me treading on eggshells. This conversation had to happen one way or another.

"Then you know about Zander."

"I want your side of the story. I want to know if you really killed your best friend. I want to know if what Zach said is true about the blood debt, and were you and Mum having an affair?"

He sighed, fidgeting in his seat again. Dante's hand tightened around mine. I couldn't look at him even though I wanted to. How would I have been able to face this without him? I already felt like I was breaking inside all over again.

"I did, lass, but what you've got to understand is Zander wasn't a good lad. He hurt your Ma. He was vicious and unkind behind closed doors. Your Ma and I weren't having an affair, I was her shoulder to cry on. Zach made assumptions and I didn't contradict him. It was easier than trying to convince him about his brother's temperament."

Did my father know Zach was the same? That he beat his own children. Dante hadn't exactly told me the whole story, but I'd gathered that from what little he'd said. Maybe he would tell me soon.

"Why did you agree to the debt?"

"I didn't want to go to prison and the police had no reason to suspect it was anything but an accident. I regret it, Lass. It was a stupid decision, but he was right there and I couldn't stop myself. Not after I saw all the bruises on your Ma. He was never going to stop and he told her he would kill her if she left."

I felt sick. If what my dad was saying was true then Dante's uncle was an awful person. It didn't mean my dad had the right to take away his life, but I understood on some level.

"There's something else, lass. Something your lad won't have told you because they don't know the truth."

I fought against the urge to check Dante's expression.

"Your Ma didn't handle Zander's death very well. We didn't speak for a year, but when she did come see me, she told me she'd been with another abusive lad and he'd kicked her out because she was pregnant."

The implications of what he just said whirled around in my brain.

"I always loved your Ma, so I told her I'd marry her and raise the baby as my own. Declan, your brother, isn't mine. I'm so sorry, Liora. I didn't want this to fall on your shoulders, but you are my first born. You were always destined to pay the blood debt."

I was so shocked, I forgot to breathe. It was only when Dante squeezed my hand that I took in a rasping breath.

"What?" I whispered. "You mean… Declan is only my half-brother?"

"Yes. He doesn't know, lass, and you can't tell him."

"Then why tell me?"

"You deserve the truth. I wish I'd never made that agreement with Zach, but his lad isn't like him. He promised me he'd take care of you. He asked me so many questions about you. He genuinely wanted to know so he could make you happy. I know what I did was wrong, but I would've never given you away if I didn't think you'd be safe with him."

My heart thumped in my chest. I'd known Dante had asked my dad things about me, but I thought my dad had told him under duress. To know my dad actually thought somewhat highly of Dante surprised me.

"He is taking care of you, isn't he?"

I was nodding before I realised it.

"Yes, Dad. He is. He's not what I expected, but I'm fine here… with him. You don't have to worry about that part. It's only really, you know, Zach, who's the issue."

He gave me a small smile. I wasn't sure how I felt about what he'd told me, only that I didn't want to be angry with him any longer. He was my dad. I was well within my rights to rant and rage at him. And I could've, but I didn't. I was just so tired of all the pain. All I wanted was to feel normal again.

I'd forgiven Dante so I could forgive my dad too. Forgive him for the shit he'd done because deep down I understood his motives. He wanted to protect the person he cared about the most. My mother. Even though it meant he had to sacrifice me. I wasn't even born when he made that promise. It wasn't until now, I realised how much it must've weighed on him.

"I'm glad, lass. I'm still sorry all the same. You'll never know how much I love you and I'm so proud of you. You're the strongest one of us all."

"Thanks Dad. Um… I should go."

I wanted to end this so I could talk to Dante and make sense of it all.

"Will… will he let you speak to me again soon?"

"Yes, I'm sure he will."

"Be sure to give him my thanks, you know, for taking care of you."

"I will, bye Dad."

"Bye lass."

I pulled my hand from Dante's and ended the call. We sat in silence for a long moment.

"You were always destined to be mine," was the first thing Dante said.

I looked over at him. His blue eyes were dark.

"You believe him?"

"What reason would he have to lie to you about something like that?"

"He wouldn't."

"Liora, I would trust your father's word over Zach's any day. You have no idea what a manipulative piece of work he is."

I shook my head.

"I think I have some idea."

"Are you okay?"

Was I? My feelings were tangled up inside. I wasn't sure if I was in shock at my father's revelations or I was just numb to it. There was one thing that was very clear to me. I needed something to focus on. Something which would give me clarity. Something only Dante could grant me. And I wanted to tell him how I felt.

I stood up, putting my hand out to him. He frowned.

"Come with me… please?"

His brow was still furrowed as he stood and took my hand.

Provoked

"Where are we going?" he asked as I tugged him out of the room towards the stairs.

I didn't answer, making him come up to the second floor with me. We stopped outside a closed door. One I knew only he had the key to.

"You want to go in there?" he asked, surprise lacing his features.

I took both his hands in mine, staring up into his beautiful face.

"I need it. You seem to think this is just what you desire, but I crave it too. I want the pain, Dante."

"Are you sure you're not trying to avoid what just happened?"

"No. I'm not. We've never had time to just let go and be with each other fully in there. That's what I want. It helps me. Gives me freedom and clarity. I want to be able to focus and not have this tangled mess running riot inside me. I want your pain. Please."

He let go of one of my hands and rubbed the back of his neck.

"Okay… as long as you're sure. Hold on."

He let go of my other hand and stepped away, going towards his bedroom. He reappeared moments later with the key in his hand. He stopped outside the door and started to unlock it. I put my hand on his arm. He looked down at me, eyes cautious.

There was only one more request I had for him.

"Can it just be you and me? No Master and Pet. Just Dante and Liora. Just us. No hiding behind names or masks."

313

Chapter Twenty Two

DANTE

My heart hammered against my chest. Why did Liora make me feel so fucking vulnerable? Always pushing. Always needing more. Could I really shed that last mask I hid behind and show her the real me? Could I let her call me Dante whilst I marked her back?

When Brent found me, I was finishing breakfast after having spent the night tossing and turning without her. Yesterday had been tough, but worth it. James and I were talking and he didn't act like he hated my guts any longer. The truth had a funny way of setting you free. I didn't want any more secrets. I was done with those. The final thing I kept back would come out soon. The one thing I had left to fight against Zach with. And it wasn't a prospect I relished at all.

I hadn't known what to expect when I got upstairs and saw her for the first time in twenty four hours. Maybe she would shout at me. Maybe she would tell me she hated me.

Neither of those things happened.

Liora held me tight, told me she missed me and that she never wanted to be away from me again. What did I do to deserve this elfin beauty? This girl with her halo of blonde hair who intoxicated me. The one who wanted my pain.

And now the real truth about Liora was exposed. She was always meant to be mine. She was Angus's only child. As crazy and fucked up as it was, I think we both felt the truth of it deep in our bones.

Liora didn't want to talk about what we'd just learnt. She wanted to play. And she wanted me to play as me. Not as her Master.

I dropped my hands from the door, leaving the key in the lock. She, of all people, deserved to see the real me. Why the fuck was I so scared? It's not like Liora didn't know who I was. It's not like she hadn't ripped open my soul and buried herself deep inside it.

I took a steadying breath. Was this the last thing we needed so we could admit all our truths? So we could let go of everything holding us back?

I raised my hands again, unlocking the door and pushing it open. I turned to her before she could step in.

"Are you sure this is what you want?"

"I've never been surer of anything."

Her green eyes told me she was telling me the truth. All I saw in them was her vulnerability. Her truth. Her determination.

"Okay. Just Dante and Liora."

She strode into the playroom, flipping the light on before she stood at the end of the bed and waited. I walked in, shutting the door behind me before I locked it. I placed the key on the drawers and stepped up to her.

She raised her hands above her head. I pulled off her jumper followed by her t-shirt. Her bra came next. I unbuttoned her jeans, sliding them down her legs and lastly, her underwear. She stepped out of them for me, resting her hand on my shoulder to steady herself.

I folded each item of clothing neatly, placing them on top of the drawers too. She let out a shaky breath. I reached behind me and tugged off my own t-shirt, folding that and placing it next to her clothes. I was left in jeans and boxers. They wouldn't come off yet. Not until she begged for my cock, which was already straining against my clothes in anticipation.

"Do you remember the safe word?" I asked.

"Tiger."

"Good girl."

I turned to her fully. She stood waiting for my instructions. Waiting for my command. My eyes scanned the room. How did I want her? What would I use? This was new. Just being me. I couldn't fail her in this. I had to do it right. I had to show her the truth behind all the walls.

"I want you on your hands and knees on the bed."

"Yes, Dante."

I almost groaned, hearing my name on her lips. She crawled onto the bed and waited for me on all fours in the centre of it. I opened one of the drawers and tugged out four leather cuffs. I brought them over to the bed and attached one to each of her limbs. At each end of the bed there was a length of rope. They all joined together under the bed around a metal loop and the ends of those ropes were at my feet. I could make each one of her limbs completely immobile if I wanted to. Pulling the rope tight so she'd be spreadeagled on the bed.

I tied each length of rope to each cuff in turn. She wouldn't be escaping any time soon. Just how much did Liora trust me? I hoped it was enough for the both of us.

"Tell me, Liora, what is it you were hoping for when you made me bring you in here?"

She looked up at me.

"I want you to let go. Show me who you are. Hurt me in the ways you need. Don't hold back with me, Dante. I can take it. All of it. Everything you have. I'm not fragile. I won't break."

My heart pounded in my chest. My cock was so hard it hurt as it strained against the confines of my jeans. I fought against the urge to touch it just to relieve the pressure.

Walking over to the wall, I selected a short riding crop. She asked for this. I hoped she remembered that before the end. I stood behind her, looking at her beautiful pale skin and her pussy on full display for me. Reaching over, I grabbed both of her hips and tugged her back so she was at the edge of the bed.

I released her and trailed the crop up her leg.

"You want my pain, hmm? You want it to hurt?"

"I want it. I crave it."

The first strike across her arse made her yelp, but she didn't cower from me. She arched her back and offered herself up to me.

"Normal girls don't ask to be punished, Liora."

Smack.

"Normal girls don't want to be hurt."

Smack.

"I'm not normal," she hissed.

Smack.

Fuck. Her skin was beginning to turn red. Several more strikes had her crying out, but not once did she say stop. Trailing the crop up her pussy, it came away glistening. I struck her again.

"You're so wet. Wet for me. Wet for my pain. You want it to hurt so you can feel again, isn't that right?"

"Yes, please. I want more, Dante, please."

There was a certain stillness in the air as I struck her. Only the hiss of the leather sailing through the air and hitting her skin pierced the silence, followed by her cries of pain. Pain she wanted. Pain she craved.

"You have no idea how many times I've thought about punishing you. Pushing you to your absolute limit until you can't take it any longer."

Smack.

"You've defied me so many times, Liora."

Smack.

"You've run from me."

Smack.

I dropped the crop, needing to feel her skin on mine and the sting my palm would bring. Her yelp as the first strike came was like music to my ears.

"You've torn down all my walls."

I wasn't careful with my strikes. My palm found all the sensitive areas I'd hit with the crop.

"You've made it impossible for me to be without you."

Her cries got louder, but still she didn't say stop. She didn't use the safe word. Liora told me she could take it and she was. I didn't think I could love her more right then, but I did. I loved how strong she was. How she'd become the girl she was always meant to be. And I loved all the power she had over me even if I'd hated it before.

"Promise me you're in this with me. Promise me you want this as much as I do."

"I do," she moaned. "Fuck, I do. Please, don't stop. I need it. I promise, Dante. I'm yours. I'm here. I'm not going anywhere."

I couldn't take it any longer. My hand went to my jeans and I tore them open just so they weren't pressing against my cock. It hurt too fucking much. Being this hard and seeing her skin so red and raw for me.

My chest was heaving as I stared down at her. Then I reached down and gripped two of the ropes, tugging on them. They ripped her arms out from underneath her. I tugged the other two ropes tight so her legs were equally spread out but she could still stay on her knees for me. I secured the ropes so they wouldn't come loose. Her cheek was pressed against the bed, her green eyes wide.

I grabbed a whip off the rack and walked around the bed. Her back was perfectly arched and ready for me. I struck, the whip hissing through the air until it met skin. The line along her back it left made my cock twitch.

Her cry echoed around the room. I knew this position was uncomfortable for her. It was stretching her arms at an awkward angle.

"Again."

I was almost startled by her voice, but I obliged, sending the whip hissing through the air.

"Please, again."

The next three strikes left deeper marks as I put more force behind the flick of my wrist.

"Please, Dante, I want you so much."

"What do you want from me?"

She whimpered as the whip landed another strike.

"I'm so wet. I want your cock inside me. I want to feel your skin against me. I want to feel the burn of each lash. Please."

"Do you think you deserve my cock, Liora?"

I struck her again, needing to see more marks on her back.

"Please, I've done everything you've said. I've taken your punishment. I wanted it. Please give me your cock. Please fuck me."

"Are you sure you've taken enough punishment? Are you holding back on me? Are you keeping shit from me?"

"N… no," she whimpered as the whip struck her.

"I don't believe you."

It sailed through the air, hissing and she bucked when it met her skin.

"I'm telling you the truth."

"Only good girls get fucked."

I struck her twice more before her next words made me freeze entirely.

"Damn it, Dante. You want the truth? The whole truth? The truth is I love you. I'm in love with you. Please, please stop punishing me and fuck me."

The whip clattered on the floor as it slipped out of my hand.

"What did you just say?"

"I said I love you."

I was around at her side and kneeling beside the bed so I could look at her face. Look into her eyes.

"Say it again," I whispered, barely able to get the words out.

Her eyes softened.

"I love you, Dante."

I'd known deep down she felt that way but hearing her say it was something else. Hearing her admit those words out loud made my heart squeeze painfully in my chest. I no longer wanted to play this game. I just wanted her.

I crawled onto the bed and uncuffed her, fumbling in my haste to free her. Her eyes were questioning as she sat up and stretched her arms out. I didn't let her speak. Grabbing her face, I kissed her and crushed her to me. Her hands found their way into my hair, tugging at the short strands.

I needed her. Needed her encasing me. I dropped my hands from her face and tugged at my jeans and boxers. She released my mouth, reaching down to help me. They were off in the next instant. I pressed her down, sinking between her legs. She didn't make any complaints about being on her back. Just opened herself up to me. Her pussy was so wet as my cock ran along the length of it. I groaned, capturing her mouth again.

Reaching in between us, I gripped my cock pressing it to her before one sharp thrust of my hips had me buried halfway inside her pussy. I pulled back and thrust inside her again, gaining another inch. She was so wet; it was almost effortless.

"Liora," I murmured against her mouth. "Fuck, you feel so good."

One more thrust and I was buried up to the hilt. She pulsed around me. It was fucking heaven. Everything about the lead up to this had been bliss. Inflicting the pain she adored so much, having her call me by my name rather than Master and her admitting she loved me. All of it bound itself around my heart.

"You're my everything," I told her, pulling away so I could look into her eyes. "Don't ever forget that."

I cupped her face, brushing her hair out of it as I leant on my elbows.

"My heart. My most beautiful and precious heart."

She reached up, wrapping her hand around my neck and the other laid on my chest. Her smile lit my whole damn world on fire.

"I'm yours and you're mine," she said.

"I'm never letting go. I hope you're prepared to have me for life."

Her smile widened, green eyes twinkling.

"I am, Dante. I love you."

Those words. They wrecked me. Destroyed me. And made me whole again.

I took her with long, hard strokes, staring down at her like she was the most precious thing in the world to me. Because she was.

Our breathing became heavier and movements erratic. Liora practically clawed at my back and curled both legs around me, allowing me deeper access.

"Harder," she breathed. "Please, I'm so close."

I was brushing up against her clit the way I was angled. Her body was taut beneath me as she began to crest the wave. I wanted to see her come apart. I needed it.

There was a pounding at the door which startled both of us. I didn't stop fucking her, but I looked over at it.

"Dante," a voice called through it as the handle rattled.

Who the fuck was that? I didn't quite recognise the voice muffled by the door.

Turning back to Liora, her eyes were wide. I wasn't going to let anyone ruin this moment because we were both so close.

"Ignore it," I told her.

The pounding got louder.

"Dante—" she began to say.

"No, you're going to come for me. I don't give a shit who it is."

She stared up at me. Her eyes told me she could do that. I thrust harder as her body tensed further and her lips parted on a silent moan.

"Dante, open the fucking door."

Now I recognised the voice. That was just fucking great. We were going to deal with a hell of a lot of shit when we got out of here, but I just couldn't bring myself to care. I was so wrapped up in my girl. In the way her pussy clamped down on my cock, signalling she was close. So fucking close.

"I want you to listen to me carefully," I told her. "No matter what happens, remember what I'm about to say."

I didn't have much time to explain, but I had to say this.

"O… Okay."

"I'm going to destroy my father. I'm going to make sure he doesn't hurt any of us ever again. What he did to me, James, the girls and our mother when we were kids was awful. He's the reason I hate people touching me. I need you to trust me. Trust what I'm going to do and why."

Her hand around my neck tightened.

"I do trust you."

"Good because I love you, Liora, and I can't live without you."

"You do?"

Her expression was so hopeful. So adoring.

"Yes, I love you so much."

I leant down and kissed her. I wasn't lying. I was in love with her and that wasn't going to change. And she needed to know that because what came next wasn't going to be pretty.

"Dante, open this door right fucking now," came the voice again.

Go to fucking hell.

"Come for me," I whispered against her lips. "Please, my heart. I need it."

If I was going to go through with the next step, I had to have something to hold onto. I needed this to keep me sane.

"Please, Liora."

She bucked and her pussy clamped down on my cock, pulsing. She turned her face from mine and cried out.

"Dante, oh, god, Dante."

She came so hard I couldn't hold back. I tried to fight it, but she was like a fucking vice and my cock erupted. I grunted, feeling the warmth of her cum and mine surrounding me as I spurted inside her.

"Fuck," I groaned.

I tried not to collapse on top of her. Her back must be raw from my treatment as well as me fucking her into oblivion. I wanted desperately to take care of it for her, but we didn't have time.

I heard a body slam into the door.

"You will open this fucking door right this instant."

I kissed Liora's forehead and pulled away. She lay there for a long moment as I got off the bed and dug through the drawers, tossing her some wipes after grabbing a couple for myself. I cleaned myself up and tugged on my clothes.

"I need you to get dressed," I said.

She'd just finished cleaning herself up. She got off the bed gingerly and I helped her into her clothes.

"Open the fucking door!"

I cupped her face, staring down at her.

"There are two things I need you to do for me when we get out there, my heart."

"Okay," she whispered.

I could see the nervousness in her expression. I dropped one of my hands and pulled something out of my pocket.

"I'm going to ask Brent to take you downstairs. Make him give you his phone and then call the police for me. I don't care what you tell them, just make sure they get here fast. Secondly, I need you to give them this."

I pressed something into her palm, curling her fingers around it.

"Can you do that for me?"

"Yes, but what's going on, Dante?"

"Just trust me. You're not going to like what I'm going to do, but I have to. It's the only way to keep us safe."

I kissed her before she could open her mouth.

"I love you," I told her when I pulled away.

"I love you too."

Taking her hand, I pulled her over to the door and unlocked it. I opened it finding Zach outside, his face a picture of irritation and Brent hovering in the background.

"About fucking time," Zach growled.

I stepped out, keeping Liora's hand held tightly in mine.

"Well I'm sorry I was busy."

Zach's eyes flashed before they fell on Liora and narrowed.

"What do you want, Zach?" I continued.

He took a step towards me, reaching out like he was going to take Liora from me. I pushed her behind my back.

"She's coming with me."

"Like fuck she is."

Zach's eyes were wild. They held that hard edge to them which told me he was close to losing his temper. And I knew what would happen when he did.

"We had a fucking agreement and as far as I'm concerned you've broken it."

I moved away from him, taking Liora with me to try put some distance between us. I needed to get her to Brent before Zach got his hands on her.

"And how do you think I did that?"

Zach pointed at me.

"Don't think I was fooled by your little act. You can't hide it from me. She's got you wound around her little finger, turning you against me."

I almost laughed as I moved closer to Brent. Liora's hands were buried in the back of my t-shirt as she moved with me.

"You've done that just fine all by yourself. Did you really think I'd forgotten about what you did to me? To them? Did you think just because I fell in line that I didn't still hate the very sight of you?"

He was a fucking idiot if he thought I'd ever let go of it. I'd done all of this so he wouldn't hurt my brother and sisters anymore. So they could live without all that pain in their lives. The pain which haunted them, especially Jen and Fi.

Brent skirted closer to us, as if realising what I was trying to do.

"Oh, I knew, Son. I've always known how weak you are. How love has turned you into a fucking pussy. That's your problem. You care about others too much."

"Yeah? Well at least I'm not a fucking sick fuck who doesn't give a shit about his own children. At least I didn't use my fists to take out my own anger and frustration on other people. You make me sick; you know that? You were never fucking fit to be our father. That's why I took them away from you. Made sure you couldn't hurt them anymore."

I'd rather be a pussy than be like him. I'd rather love freely and deeply than be twisted by anger and hatred.

Zach started towards me and I shoved Liora at Brent, who caught her up in his arms and took her towards the stairs. I looked at him.

"Take her downstairs and don't come back up here."

He gave me a sharp nod.

"You give her to me, Brent, right fucking now," Zach seethed.

"No, Zach," I said. "You're not having her. You're never getting your hands on her."

Brent picked Liora up who started struggling.

"You broke the fucking agreement. She is mine."

He started towards Brent and Liora, but I moved into his path, stopping him in his tracks.

"You're not touching her. Take your shit out on me if you want a fucking punching bag, but she is not your plaything."

"What? Dante, no, what are you doing?" Liora cried out.

Zach's eyes widened a fraction as he stared at me.

I was slightly taller than him, but that didn't mean I was any less intimidated by him. I always had been. The number of times he hurt me guaranteed that. Made me feel weak and helpless with his fists.

"Take her downstairs, Brent."

"Dante, don't. Please, don't."

I didn't look back at her. I couldn't because I would fucking break. Sacrificing myself for her was the only way. I hoped she'd call the police. I hoped she would get them to come here in time because otherwise, my gamble wouldn't pay off.

"Dante!" I heard her screams echoing off the walls. "Let go of me. Dante!"

I love you, Liora. Please, my heart, save me.

"Are you sure you want to do this?" Zach asked.

"Do your fucking worst."

He raised his hand and I stood there, waiting for the first strike to come.

Chapter Twenty Three

LIORA

I struggled in Brent's grasp as he pulled me down the second flight of stairs to the ground floor. What the hell was Dante doing? Was he crazy? He couldn't do this. Couldn't let Zach hurt him in place of me.

"Let go."

"No. You need to calm down," Brent told me as we reached the bottom of the stairs.

"He's going to hurt him."

"I know he is."

"We have to stop him."

"You heard what he said. Told us to stay down here."

I had, but it didn't matter. We had to stop Zach hurting him. Dante didn't need to go through that again. He might not have told me everything, but I knew Zach had beat them all as children. And I was relatively sure Dante suffered the worst of it.

"Please, Brent, please."

He set me on my feet and held both of my shoulders, keeping me locked in place as he looked down at me.

"No. I made a promise to D a long time ago that I'd do exactly what he asked me to without questioning his decisions. I trust him and you need to as well."

I clenched my fists. Something dug into my palm. I opened my hand and looked down at it. It was a memory stick. Dante had given me a memory stick. Then I remembered what he told me to do.

"Give me your phone, Brent."

"What?"

"Give me your phone right now."

"Why do you want it?"

"Dante told me to phone the police before we came out of the playroom so give me the fucking phone."

I was losing my shit here. Zach was likely already hurting Dante and I couldn't let that continue. He'd told me to make sure they got here fast. I wondered what was on the memory stick and why it was so important, but I didn't have time to think about it.

Brent let go of me and fumbled with his pocket before he pulled out his phone and handed it to me. I expected him to grab me again, but he didn't. He looked just as worried as I felt. The thing is, I didn't know if Dante was going to be okay, but I also knew he wouldn't forgive me if I went back up there without the police here.

I gripped the memory stick in one hand and dialled 999 with the other.

"Hello, emergency service operator. Which service do you require?"

"The police," I replied.

"I'll connect you now."

The hair at the back of my neck stood up. How was I going to convince them they needed to get here as fast as possible? I should just tell them the truth. That my boyfriend's father was beating him.

I was put through to the operator and they asked me the address of the property and my name which I gave them.

"Thank you, Liora, what's the nature of your emergency?"

"My boyfriend's father came to our house and started threatening us. My boyfriend sent me and his friend downstairs, but I think he's going to hurt Dante."

"Okay, do you know what's happening upstairs now?"

"No. It's quiet, but I think Zach is hurting Dante, no, I'm sure of it."

"Is Dante your boyfriend?"

"Yes and Zach is his father."

I was trying to stay calm and answer the questions but my fear for Dante was eating me up inside. I wanted to tell them to get here right now because I couldn't stand it.

"Okay, Liora, can you tell me exactly why you think Zach would hurt his son?"

"Zach threatened to take me away and Dante wouldn't let him."

"Has Zach been abusive towards Dante in the past?"

"Yes... I don't know all the details, but I know there's a history of domestic abuse. Please, I'm so scared for him. Zach is crazy. I'm worried he'll go too far and kill Dante."

I seriously hoped the police were on their way now because I wasn't coping with this very well. I was shaking so hard I almost dropped the phone.

"Are you aware of Zach having any weapons or mentioning them?"

"No."

"Can you give me Zach's full name please and date of birth?"

"Zachary Benson and I don't know how old he is, maybe sixties. He owns Bensons, you know the fashion house."

"Thank you, can you tell me Dante's full name and date of birth?"

"Dante Benson. He's twenty seven but I don't know his birthday. Are the police on their way?"

"Thank you. Yes, we have a unit on their way now and they will be with you as soon as they can."

"Okay… thank you. I'm so scared."

That's when both Brent and I heard a sharp howl of pain from upstairs. I almost bolted up the stairs, but Brent put a hand on my shoulder.

"Can you tell me what's happening now, Liora?"

"We just heard a cry of pain. Oh god."

I burst into tears, unable to hold back my emotions any longer. I shoved the phone at Brent before I crumpled to the floor. I vaguely heard him talking to the 999 operator. After everything we'd just shared together in the playroom and now this shit was happening. My back hurt, but I barely felt it. I was so worried for Dante.

"I can't confirm he's hurt, but yes, I think we need an ambulance too… Yes, she was right, there is a history of domestic abuse, but it was never reported."

Another howl came from upstairs and my heart shattered in my chest. I couldn't do this. I needed to get to Dante. I had to stop Zach. I crawled towards the stairs before Brent could stop me.

"Liora!"

"No," I sobbed. "Let me go to him."

"Look, are they almost here? I need to stop her going upstairs before she gets hurt too."

I couldn't stand up, but I dragged myself up the stairs.

I'm coming for you, Dante. Please hold on. Please.

There was a sharp rap at the door. I looked behind me as Brent moved towards the it. Two uniformed officers stood outside.

"Sir, are you the one who made the call?"

"Yes, I'm Brent, please, they're upstairs on the top floor."

The police walked in and noticed me on the stairs. One of them strode towards me.

"Ma'am, are you okay? Are you hurt?"

"No," I sobbed. "No, but you need to get to Dante, please."

The officers looked at each other before they turned to Brent.

"I'll take care of her, please, they're on the top floor," Brent replied.

The officers walked by me and up the stairs.

"Brent, please, we have to go after them."

335

He shook his head but came over to me and picked me up off the floor.

"D is going to kill me for this."

"Just take me upstairs, please."

I was a mess and I had no idea what we were walking into. I'm pretty sure the police would've wanted us to stay put, but nothing would stop me from getting to Dante. Brent set me on my feet and held my hand. I practically dragged him up the stairs with me, desperate to make sure Dante was okay.

When we got up to the second floor, my heart fractured in my chest. Zach was in handcuffs with one officer holding him back whilst the other was kneeling on the floor next to Dante.

"Oh god, Dante!"

Brent wasn't able to stop me as I ran towards them. The officer turned at my approach.

"Ma'am, you need to stay back."

I dropped to my knees next to him, completely ignoring what he said and looking over Dante. His right eye was already swelling up and his lip was split. He looked like he'd been ten rounds in a boxing ring.

"Why? Why did you do this?"

He opened his good eye, staring up at me.

"Liora," he croaked, reaching for me.

I took his hand, placing a kiss on top of it. He was okay. He was alive. My heart thumped against my chest. He looked like hell, but he was still breathing and talking.

I turned to the officer.

"Is an ambulance on its way?"

His expression softened.

"Yes, ma'am and more officers. We will need to take a statement from you when they arrive."

I remembered the memory stick in my free hand.

"Here, you'll need this," I said, sticking my hand out to him.

I dropped the memory stick into his hand.

"What is this?"

"Evidence," Dante croaked.

I stroked his hand.

"Shh, don't try to talk," I told him.

"No, I… I have to. Cold case, my mother… her… her murderer was never found. What's on there… proves it was my father."

What? What the hell did he just say?

"Sir, that's a very grave accusation."

"You fucking bastard," Zach roared.

I looked back and found the other officer struggling to hold Zach back.

"Sir, you need to calm down."

The officer next to me sprung up and went to help after he tucked the memory stick into his pocket.

"We should take him downstairs."

"I'm going to kill you, I'm going to fucking kill you," Zach screamed.

The two officers ended up pinning Zach to the floor as he kept bucking and shouting.

"You're no fucking son of mine, you hear me!"

"Sir, I suggest you calm down."

The doorbell rang. Brent looked over at me before he disappeared downstairs to answer it. I hoped it was the ambulance and more officers. I turned back to Dante, knowing the two officers had Zach under control.

He was staring up at me with no small amount of pain in his eyes.

"Where does it hurt?"

"Everywhere."

I shifted closer to him, carefully laying my other hand on his cheek.

"Is what you said true?"

"Yes."

Tears rolled down my cheeks. Zach had murdered his mother. His own wife. And if Dante had evidence of it then he'd known about it for a long time.

"I was there," he croaked. "He made me watch. She told me he would, that he was so close to doing it. I couldn't stop him. He tied me up, but she knew. She set up a camera to film it and told me to keep it safe until the day I could use it against him. Told me one day, I'd have to tear him down."

My heart broke all over again for him. For his mother. For everything they'd all had to endure. I stroked his hair back.

"Shh, don't talk any more."

I heard footsteps and the next moment, I found two paramedics next to me.

"We need to look him over now," one of them said gently to me.

I let go of him, moving back so they could attend to him. His good eye tracked my movements. All I could see is the love he had for me and it tore at my soul.

'I love you, my heart,' he mouthed at me.

I put my hand on my heart, unable to speak any longer. I found Brent had squatted down next to me and put an arm around my shoulder. I buried my face in his chest and sobbed, unable to help myself. It was all too much. I'd tried to stay strong, but I was broken. Seeing Dante hurt killed me.

"Shh, Liora, he's going to be okay, I promise," Brent murmured.

I sat in the chair next to Dante's hospital bed. He looked so broken with his swollen eye and split lip. He had bruises all over his chest. I'd seen them when they were working on him. He was asleep now. I was glad of it. He needed rest after what Zach had done.

I was pissed off with him for sacrificing himself in my place. He hadn't needed to do that, but then again, the police had locked up Zach and weren't letting him out after what they'd seen. I honestly didn't care what they charged him with as long as he didn't get his hands on Dante again.

I heard someone come in the room and I looked over at the door. James was standing there, his blue eyes wide. Brent must've called him. He'd gone back to the house when I refused to leave Dante's side. We'd both had to give statements to the police, but mine was conducted here at the hospital whilst they attended to Dante.

After Dante was seen in A&E, Brent had insisted he be moved to a private hospital nearby and wouldn't take no for

Sarah Bailey

an answer. At least it meant they wouldn't kick me out of his room and he wasn't being disturbed by other patients.

"Hey," I said, my voice quiet.

James came further into the room.

"Is he okay?" he asked, his voice just as quiet as mine.

"The doctors said he'll be okay, but he's in a lot of pain. He just needs to rest."

"What happened? Brent didn't really explain."

"We should talk about this outside so we don't disturb him."

James nodded and I got up and followed him out. I was exhausted, but James deserved to know the truth.

"Are you sure he's going to be okay?"

"Yes, it looks worse than it is. Honestly, I'm really pissed off with your brother, but right now, I'm just glad he's safe."

He put a hand on my arm, giving it a squeeze.

"Brent said Dad is locked up."

"Dante let Zach beat the shit out of him to save me."

"He what?"

Tears welled in my eyes. I was done crying, but I couldn't help it. My heart bled for my boyfriend. He'd suffered far too much in his life. Especially with what he'd told me about their mother. It reminded me that James must not know. How would I break it to him? Did Dante want to tell him? I had no idea how to handle this.

"Exactly. Zach came around and started shouting at us, telling Dante he broke their agreement and he was taking me. Dante made Brent take me downstairs and basically told Zach if he wanted to use him as a punching bag he could, but Zach wasn't getting me."

340

James dropped his hand and looked down at the floor.

"Did Dante tell you what Dad used to do to us?"

"Not really. I mean I've guessed a lot of it."

He sighed, rubbing the back of his neck like I constantly saw Dante doing. It made my heart ache. I looked over through the window at the man who I loved with every inch of my being. He was still asleep, but the sight of him broke me all over again.

"Dante protected me and the twins from the worst of it. He told me everything yesterday. That's why he took us when he turned eighteen, to stop Zach hurting us all. He beat the four of us and our mother."

I looked up at him. His face was tense and I could see the worry behind his eyes.

"There's something Dante needs to talk to you about when he wakes up. It's about your mother, but it's not my place to say."

He nodded.

"Do you think the police will let Dad out?"

"After what happened and what Dante gave them? No."

"What Dante gave them?"

"He has evidence of stuff from your childhood. It's what he needs to speak to you about. I can't say any more. I'm sorry. I don't know the whole story anyway. He only managed to say a few things to me before the paramedics came. I was so scared. Zach could've killed him."

James stepped closer to me and put his arm around my shoulders, giving me a squeeze as we both stared through the window at Dante.

"I can't say I'm unhappy he's locked up."

"Me either."

I sighed. Whatever happened next, I just hoped we wouldn't have to go through this again. I couldn't stand seeing Dante hurt.

"I should go be with Dante in case he wakes up," I said.

"Is it okay if I sit with him too?"

"Sure."

I didn't mind the company, but I was dead on my feet. We both went back in the room. I sat in the seat closest to Dante and held his hand whilst James sat next to me.

I wasn't sure how much time passed. The police came and went, speaking to James whilst I kept a watch on his brother. The nurses had tried to tell us visiting hours were over, but I wasn't having any of it. At some point, I dropped my head on the bed next to Dante with his hand still in mine. I could've sworn I felt a blanket being put over me before I fell away into oblivion.

I could only hope Dante would wake up soon and that he really would be okay.

That we'd get through this.

And that Zach would be out of our lives forever.

Chapter Twenty Four

DANTE

I ached everywhere. The doctors had given me painkillers, but my face and chest burnt with the pain. I opened my good eye. It was dark in the room but I could still see from the light streaming in through the window from the corridor.

Someone was holding my hand. I looked down. Liora's blonde head was resting on the bed next to me, my hand clasped tightly in hers. Was she allowed in here at this time? Why did I even care? Having her here made my heart thump. I reached over and stroked her hair even though it aggravated my chest and hurt like hell.

She stirred. I dropped my hand and she sat up, blinking. A blanket dropped off her shoulders onto her chair.

"You're awake," she said.

"Mmmhmm."

"How are you feeling?"

"Sore."

Tears welled in her eyes. I reached out for her, wincing at the pain and cupped her cheek.

"Hey, don't cry, I'm okay."

"If you weren't so hurt, I would hit you. That was idiotic and reckless."

I blinked. I knew she'd be upset but I didn't expect her to be this angry with me. Her eyes blazed even though tears were falling and she looked like she wanted to strangle me.

"Liora, I—"

"No, I'm not finished. If you ever, ever do anything like that again, I won't be responsible for my actions. Do you hear me? Damn it, Dante, I was so scared."

Her face crumbled and I felt like the world's worst boyfriend. I'd done it so she would be safe. So the police would have a reason to arrest my father. So they could see how violent he was and therefore the evidence I had against him wouldn't be dismissed so easily. They were surely going to question why I hadn't come forward before. It was a huge risk, but one I felt necessary to take.

"Come here, my heart."

I let go of her hand and put my arms out to her.

"No, I don't want to hurt you any further."

"If you won't come to me, I'll get out of this bed and come to you."

"What? No, you can't do that. Stop being an idiot."

"Then come here and let me hold you."

She huffed but stood up and crawled onto the bed with me. Carefully, she let me wrap my arms around her as she laid her head against my chest. I ignored the pain, feeling contentment wash over me having her right there.

"I'm sorry," I told her, kissing the top of her head. "I know it was stupid and reckless, but I really am okay."

"The police were here, but you were sleeping. I told them to come back in the morning."

"Since when did they allow visitors to stay with patients?"

"They don't. I refused to leave. I may have scared the nurses. James told them to leave me be."

"James was here?"

I hadn't expected him to turn up.

"Yes, he was here for a couple of hours. He also spoke to the police. He's really worried about you."

"What did the police say?"

"They're going to charge Zach with assault, I think they said ABH, especially since the officers heard him threatening to kill you and investigate the other allegations you made against him. I'm sure they'll talk to you about it tomorrow."

At least it meant they were taking it seriously. I'm sure I was going to have to spend a lot of time talking to the police about what he'd done, but it was worth it. Zach needed to be put away so he couldn't come after us. He needed to rot for everything he'd done to me, to James, to Jen and Fi as well as our mother.

"I'm sorry, my heart."

"I was so scared for you. So, so scared he'd kill you."

Honestly, I thought he was going to. The number of times he hit me blurred together and I'd stood there and taken every punch. Every kick after I'd fallen to my knees. He'd ranted and raved at me, but I barely heard him. All I could think about was Liora. She was safe and I'd told her to call the police.

"I knew you'd save me."

"If the police hadn't got there so fast, then I might not have."

"You can't think like that. I'm here. No lasting damage. How is your back?"

She lifted her head from my chest, staring at me.

"You're asking me that when you're the one lying in a hospital bed?"

I tried to smile, but it hurt too much.

"Is asking after the woman I love a crime?"

"I'm fine, Dante. I mean it stings, but I don't care about me. I care about you. You're the one who got beaten up."

I frowned. I always made sure she was cared for after I inflicted any sort of punishment on her delicate skin. That wasn't going to change just because I was hurt.

"You tell Brent to put cream on your back."

"Excuse me?"

"Liora, I should've done it before we left the room and you need to tell Brent to come get you because you should be at home in bed."

"No."

"No?"

Why was she being so stubborn? She would wear herself out completely if she stayed here.

"I don't want Brent to see me half naked all over again and I'm not leaving you either. Don't you understand? The last time I left you, he hurt you. How can you ask me to go now?"

My heart fractured in my chest.

"I'm safe here, my heart."

"Don't make me go," she whispered. "Please."

"Okay, but you need to get some sleep."

"I can't sleep on the bed with you."

"Don't argue."

"But the nurses will come and tell us off."

"I don't care."

I started to shift to the side, wincing. She put her hands on my shoulders, holding me in place.

"Dante, you'll hurt yourself further. Let me help you."

I didn't make any complaints as she carefully helped me move over before she curled up by my side with my arm wrapped around her.

"You're very bossy," she told me, stroking my stomach gently.

"And you're stubborn."

She was silent for a long moment and all I could hear was the sounds of the hospital and Liora breathing.

"I love you," she whispered.

"I love you too."

I looked down at her. She'd closed her eyes, her hands resting by her head. Even though everything hurt and I wished I'd never moved, having her right next to me was soothing. So I closed my eyes too and let exhaustion carry me under.

I managed to convince Liora to let Brent take her home in the morning. The nurse lectured me about having let her sleep on the bed with me when she found us first thing. Liora wasn't even meant to be with me overnight. Neither of us paid the nurse much mind, but I did ache all over so I supposed she did have a point.

The police came after Liora left, which I was glad about since I didn't want her worrying further. She was on edge enough as it was. They informed me Zach would be charged with Actual Bodily Harm for his assault on me yesterday. He was being held pending their further investigations into the evidence I'd provided them with on the memory stick. His threats to kill me were enough for them to deny any sort of bail.

I spoke to them in length about why I'd let him do it and what happened in the past. They told me they'd need a written statement and they would be speaking to my siblings too. I was worried they'd push me on why I'd kept this a secret for so long, but they never once made me feel like it was my fault or place any blame at my door. A lifetime of abuse, intimidation and threats was enough to make anyone stay silent.

I was alone for a while when they left. The reality of what happened crashed down on me all at once. After all these years of living in fear, Zach was finally somewhere he couldn't hurt me, James, Fi or Jen any longer. And I was going to fight tooth and nail to make sure he stayed there.

Maybe I should've done this a long time ago, but if I beat myself up over all my mistakes, I'd spend eternity being miserable. I had a lot to live for now and I wanted a life full of laughter. To rebuild my relationship with my siblings. And most of all, to make Liora happy.

When the doctor came to say I could be discharged the next day, I was happy to be going home. It was a miracle I wasn't hurt worse. They'd wanted to make sure I didn't have any sort of concussion or further internal injuries. A few bruised ribs, black eye and a split lip. No internal bleeding.

Brent picked me up. I told him to make Liora stay at home since she hadn't gotten any sleep with me not being there.

"D, I appreciate she's your girlfriend and all, but she's been driving me fucking crazy," he told me as he walked with me up the steps to the house.

"She has?"

"She wouldn't eat. She wouldn't sleep. Spent the entire time fretting about you and I swear she told me to take her back to the hospital at least twenty times."

The door was thrown open before I could respond. Liora stood on the threshold, her green eyes wide before she promptly burst into tears.

"Hey, hey, no crying," I said as I stepped in.

I carefully pulled her into my arms and held her whilst she sobbed on my chest

"I'm s…s…sorry."

"Shh, my heart, it's okay."

I kissed the top of her head. Brent walked in and rolled his eyes.

"Come on, Liora, we've got to get him upstairs for bedrest. Doctor's orders."

She pulled away, glaring at Brent. He put his hands up.

"Don't look at me like that."

I shook my head, shutting the front door and taking her hand. I was perfectly capable of walking up two flights of stairs, but she kept checking on me like I was a fragile flower.

Not wanting to upset her further, I didn't say anything until we reached the bedroom.

"Liora, Brent said you haven't eaten or slept."

"I'm not hungry."

She started to help me out of my coat. It still hurt to move around too much so I was grateful, but she couldn't just avoid the topic. I let her fuss over me and get me settled in bed, then I stopped her from moving away.

"This is what's going to happen. Firstly, you're going to stand here and let me put cream on your back, secondly, you're going to eat something and then you're going to get in this bed with me and get some sleep. Is that understood?"

"But you're hurt."

"No fucking buts. How are you going to take care of me if you're not taking care of yourself?"

She bit her lip and said nothing.

"Right, I thought so. Now, take your clothes off."

I sent a quick text to Brent asking him to get the chef to make her lunch whilst she took her t-shirt and bra off. She sat with her back to me. It didn't look too bad, but I knew she hadn't been taking care of it.

"Aftercare is very important," I told her as I took the cream from the bedside table and squeezed some out into my palm. "I don't want to hear any more about me being hurt from you. I'll heal in time."

"I'm only letting you do this so you'll let me look after you."

I shook my head as I applied the cream to the fading lash marks.

"I was always going to let you take care of me. Who doesn't want their girlfriend to act as nursemaid?"

She stiffened.

"I'm your girlfriend?"

"What else did you think you were?"

"You've just never said it in front of me… at least not since it became real."

I finished with her back.

"You need to stand up so I can do the rest. Do you want me to say it more often?"

She stood, shaking her head as she tugged down her jeans and underwear.

"No… I prefer your term of endearment for me."

I started applying the cream to her behind and the tops of her thighs.

"My term of endearment? Which one would that be?"

I knew exactly what she was referring to, but I wanted to hear her say it.

"Dante…"

I said nothing, setting the cream down when I finished up. She turned to me, looking a little wary.

"I like it when you call me your heart."

"Well good, because that's what you are. Now go put some pyjamas on."

She tugged her jeans off before going over to the cupboards and selecting a pair of shorts and one of my t-shirts. I didn't say anything as she came back over and got in bed next to me.

"I forgot to tell you Jen and Fi will be here in a bit," she told me as she kissed my shoulder.

"They will?"

Why were my sisters coming over? I'd known Brent told them what happened and the police were going to speak to them, but they hadn't come to see me in hospital.

"They said they wanted to talk to you about Zach."

There was a knock at the door before it opened and the two of them walked in followed by Brent with a tray.

"Dante," Jen said, coming over to the bed with Fi. "You look like shit."

"Should I say thanks?"

They both sat down at the foot of the bed. Brent gave the tray to Liora before retreating. I eyed her. She started eating so I turned back to my sisters.

"Dad really did that to you?" Fi asked.

"Yes. Have you spoken to the police?"

"We did… that's what we came here for. We told them what he did to us and that we'd testify against him if it comes to it," Jen said.

"You will?"

"You know we hate him. You're not the only one who's put up an act for all these years. We just can't believe you finally did something about it."

"Did you tell her about it?" Fi said, pointing at Liora.

"I didn't tell her what he did to you, no. Haven't really had a chance to explain everything yet… but James knows now."

I wanted to. It was difficult when people kept interrupting us though.

"Why didn't you tell us he murdered Mum?"

"I couldn't. He threatened to kill all three of you if I told anyone."

"Why now?"

Because I met the love of my life and Zach stood in the way of our future.

How could I tell my sisters the truth? Would they even understand that love has a fucking strange way of changing you? Even though I loved them and James, it wasn't the same kind of love I felt for Liora. I would die to keep her safe.

"He did it for me," Liora said before I had a chance to open my mouth. "To protect me, and he's spent how ever many years trying to protect you two and James too. So don't get pissed off with him for not telling you the truth until now."

The girls stared at Liora for the longest moment.

"I like her," Fi said. "Is this serious? You better not send her back to Scotland."

What the fuck? My sisters liked Liora. What planet was I on?

"Of course it's serious," I said, frowning at them.

"Well, excuse me, you don't exactly have a stellar track record when it comes to women," Jen said, rolling her eyes.

The twins could be incredibly blunt and sarcastic when they wanted to be.

"This is different."

"Oh, I can see that," Fi said, eyes softening suddenly. "It's like we said at the gala... you're in luuurrve."

I almost put my head in my hands. They also had the ability to act like they were teenagers all over again instead of twenty five.

Liora grinned before she set the tray on the bedside table.

"So, has our brother been a complete bastard to you or is it just his siblings he decided to act like a dick to?" Jen said.

"He's fine, most of the time," Liora said, her green eyes twinkling.

"You two need to mind your own fucking business," I interjected before the twins could reply.

"Aww, down in the grumps today," Fi said.

Now I wanted them to leave, but I wouldn't kick them out. Not when they were smiling and ribbing me. I'd missed this. Missed having my siblings look at me without distain or irritation.

Jen poked Fi in the ribs.

"He's allowed to be grumpy, he can't see properly."

I shook my head. They were right. The swelling still hadn't completely gone down so I still only had partial vision.

"We should probably leave you two in peace. We'll go harass Brent. You mind if we stay?"

"As if I'd ever kick you out," I muttered.

The twins grinned, jumping off the bed. One of them took Liora's tray and before she could protest, they were out of the door, closing it behind them.

"They're…" Liora started.

"A pair of troublemakers," I finished for her.

"I wasn't going to say that."

"You were thinking it."

She smiled, tucking herself under my arm.

"How are you really feeling?"

"Sore."

"Did the doctor give you anything for the pain?"

"Mmmhmm, it's in my coat pocket, but I can't take any until later."

She took my hand and kissed it before laying her head on my shoulder.

"Will you tell me what happened to… your mother?"

I sighed. It was something I'd been meaning to do. It was just hard to talk about that day. Especially when I had a video to remind me exactly what happened.

"Zach used to hurt her all the time and when he got bored of hurting her, he started hurting me too. And when he realised how much I loved her, he hurt her in front of me as punishment for being a disappointment to him. He's always been a very jealous man. I think he hated how much she doted on us."

She looked up at me, green eyes full of compassion.

"I was fifteen when it happened. He'd tied me to a chair on several occasions but I thought nothing of it until he brought in a plastic sheet and then her. I'll spare you the details, but know it wasn't pretty. He wrapped her up in the sheet and dumped her body in the Thames. She was found two weeks later and by that time, it was hard for the police to determine much. We were all questioned, but Zach's friend, you know Marcus who you met at the party, he gave him an alibi so he was never really a suspect."

"How did she know he was going to kill her?"

"I don't know. She wouldn't tell me, only that she had set a camera up in his office. After he took her, the girls found me in there and untied me. I didn't tell them what happened, but they kept asking where Mum and Dad had gone. I shooed them out of the room and grabbed the camera before Zach came back. I've kept it safe all this time. And every time he hurt us, she'd make me sit so she could take pictures of the bruises and she'd document her own. I think she knew one day I'd need it."

Liora reached up and cupped my face gently, she had tears in her eyes.

"I'm so sorry."

"It's okay. He can't hurt us anymore, that's all that matters."

And it did. Even after everything Zach had done. I just wanted to put it to bed. To move on with my life because I had Liora and she meant everything to me.

"If this goes to trial, it will be horrible for the four of you to have to testify against him."

I shook my head.

"I don't care. He deserves to be put away for it and if that's what it takes, then that's what it takes."

She didn't look convinced, but she just dropped her hand and laid her head back on my shoulder.

"Do you think he'll implicate my father?"

"Not if he knows what's good for him. Who would believe him anyway? It's Angus' word against his."

She didn't say anything further. I hoped I'd reassured her everything would be okay. Only time and speaking to legal counsel would tell.

All I knew is I would stop at nothing to make sure Zach remained behind bars.

Chapter Twenty Five

LIORA

*D*ante was most definitely going to kill me. When he found out what I was doing, he would lose his shit, but I had to. I just had to.

Zach had been formally charged with murdering his wife along with further charges brought against him for child abuse, child sexual abuse and others. He was facing life imprisonment. The problem was he hadn't pleaded either way yet. I didn't want this going to trial for Dante's sake.

He was healing, but his ribs still bothered him. He'd spoken to his legal counsel several times about how things would proceed now the police had charged Zach. They were sure he would be convicted based on the evidence, although some of the charges were tenuous.

I didn't want to take that chance.

That's why I'd requested permission to visit him in prison without Dante's knowledge. And permission had been granted. Even Brent had no idea I was here.

Walking into the visiting room, I sat down in front of the glass screen and waited. Two prison guards brought Zach in. He looked thinner and had dark circles under his eyes. He was being kept in solitary for his own safety due to the high profile nature of his case.

He didn't say anything to me as he sat down.

"Hello, Zach."

His lack of acknowledgement bothered me, but I had to press on. I came here for a reason.

"I guess you want to know why I asked to see you."

This entire thing was crazy. I shouldn't be here. I shouldn't be about to ask him to do this, but my fear for Dante overrode any concerns I had about seeing Zach again.

"I know you don't have a good bone in your body nor do you give a shit about your son, but I'm going to ask this anyway. I want you to plead guilty to all the charges. I want you to spare your kids from having to testify against you. From having to go through a lengthy trial."

After hearing about what Zach had done to his wife and kids, I just couldn't take it. I didn't want Dante reliving that. He might be determined to see Zach burn, but I could see how much pain this whole thing caused him. He'd suffered enough. Too much even.

If Zach was perturbed by what I'd just said, he didn't show it.

"You know, your friend, Marcus, he's been arrested for providing a false statement about your whereabouts. It's over now. All of it."

He sat back in his chair, regarding me with a neutral expression. I wasn't going to be intimidated by him any longer.

Provoked

When I'd first seen Zach, he'd reminded me of a tiger. He didn't any longer. All I saw was a weak man who used his fists to intimidate other people.

"I don't care if you don't say anything to me. I only came to ask you to do this because I love your son and I don't want to see him suffer any further. I didn't come empty handed either."

That seemed to catch his attention as he sat forward again, spreading his hands as if to say 'what do you have?'. I'd known coming here without something to give him, it would make it fruitless. A man like Zach dealt in an eye for an eye. He had forced my father into agreeing to a ridiculous blood debt after all.

"I don't expect any assurances from you because I know I'll get none."

He inclined his head. The first acknowledgement he'd given me since I'd got here.

"What I have to offer is information. You see, I had a little chat with my father. I know all about Zander."

His eyes narrowed momentarily before his expression cleared again. I couldn't say anything incriminating in this room, so I had to tread carefully.

"It was always meant to be me. Declan isn't my father's son. Don't worry, he's not Zander's either. Just some deadbeat who kicked my mother out when he found out she was pregnant. You know your brother used to hurt her right? Just like you hurt your wife and children. That's why everything happened. My parents weren't having an affair. He did what he did to protect her from the abuse. Just like your son took away his siblings to protect them from you. You can choose to believe me or not, but I know my father. He's never had any reason to lie to me."

I didn't know what Zach made of my pronouncement because his expression remained the same.

"Just plead guilty, Zach. That's all I'm asking. Don't put Dante, James, Fiona and Jennifer through any more pain. You've done enough to them already. They deserve to put this behind them and find happiness."

I stood up. Zach wasn't going to say anything to me and there was no point me prolonging this. I nodded at the two prison guards who moved towards Zach. He got to his feet, giving me a hard stare. I turned to leave when his voice rang out.

"You love him even after he was complicit in what happened to you?"

I stood with my back to him for a long moment.

"When you really love someone, you forgive them for the things they've done wrong and accept them for who they are without conditions. I love Dante because he's compassionate, caring and puts other people above himself. He could've given up completely after what you put him through, but he didn't. I don't expect you to understand that since you're devoid of all those things."

I started to walk towards the door.

"I don't admire many traits in other people, but you were brave to come here alone. I don't suppose he knows, does he?"

"It doesn't matter. You'd be surprised by the lengths I would go to, to protect the person I love. Goodbye, Zach. Excuse me if I don't wish you well."

"Goodbye, Liora."

I opened the door and left the room with no idea whether Zach would do as I asked him to or not. It was worth facing him regardless. He'd been a monster to me all this time, but now I saw him for what he was. A pathetic excuse for a human being who didn't deserve his children or anything else he'd had in his life.

And now I had to go tell my boyfriend what I'd done. That to me was far more terrifying than seeing Zach behind bars.

"Where have you been?"

Dante was waiting for me as soon as I walked in. I'd taken the tube and the bus to get to and from the prison. I took off my coat and shoes, hanging them up in the cupboard.

"I went to see Zach."

"You what?"

I turned to look at him. His blue eyes were dark.

"I went to see your father in prison."

He strode towards me, gripping me by my shoulders and almost shaking me.

"Why would you do that? For fuck's sake, Liora, he's dangerous."

I shrugged him off.

"Have you taken your painkillers?"

"Don't avoid the question."

"I'm not, but the doctor said if you're going to recover properly you need to make sure you're taking them if you're going to be up and about."

"Yes, I took my fucking painkillers, now you're going to tell me what the hell you're playing at."

I took him by the hand and led him upstairs to the living room. He looked like he was about to blow a fuse and I was worried about him. His eye was better now, so he could see properly again. His ribs were still bothering him although the bruising on his chest was starting to fade. I made him sit down on the sofa before I knelt at his feet, taking both his hands.

"Why didn't you tell me?" he asked before I had a chance to say anything.

"You wouldn't have let me go."

"Liora—"

"Don't. I asked him to plead guilty to the charges so you won't have to go through a trial. I'm worried about you. After everything you've had to deal with, that shouldn't be another thing to add to the list. I did it because I love you so don't be angry with me, please."

He was silent for a long moment, his blue eyes searching mine. My heart ached. All I wanted was for him to be free of his father completely.

"You asked him to plead guilty?"

"Yes and in exchange I told him the truth about Declan. I don't expect him to do what I asked, but I went anyway."

"What did he say?"

"Nothing really. He just asked how come I could still love you even after you were involved in me being taken and said I was brave to come alone."

He stiffened, pulling his hands out of mine. His withdrawal hurt me far more than it should've. His expression turned and it looked like he was about to break inside entirely.

"I should've said this before, but if you want to leave me now, you can. I'm not going to force you to be here any longer."

I almost fell backwards onto my hands.

"What?"

"I said you can go back to Scotland if that's what you want. You're not a prisoner any more. You're safe to leave."

I wanted to shake him. What the fuck did that mean? Didn't he want me here any longer?

"What makes you think I want to leave?"

"After everything I did to you and what my family has put you through, why would you want to stay? All I've done is prevent you from doing what you love. From being truly happy."

I shook my head before I stood up. He was fucking dense if he really believed that.

"What the fuck, Dante?"

"What? It's the truth."

"Has everything we've shared together meant nothing to you?"

He frowned.

"It means everything to me. You know I love you."

"Well, you're not acting like you do right now."

He grabbed my hands, holding them tightly in his.

"I don't want you to go, Liora. I'm trying to give you a choice."

I ripped my hands from his and strode away to the windows. Did he think *I* didn't think I had a choice? I've always had a choice. I decided from day one to stay with him. At first, it'd been because I knew I couldn't leave or Zach would come after me, but soon it became because of Dante. Because I couldn't live without him. And now he was telling me he could live without me.

"Are you really saying you'd want to be without me?"

"What? No. That's not what I'm saying at all. This is all coming out wrong."

"Then explain it better."

"Liora…"

I turned back to him. I could see the pain in his eyes. It broke my heart.

"I just went to see your goddamn father to try to appeal to his better nature, not that he has one. I did it for you. For you. Because I love you. I love you so fucking much. What have I done to make you think I'd ever want to leave you? Huh? Because I'd like to fucking well know."

He stood up, walking towards me.

"Nothing."

"Then what the fuck is this?"

"You deserve more than all of this. More than me. I took you away from your dreams, Liora."

He stopped in front of me. I stared up at him, feeling like my heart was in a vice.

"I love you enough to let you go if I have to."

I wanted to shove him. To shout, rant and rave at him. But Dante was still in pain and I couldn't stand to see him looking like a little lost puppy. I reached up, holding his face in both of my hands.

"I never imagined I'd ever meet someone who makes me feel the way you do. I'm not giving up my dreams. I have new ones. Ones that involve you. I can still do what I love and be with you. I'm not giving up anything by following my heart. Don't you get it? You're the one. You've always been the one."

I didn't give him a chance to respond, going up on my tiptoes and pressing my lips to his. I was gentle about it, but I couldn't not. His hands came up to cup my face too. I shouldn't have worried about being gentle because he kissed me like he was drowning in me. It was desperate, both of us pouring out our frustration and pain.

When we finally drew apart, both of us were panting.

"You mean that?" he whispered.

"Yes, idiot. I love you."

"It would kill me if you left me."

"Then stop trying to push me away."

He smiled, running a thumb over my cheek.

"You're the best thing that ever happened to me, you know that? I love you so fucking much."

I couldn't stop the smile on my face. Even if he'd pissed me off, I couldn't stay annoyed. He was my everything. The person who'd shown me true passion, desire and love. I felt half alive before I met Dante. Now I was free. I was who I was always meant to be.

"If you weren't still hurt, I'd suggest we move this to the bedroom."

He raised an eyebrow.

"The doctor didn't say anything about not engaging in that kind of strenuous activity."

"Dante!"

He took me by the hand and brought me back over to the sofa, sitting down and pulling me into his lap so I was straddling him. His hands went to my blouse, unbuttoning it.

"Are you sure?"

"Am I sure if I want to have sex with my girlfriend who I've not been able to touch properly because she's been too scared she'll hurt me? Are you really asking me that?"

"You're still injured."

He grinned wickedly, a twinkle in his blue eyes.

"If you're so worried about me, then you're welcome to do the heavy lifting."

I bit my lip.

So that's why he's made me sit on him.

I didn't stop him as he finished unbuttoning my blouse before he tugged it off me and flung it halfway across the room followed by my bra.

"Now… this is a sight I've missed."

He leant down, capturing a nipple in his mouth whilst his fingers found the other. I moaned, unable to help myself. I'd missed his touch so much. My hands tangled in his dark hair, holding him to me.

"So beautiful," he whispered against my skin as he kissed his way over to my other breast.

His other hand ran up my inner thigh, causing me to buck against him.

"Take them off. I want you naked."

He released me so I could move off him. I unbuttoned my jeans, tugging them down along with my underwear.

"What about you?"

"Do you really want to see your poor injured boyfriend?"

"Don't you try play that card with me."

He smiled as his hands went to his shorts and he tugged them off along with his boxers. I straddled him again and carefully helped him take his t-shirt off so I didn't jostle his ribs too much. He stared up at me.

"Are you sure this doesn't bother you?"

I stroked his chest where the bruises were fading.

"What kind of woman would I be if I was put off by this? You only have those because you were protecting me. Besides, I've been helping you change for over a week, have I once looked at you like I was repulsed?"

"Well, no."

"Then shut up and kiss me."

"I thought I was the one who made demands."

I shook my head.

"No, you're an invalid today so it's my turn to be in control."

I didn't let him say anything else. I kissed him, trying to let my worries about hurting him fade into the background. Having him against me, his bare skin on mine set me on fire. His hands banded around my back, pulling me closer. I rocked back and forth against his cock, causing him to groan in my mouth.

Reaching between us, I held his cock so I could sink down on him, inch by inch. He felt so good. So, so good. He released my mouth, leaning back so he could watch me. His hands wrapped around my hips even so. I gripped his forearms, not wanting to aggravate his chest. I rose and fell on him, setting a steady rhythm.

"You look so fucking sexy right now," he said, his eyes blazing with heat.

"Are you sure I'm not hurting you?"

"Even if you were, I wouldn't care. You feel so good, so don't you dare stop."

I had no intention of doing so. He felt amazing too. I was so in love with Dante. Every part of him. Especially this. When we were together and the world just fell away. It was just me and him. Nothing else mattered.

His hands on my hips tightened, guiding me, showing me he wanted more. Faster. Harder. I let Dante set the pace even though I was meant to be the one doing the work. We held eye contact with each other. The love I had for him reflecting back at me.

Each thrust sent me closer to the edge. Each time he grunted and I moaned, I knew we were losing ourselves to each other. My hand fell from his forearm. I stroked myself, needing to find oblivion. His eyes were on what I was doing as I continued to ride his cock.

"Fuck," he groaned. "Come for me, my heart."

His words sent me over the edge. It rushed over me as I trembled. The feeling of bliss. Spots formed in my vision. My hand tightened around his forearm, nails digging into his skin. I cried out his name over and over. I crested the wave and drowned in the sensations.

I was pretty much a panting mess when I came back down to earth. All of my pent up tension and concerns left me. I'd been on edge for weeks, but now I felt like a huge weight had been lifted off my shoulders.

Dante pulled me towards him, kissing me gently.

"You always look so beautiful when you come," he murmured against my lips.

"Hush you."

"What? You do. I'll never get over the sight of it."

I took his hands, pinning them to the back of the sofa.

"It's time I took care of you."

He raised an eyebrow but said nothing. I rose and fell on him again, increasing the tempo until he was groaning and struggling against my hands. I let his go and he gripped my hips, forcing me down on his cock.

"Fuck, I'm so... fuck."

He grunted, resting his head on my shoulder as I felt him let go and his cock pulsated inside me. He held me close until he stopped trembling.

Sitting back, he stared up at me with a lazy smile.

"Mmm that was worth the wait."

"Are you sure?"

"I'm sure I want to do that again."

I grinned, shaking my head.

"I will agree, pending one condition."

"What's that?"

"That you promise me you'll tell me if it hurts."

He rolled his eyes.

"Fine. My ribs hurt now, but please don't start fussing over me."

"Dante…"

He cupped my face.

"No, my heart, I'm not going to let you start worrying about me all over again. I'm fine. I love you. I love being inside you and I'm not giving it up for the world. Do you understand?"

He looked so hopeful and I couldn't crush him like that. Not when he'd been through enough already. I had to stop treating him like he was going to break any second. It wasn't fair on him. He'd heal. The doctors had assured us he was going to make a full recovery.

"I understand."

"Good."

He was about to kiss me when his phone rang. I shifted, grabbing his shorts off the floor and digging it out for him.

"Hello? Oh, hi, yes... He has? That's unexpected... I see... Yes, thank you for letting me know... Okay. Sure... Great. Speak soon."

He hung up and stared up at me.

"Who was that?" I asked.

"My barrister."

"What did he have to say?"

"Zach has pled guilty to all charges. All of them. We have to wait for sentencing of course, but it means he's not getting out any time soon and we don't have to go to trial."

I smiled, wondering if it was my visit that made him do it.

"We're free, Liora. I'm... free."

"You are."

He wrapped his arms around me, pulling me into him.

"Thank you. Thank you for being you and doing something incredibly reckless by going to see him. I love you, Liora. Never forget that."

Provoked

"I won't. Don't forget I love you too."

Epilogue

DANTE

I leant against my car, watching her walk towards me. Her hair was braided down each side and tied up at the ends. She looked tired but happy.

"Hey you, how was your first day?" I asked as she drew near.

"Tiring, but really good."

After a long wait, she'd finally managed to secure a volunteer keeper position at London Zoo. She was hoping in the future it might lead to a permanent position, but for now, she was happy to be working with animals.

I wrapped my arms around her and dropped a kiss on the top of her head.

"I'm so proud of you."

"I'm only a volunteer."

"So what? You're still a zoo keeper now, just like you've always wanted to be."

She pulled away, grinning up at me.

"I am."

I opened the car door for her and she got in. I shut it and went around to the driver side, getting settled in, starting the car and pulling away.

"You didn't have to come get me. I could've caught the bus."

"I did. You worked hard all day. Tell me, which animals did they let you look after?"

"I was shadowing this other keeper, Tom. We were with the giraffes and zebras. He's really nice."

"Nice, eh?"

She looked at me with a raised eyebrow.

"Jealous much?"

"Me? Never."

I grinned, eying her for a moment before turning back to the road.

"How was your day?"

"If you call dealing with buyers all day fun, then my day was fine."

One surprise James, the twins and I had was Zach gifting us all the shares to his company. We were now the major shareholders of Bensons. The four of us were working towards restoring the brand's name in the wake of our family scandal. It'd taken us eight months, but things were looking up now.

"Was it really that bad?"

"No, fashion types are just… over dramatic."

She snorted.

"No, really?"

I ruffled her hair and she shoved me off.

"Pay attention to the road."

I rolled my eyes. We were waiting at traffic lights so it wasn't exactly like I was endangering anyone.

I'd let most of my staff go, including my driver. Mostly because Liora and I wanted the house to ourselves. Brent still lived in the basement and we had a maid who came a couple of times a week.

When I pulled up outside the house, Liora looked like she was dead on her feet as she got out the car. I wrapped an arm around her as we walked up the steps.

"Too tired to celebrate?" I asked.

"No... Wait, we're celebrating?"

"Mmmhmm."

I let go of her to unlock the door and pulled her inside. After she kicked off her shoes, I brought her through the kitchen into the conservatory.

"Surprise!"

Brent, James, Fi, Jen, Avery, Aiden, Declan and Liora's parents were all gathered in the room. I'd been planning this for weeks. Getting her brother to agree to come down was a pain, but he'd finally relented after Heather had told him he had to support his sister. He didn't like me, but Liora didn't really give a shit what he thought. And to be honest, neither did I.

We'd had Avery and Aiden around to dinner several times with James. I'd missed her. I would always see her as my little sister. Even though her husband was sort of intense, he and I got along okay.

Liora's eyes bugged out and she looked up at me.

"What's this?"

I dug my hand into my pocket before taking one of hers.

"Well… they're here because I wanted to ask you a very important question."

Her expression went from confused to shocked in a matter of seconds. I took the opportunity to drop to one knee.

"Liora, I love you. You're beautiful, smart and you keep me on my toes. I can't imagine spending my life with anyone else. Will you marry me?"

I dropped my hand so I could open the box. There sat a platinum band with an oval sapphire surrounded by diamonds. She told me once she loved the colour of my eyes.

"Dante," she whispered. "Are you crazy?"

I shook my head, smiling up at her. She put her hand out to me. I took the ring out and slipped it on her finger. She tugged me off the floor and stared up at me.

"Is that a yes?"

"Yes."

I leant down and kissed her. She squirmed away from me after a moment, her cheeks going red. She gave me a shy smile before running over to her parents and hugging them. Everyone else came forward to congratulate us. Before I knew it, an hour had gone by and I hadn't had two moments alone with Liora. I was standing with Avery and Aiden after she'd cornered me.

"So, marriage, eh?" she said.

"What? It's been over a year, not like you two tying the knot after, what was it, six months?"

She stuck her tongue out at me, curling her hand around Aiden's waist.

"You know why that was."

I nodded slowly. She'd told me a while back a lot of the real story behind the scandal involving her family. We'd swapped stories. What with Avery growing up with us, she already knew enough about Zach as it was. I suppose I had something in common with her husband having both grown up with abuse surrounding us. In that respect, Aiden and I had an understanding. A past marred by violence except we'd dealt with it in very different ways.

"Besides, everything worked out for the best, didn't it?" she continued. "Say, James will kill me for telling you this, but he's seeing someone."

"He is?"

"Mmmhmm, her name is Cassie."

Hold on, she's not talking about Cassie from Accounting? She's way out of his league.

"And does Cassie happen to work with us?"

Avery grinned and gave me a wink. I looked over at my brother who was deep in conversation with my sisters.

"Well, who'd have thought. My brother, the dark horse."

She laughed, shaking her head when I turned back to the two of them.

"Don't you go telling him I told you."

I put my hands up.

"Your secrets are safe with me. Anyway… have you two come up with a name yet?"

Avery looked up at Aiden who reached out and put his hand on her small bump. She'd only just started showing.

"No, but we have decided her middle name."

I raised an eyebrow.

"If I had my way, she'd be called Afie Elizabeth Lockhart," Aiden said.

"And you don't agree?" I said, nodding at Avery.

"Someone is taking the A theme too far," she replied, grinning up at her husband.

"Well I like Afie, but I suppose you'll have to see when she arrives."

"See, it is a good name," Aiden said, rubbing her stomach.

"If you're going to start with the PDA, then I'm backing away."

Avery gave me a sharp look, but she knew I was only teasing. The two of them were still all over each other when they thought no one was looking. It was cute but a little sickening how in love they were. Even I wasn't that bad with Liora, which reminded me, I should check on her.

I looked around and found her talking to Brent. Giving Avery and Aiden a nod, I went over to her and took her hand. Winking at Brent who rolled his eyes, I pulled her away into the kitchen. She looked so radiant. Her green eyes were shining with happiness. Cupping her face, I smiled.

"Are you sure you want to marry me?"

"I love you, Dante. I've told you a million times, you're the one. And this ring is so beautiful. I can't believe you got me a sapphire. Honestly, I didn't think you were paying attention when I said they remind me of your eyes."

"You wound me. I always pay attention when you're talking to me."

She grinned, going up on her tiptoes so she could kiss me.

"How long is everyone staying?"

"Well, your family is staying here, but I don't know about everyone else. I was going to order an Indian in a minute. Why?"

She wrapped her arms around my neck, rubbing her nose against mine.

"I was wondering if anyone would notice if we slipped away upstairs."

I raised an eyebrow.

"I thought you were tired."

"That was before you asked me to become your wife. I want to celebrate with you in private."

I looked over at our guests. No one had noticed we'd left the room. I pulled her arms down and took her hand.

"If we sneak away now, I think we have half an hour tops before someone comes looking for us."

"Well, we better make the most of it then."

She tugged my hand, checking the conservatory before we hurried out of the kitchen. I looked down at her as we ran up the stairs. Liora had just agreed to become my wife. I couldn't think of any better way for us to celebrate than in the playroom.

As I stared down at her after we'd made love, I knew I'd never be happier than when I was with her.

"Liora, you're my one too."

Acknowledgements

Thank you so much for taking the time to read this book. Where do I even start with these two? The journey to tell Dante and Liora's story has been a long one for me. I started their book when I was writing Sacrifice for Aiden and Avery. I wanted to tell the Benson's story having had Avery and James drop clues throughout the Corrupt Empire trilogy. So when Dante started talking to me, I dived right in so I could learn more about him and his love interest. This helped me shape James' background whilst I was writing Sacrifice and Revenge. And gave me scope to give a glimpse into Avery and Aiden's future together as well.

This story took me on an unexpected journey and I wouldn't say it was easy to write these two characters at all. Dante was such a complex character for me. All he wanted was to protect those he loved even if it cost him everything. His backstory blindsided me and ultimately writing it was absolutely heart breaking.

I'm firstly going to thank all my readers for joining me on this journey with these characters. Thank you for sticking with me and taking a chance on my books.

Thank you to my Twitter family (Sean, Jordan, Gil, Katie, Kenny, Paul and Corry) and everyone who supports me across my Social Media platforms. You guys make every day easier and remind me of what I'm working towards. This has been a really tough road for me so having that support is appreciated. A hugely special shout out to my Twitter ladies – Elle Linder, Rebecca Hefner, Carmen Adams, Jess Shaut, Brittany Kelley, Marla Machado, J.C. Paulson, Mikki Noble, Lotte R. James, Jennifer Nichole and so many more (sorry if I've forgotten anyone, but you are loved). You all give me life!

Huge enormous thank you to my Savage Slytherin Sister – Sabrina. You encouraged me to write this story and breathe life into Dante and Liora. I can't do without you in my life!

And last but not least, thank you to my husband for putting up with me writing all the time. You made this all possible and words cannot express my gratitude.

About The Author

Born and raised in Sussex, UK near the Ashdown Forest where she grew up climbing trees and building Lego towns with her younger brother. Sarah fell in love with novels when she was a teenager reading her aunt's historical regency romances. She has always loved the supernatural and exploring the darker side of romance and fantasy novels.

Sarah currently resides in the Scottish Highlands with her husband. Music is one of her biggest inspirations and she always has something on in the background whilst writing. She is an avid gamer and is often found hogging her husband's Xbox.

Made in the USA
Coppell, TX
30 April 2022

77231129R00225